"Here's to you, Libby, darlin'. Now that you know who I really am, what do you intend to do about it?"

He didn't have a clue how she'd found out, but it had been bound to happen from the second he'd introduced himself to her as an architect. What kind of fool was he, thinking he'd find "regular love" wearing a disguise?

He really couldn't blame Libby one bit for being so angry, as would he if it had happened in reverse. But it wasn't the worst lie that had ever been told. Hell. What if he'd actually been an architect who tried to pass himself off as David Halstrom? Surely that would have been a larger crime and would have angered her even more.

He drained his glass, refilled it, then sat on a leather couch, staring south, wondering what to do next. For the first time in his life, David didn't have a clue.

The Tycoon's Secret
by Kasey Michaels

"It's all about that money, isn't it? You're just used to getting your own way."

"Wealth has its perks, I won't deny that. So, how am I doing? Convinced yet?"

She didn't say anything else for a few tense moments, moments during which they both, he was sure, readjusted the conversation to where all of this verbal foreplay was *really* heading.

When she finally spoke again, he knew they were both on the same page.

"I don't have a price, Sam," she warned him tightly.

"We all have a price, Ms Halliday. It just isn't always money."

Available in September 2009
from Mills & Boon® Desire™

The Magnate's Takeover
by Mary McBride

&

The Tycoon's Secret
by Kasey Michaels

Dante's Wedding Deception
by Day Leclaire

&

Mistaken Mistress
by Tessa Radley

The Desert King
by Olivia Gates

&

An Affair with the Princess
by Michelle Celmer

THE MAGNATE'S TAKEOVER

BY

MARY McBRIDE

THE TYCOON'S SECRET

BY

KASEY MICHAELS

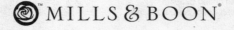 MILLS & BOON®

First published in Great Britain 2009
Harlequin Mills & Boon Limited,
Eton House, 18-24 Paradise Road, Richmond, Surrey TW9 1SR

The publisher acknowledges the copyright holders of the individual works as follows:

The Magnate's Takeover © Mary McBride 2008
The Tycoon's Secret © Kathryn Seidick 2008

ISBN: 978 0 263 87110 4

51-0909

Harlequin Mills & Boon policy is to use papers that are natural, renewable and recyclable products and made from wood grown in sustainable forests. The logging and manufacturing processes conform to the legal environmental regulations of the country of origin.

Printed and bound in Spain
by Litografia Rosés S.A., Barcelona

THE MAGNATE'S TAKEOVER

BY
MARY MCBRIDE

When it comes to writing romance, historical or contemporary, **Mary McBride** is a natural. What else would anyone expect from someone whose parents met on a blind date on Valentine's Day, and who met her own husband – whose middle name happens to be Valentine! – on 14th February as well?

She lives in Saint Louis, Missouri, with her husband and two sons. Mary loves to hear from readers. You can write to her c/o PO Box 411202, Saint Louis, MO 63141, USA, or contact her online at McBride101@aol.com.

Dear Reader,

What fun it was to work on this series with three great pals who are also terrific writers – Joan Hohl, Leslie LaFoy and Kasey Michaels. In the planning stage, we really kept the internet buzzing with our back-and-forth e-mails.

Here's hoping we've managed to bring you four terrific stories about people who all deserve to win a million dollars.

Happy reading!

Best wishes,

Mary McBride

Prologue

Well, my darlings, it's almost Halloween and I have oodles of treats and goodies for you. Shall we talk about the RB again? That oh-so-generous and oh-so-mysterious Reclusive Billionaire is believed to have struck again, anointing a candidate somewhere in the Midwest—that would be Fly-Over Country for most of you, my dear readers—with his largesse.

Alas, our information does not extend beyond mere geography at this date. Surely someone out there in the vast Heartland has a clue that he or she would be more than delighted to share. Call me, darling. I am, as they say, all ears.

Sam Balfour slapped the newspaper on the desktop as if he were swatting a fly. "This woman is worse than a rabid bloodhound," he said.

S. Edward Balfour IV, otherwise known as Uncle Ned, glanced up from his own newspaper. "She's persistent, I'll grant you that. We could use a few more like her on our team."

"Our team, as you so casually put it, Uncle Ned, is about to be exposed by this harpy. Doesn't that worry you in the least?"

"No," his uncle said. "Actually, I have other things to worry about. Here." He handed a large book across the desk. "Take a look at this. Tell me what you think."

Sam, still grinding his teeth, flipped through the pages, mostly photographs of old derelict motels in the Midwest. "They're nice pictures," he said, "if you like things like that."

"I do," his uncle said as he reached into his desk drawer to produce a green folder which he passed to Sam. "Take care of this for me, will you?"

"You're crazy, you know, to continue with this little game," Sam cautioned him.

His uncle merely smiled. "I suspect we're all a bit crazy, one way or another. Read through the folder, Sam. Then see that the usual check reaches Miss Libby Jost no later than Friday."

Sam could only sigh. Here we go again…

One

"Here's to you, you magnificent building."

Libby Jost stared out the window and raised her wine glass once again to toast the nearly completed 20-story convention hotel on the other side of the highway just west of St. Louis. Now that it was autumn and the trees were nearly bare, and even across six lanes of traffic, the bright lights of the Halstrom Marquis flickered like rubies in what was left of her red Chianti.

"And here's to you, Mr. Halstrom, whoever you are and if you really do exist. Welcome to the neighborhood." She swallowed the last of the wine, and then a silly, not-too-sober smile played at the edges of her mouth. "What took you so long?"

She put down her empty glass, stood up and then immediately realized she had celebrated a bit too much. Way too much, in fact, for a person who rarely drank at all. Her last drink, incidentally, had been an obligatory glass of champagne on New Year's Eve. She was definitely out of practice, she decided, and figured it was time for a very sobering slap of cold October air, so she flipped the main switch for the outside lights and wobbled out the door.

Once outside, Libby glanced up at the ancient neon No Vacancy sign flickering above the office door. How sad was that? she thought. After all these years, all these decades, it was probably some sort of miracle that the *V,* two *c*'s and half of the *y* still managed to faintly sputter. The mere sight of the sign might have completely depressed her a few months ago, but it didn't tonight. It didn't bother her at all because she knew there would be a brand-new, far better sign very soon, and instead of perpetual vacancies, the old Haven View Motor Court would once more be full of guests and good times.

Again, as she'd done a thousand times these past few weeks, she gave silent thanks to the anonymous Santa Claus who'd sent her a check for fifty thousand dollars in appreciation of her recent book of photographs of old, downtrodden motels in the Midwest. Libby Jost was, first and foremost, a serious photographer who had worked for the St. Louis newspaper for nearly a decade. She'd garnered numerous awards in the past, but most of them came in the form of plaques or framed certificates usually accompanied by long, boring speeches and polite applause. She'd gotten a check for two hundred bucks once for a photo of the Gateway Arch in morning mist, but never anything close to fifty thousand dollars.

The huge, unexpected check not only sustained her pride in her work, but it also provided her the wherewithal to help her aunt Elizabeth, the woman who had raised her here at this run-down motel after the death of her parents in a car accident when Libby was just a toddler.

Aunt Elizabeth hadn't asked for her help, but then she didn't have to. As soon as Libby realized that the fifty-thousand-dollar gift wasn't a joke or a stunt of some kind, but was indeed good as gold according to her bank, she arranged for a leave of absence from the newspaper and began making plans to revive the derelict motel. It was her aunt's dream, after all, and Libby felt she owed it to her to keep that dream alive as long as she possibly could.

And while she was giving thanks, she directed a few of them to the Halstrom Marquis, which soon would be sending its overflow customers across the highway to the newly remodeled, all spiffed-up, ready-to-go Haven View.

Libby was determined to make it happen. The anonymous Santa had given her the money to set it all in motion. She had taken her time to nail down her plans and to budget the money properly. Now she was ready to begin.

Stepping out onto the pebbled drive that wound through the dilapidated little tourist court, she noticed that one of the lampposts was dark. Damn. If it wasn't one irritation, it was another. Exterior bulbs had gotten so expensive, even at the discount stores, and they seemed to burn out way too frequently these days.

Maybe she could let one light go dark for awhile. Maybe no one would even notice. There weren't any guests here, for heaven's sake. But, after another glance at the magnificently illuminated hotel across the highway, Libby sighed. Got to keep up with the Joneses now, she thought, or with the Halstroms as is in this case. She went back into the office in search of a ladder and a light bulb.

Well, this wasn't one of the best ideas she'd ever had, Libby thought ten minutes later as she wobbled and swayed high up on the ladder while trying to juggle a large glass globe, a dead light bulb, a fresh light bulb and the four screws from the lamp. If anything, it was a terrible idea. She could see the paper's headline already: *Woman, inebriated, expires under lamp.*

And if it wasn't a disaster already, it surely became one when a car engine growled behind her, headlights flooding the parking lot and tires biting into the loose gravel of the driveway just behind her. A customer at this time of night? That wasn't at all likely. The motel hadn't had a single customer in three or four weeks.

She tried to look over her shoulder to see who or what it was, but the fierce headlights blinded her. When she heard the car door whip open and then slam shut, her heart leaped into her throat and made it impossible to shout or scream.

This was not good. Not good at all. It was terrible. A strangled little moan broke from her lips.

Then Libby lost her grip and the globe and the light bulbs crashed onto the ground below her, and she was about to crash down, too, on top of all that broken glass when a deep voice said, "Hold still."

Two hands clamped around her waist.

"I've got you," he said. "You're okay. Just relax and let go of the ladder."

Libby, in her total panic, tried to jerk away from his grasp and she held on to the lamppost even tighter than before.

"Dammit," he growled, tightening his grip on her waist. "I said let go. It's okay. I've got you."

He did, indeed, have her.

What else could she do? Libby dragged in a breath, held it and then let go of the lamppost, wondering vaguely if her life was going to flash before her eyes now that it was about to end.

It felt like falling into a giant bear hug. The arms that caught her were warm and encompassing. Then glass crunched under the bear's feet as he turned, took several strides and finally and oh-so-gently set her down.

She was safe, but only for a second. The bear turned on her, his eyes flashing. "What the hell were you doing up there?" he growled. "You could have broken your damn neck."

Libby's heart was pounding like a jackhammer. Her legs felt like jelly, and she was still not exactly sober. Far from it, in fact. But now, instead of feeling tipsy and scared to death, she felt tipsy and mad as hell so she yelled back at the bear, "Well, it's *my* damn neck."

He merely stared at her then, stared hard, as if he were memorizing every feature and angle, every crook and cranny of her body, or else perhaps he was merely calculating the calories there just in case he decided to take a bite out of her.

Belligerently, Libby stared right back, into a face that struck her as more rugged than handsome. Even in the semidarkness of the driveway, she could tell that his eyes were a deep hazel and the line of his chin like granite. He was fairly good-looking, for a bear. She wobbled again, struggling to keep her balance and wound up standing even closer to him. He smelled divine, even though she was too tipsy to identify the scent. Then he smiled. It was a sudden, wonderful surprise of a smile that carved out sexy lines on both sides of his mouth.

"It's a lovely neck," he said, reaching out to touch the hammering pulse in her throat.

Libby blinked. "Thank you," she said. "I think."

Whatever hostility that had flared up so suddenly between them seemed to vanish into the cool night air. She glanced at his car—a dark, sleek Jaguar—and was fairly well convinced that this guy wasn't a thug or a rapist or, for that matter, a paying customer. People who stayed at the Haven View these days tended to drive dirty pickups and dented sedans.

But before she could ask the Jaguar guy just who or what he truly was, he asked her, "Is the boss around?"

Libby almost laughed. Her whole life she'd looked far younger than she actually was. Now, even at age thirty, she could still easily pass for nineteen or twenty. And obviously she didn't look like a "boss," either, in her current panicky and slightly inebriated state.

Well, in reality she wasn't the actual boss here. The Haven View Motor Court belonged to her aunt Elizabeth, after all, as it had for the past fifty years, but while her elderly aunt was in a nursing home recovering from a broken hip, Libby was most definitely in charge.

"The boss," she said, "is currently under the weather, which means I'm temporarily in charge around here." She attempted to stand a bit taller, a bit more steadily, even as her vision seemed to be blurring. Hoping to appear professional in spite of her condition, Libby stuck out her hand. "I'm Libby Jost. What, may I ask, can I do for you?"

His lips curled into another stunning and sexy grin. "I don't think you can do much of anything for anybody at the moment, little Libby." His hand reached out to steady her. "What do you think?"

What did she think? She thought she heard a bit of a Texas twang in his voice, and then she thought she was going to be very, very sick right here in the parking lot if she didn't make it to the office in time.

"Excuse me," she mumbled, then ran as fast as her wobbly legs would allow.

Well, it wasn't the first time he'd encountered a pretty woman who'd had too much to drink, David Halstrom thought, but it was certainly the first time he'd witnessed a woman four feet off the ground clinging to a lamppost or one who looked like an inebriated fallen angel. She was so damn pretty, even in the dim lamplight, with her strawberry blond hair and her spattering of freckles that he'd almost forgotten why he'd come to this derelict hellhole in the first place.

He sighed and supposed he ought to check on her so he walked in the direction of the buzzing, nearly burned-out vacancy sign. He knocked on the door, waited a moment and when nobody answered, he entered what appeared to be the office of this dump which she claimed to manage. Hell. It was already pretty clear to him that she couldn't even manage herself much less a run-down tourist court.

The office was as tawdry as he expected, like something right out of the 1950s if not earlier. It didn't surprise him a bit to see a small black-and-white television with foil-wrapped rabbit ears wedged into a corner of the room, right next to a windowsill lined with half-dead plants. Good God. Did people actually stay here? Did they *pay* to stay here?

There was a floral couch against one wall. On the table in front of it sat a straw-covered bottle of Chianti and an empty glass. The caretaker's poison, no doubt.

He knocked softly on a nearby door, then he opened it a few inches and saw a dimly lit bedroom that wasn't quite as tattered as the lobby. There was a faint odor of lavender in the small room, and in the center of the bed, beneath the covers, he recognized a Libby-sized lump.

Good, he thought. She'd sleep it off and tomorrow she'd have a headache to remind her that cheap wine had its perils.

"Sleep well, angel," he whispered. "When you lose this job, you can come to work for me."

He quietly closed the door and returned to the parking lot.

A quick walk around the dismal property only served to confirm all of David's suspicions. The place was a total wreck in dire need of demolition, which he would be more than happy to arrange. He got back in his car and headed for his hotel on the other side of the highway. As he drove, his thumb punched in his assistant's number on his cell phone.

Jeff Montgomery was probably in the middle of dinner, he thought, but the call wouldn't surprise him nor would David's demand for instant action. The young man had worked for him for five years and seemed to thrive on the stress and the frequent travel as well as the variety of tasks that David tossed his way, from *Make sure my tux is ready by six,* to *Put together a proposal for that acreage in New Mexico.*

This evening David told him, "I need to know everything there is to know about the Haven View Motor Court across from the hotel. Who owns it? Is there any debt? What's the tax situation? Everything. And while you're at it, see what you can dig up on a woman named Libby Jost. Have it on my desk tomorrow morning, Jeff. Ten at the latest."

"You got it, boss" came the instant reply. David Halstrom was used to instant replies.

He was used to getting precisely what he wanted, in fact, and he figured he'd own the ramshackle Haven View Motor Court lock, stock and barrel in a few days, or a week at the very most. And if he didn't exactly own the fallen strawberry-blond angel by then, at least she'd be on his payroll.

Two

At ten o'clock the next morning Libby, in faded jeans and a thick white wool turtleneck, wasn't at all surprised that she had a splitting headache while she followed the painting contractor around Haven View. She couldn't even bear to think about the previous night, even as she wondered what had happened to the handsome bear.

As on most days, a camera hung from a leather strap around her neck because a dedicated photographer never knew when a wonderful picture might present itself. This morning, however, the camera strap felt more like a noose while the camera itself seemed to weigh a lot more than it ever had in the past. She was grateful the contractor didn't walk very fast, which allowed her to sip hot, healing coffee while she tried to interpret his expressions.

Sometimes the man's sandy eyebrows inched together above the bridge of his nose as if he were thinking, *Hmm. This old wood window trim might be a little bit tricky. That won't be cheap.* Other times he narrowed his eyes and bit his lower lip which Libby interpreted as, *There's not enough paint in the state of Missouri to make this crummy place look better.* Once he even sighed rather dramatically and then gazed heavenward, which probably meant he wouldn't take this job no matter how much she offered to pay him.

Finally, the suspense was more than she could stand, not to mention the imagined humiliation when he told her the place wasn't even good enough to paint, so she told the man to take his time, then excused herself. She headed back to the office, pausing once more to look around the foot of the lamppost to make sure she'd picked up every shard of broken glass from last night's sorry incident.

She had almost reached the office door when she heard the familiar growl of a certain sleek automobile. As she turned to watch the dark-green vehicle approach along the gravel driveway, Libby swore she could almost feel the sexual throb of its engine deep in the pit of her stomach. Oh, brother. She wasn't going to drink Chianti again for a long, long time.

Or maybe she was just feeling the deep shame of losing control the way she had the night before. Whoever the guy was and whatever he wanted, his opinion of her must be pretty low. If nothing else, she thought she owed the guy an apology along with a sincere thank-you for rescuing her from all that shattered glass.

She also thought, while staring at his fabulous car, that the vehicle was undoubtedly worth more—way more—than her fifty-thousand-dollar surprise fortune. How depressing was that? Still, it certainly piqued her interest in the man behind the wheel and whatever intentions he might have.

As if by reflex, she put her coffee mug on the ground and lifted her camera, shoving the lens cap in her pocket and glancing to make sure the aperture was set where she wanted it for this relatively bright morning. She snapped him exiting the car.

He seemed taller and more muscular than she remembered from the night before, but that face matched her memory of it perfectly. It was tough. Rugged. Masculine as hell. It was a countenance far better suited to a dusty pickup truck than a shiny luxury sedan.

His face, however, was shielded by his lifted hand as he approached her. Damn. She really wanted to capture those great Marlboro-Man features, especially his wonderful smile lines, but he kept them hidden as he approached.

She lowered the camera. He lowered his hand.

"How are you feeling this morning?" he asked.

Sensing the smirk just beneath his affable grin, Libby quickly forced her lips into a wide, bright smile as she responded, "One hundred percent."

He cocked his head and narrowed his autumn-colored eyes, scrutinizing her face. "Really?"

"Well…" Libby shrugged. The man knew all too well what her condition had been the night before. She had nearly thrown up on him, after all. There wasn't much use denying it. "Maybe ninety-five percent. Actually it's more like eighty-five percent, but definitely trending upward."

"Yeah," he said, bending to pick up her coffee, then placing the mug in her hand. "Booze tends to do that more often than not." Now his gaze strayed from her face, moved down past her turtleneck, paused at her breasts for a second, then focused on her Nikon. "What's the camera for?"

"I'm a photographer." She took a sip from her mug.

"I thought you were a motel sitter."

Libby laughed. "Well, I'm both I guess. I'm Libby Jost." Locals more often than not recognized her name from the photographs in the paper, but it didn't seem to ring even a tiny little bell for Mr. Marlboro Man. She extended her hand. "And you are…?"

"David," he said, reaching out to grip her hand more tightly than she expected. "I'm…" He frowned slightly, then angled his head north in the direction of the hotel across the highway. "I'm the architect of that big shiny box."

At that particular moment the big, shiny, mirrored façade of the Halstrom Marquis was full of lovely blue autumn sky and a few crisp white clouds. Libby loved it more every time she looked at it, she thought.

"It's stunning," she said. "You did a truly spectacular job. And I confess I love taking pictures of it. It's a completely different building from one day to another, even from one minute to another. Today it's like a lovely perpendicular piece of sky."

"Thanks. Just a few more weeks until the grand

opening. Would you like an invitation?" He chuckled rather demonically. "I'm sure the liquor will be freely flowing, if that's any incentive."

Libby rolled her eyes. "I've sworn off. Trust me. But I'd love an invitation. Thank you."

"You've got it." He plucked a cell phone from his pocket and mere seconds later he was directing someone to put her on the guest list. "No, that's all right. Don't worry about the spelling right now. No address necessary," he said. "I'll deliver it personally."

For some odd reason his use of the word *personally* and the way he locked his gaze on her when he said it suddenly caused a tiny shower of sparks to cascade down Libby's spine. She took a quick gulp of coffee, hoping to extinguish them.

This guy was good, she thought. He was good not only with buildings, but with women, too. At least his technique seemed to be working fairly well with her at the moment. She swallowed the rest of the coffee.

She was so conscious of her sparkling, sizzling innards that she didn't even realize the painting contractor had walked up behind her until he cleared his throat rather loudly and said, "Here's your estimate, Ms. Jost. I guess you know it's a pretty big job, considering the age of the place and all. My numbers are there at the top,." He pointed with a paint-crusted fingernail. "You just give me a call whenever you decide."

"All right. Thank you so very much for coming. I'll definitely be in touch." She was thrilled—amazed actually—that he was willing to take on the work.

The man had turned and walked away as Libby

flipped a few pages to glance at the all important bottom line. Reading it, she could almost feel her eyes bulge out like a cartoon character's. She didn't know whether to scream or to faint dead away or to throw up—again—right there in the driveway. She might just do all three, she thought bleakly. This was terrible.

He wanted thirty-seven thousand dollars for all the painting and patching that needed to be done, which would leave her the not-quite-staggering sum of thirteen thousand dollars for additional, equally necessary repairs and renovations like plumbing fixtures, tile, carpeting, new beds and bedding and lighting, not to mention a bit of advertising and a new damn sign over the office door. She'd had no idea, none whatsoever, that her dreams were so damned expensive and so dreadfully, impossibly out of reach.

Libby was so stunned, so completely stupefied that she was only vaguely aware that David had taken the paper from her, and then the next thing she heard was a gruff and bear-like curse followed by the sound of tearing. Her painter's estimate, she observed, was now falling to the ground in little pieces, like an early, quite unexpected snow. It was a good thing she didn't want to hang on to it, she supposed.

"This is absolute bull," David said. "It's worse than highway robbery. I'm betting the guy doesn't even want the job, Libby, and that's why he jacked the price up so high. He probably just wanted to scare you off."

"Well, it sure worked," she said, trying to accompany her words with a little laugh. A very little laugh. "Gee, now I can hardly wait to see if the plumbing guy and the electrician try to scare me, too. I can imagine it already. It'll be just like Halloween here every day of the week. Trick or treat!" There was a small but distinct tremor in her voice that her sarcasm couldn't even begin to disguise. At the moment, quite frankly, Libby didn't care.

"Look," David said. "I can get my guys over here for two or three days or however long it takes. They can do the painting for you for a tenth of that amount. Even less than that, I'd be willing to bet."

"*Your* guys?" Libby's headache took the opportunity to make a curtain call just then. She closed her eyes a moment, hoping to banish the unwelcomed pain. "I don't understand this at all."

David was already opening his phone as he responded to her. "Painters. From the Marquis."

"But you're the architect." She blinked. "How can you…"

"Architect or not, I just happen to be the guy in charge over there right now," he said, sounding most definitely like a guy in charge.

"But…"

He snapped the phone closed and gave her a look that seemed to question not only her ability to make a decision, but her basic intelligence as well. "Look," he said. "It's really pretty simple. Do you want the painting job done, done well at a reasonable price, or not? Yes or no."

This was obviously a man who made lightning-quick decisions, Libby thought, while she tended to procrastinate and then a bit more just to be absolutely sure or, as in most cases, semi-sure. Procrastinating had its benefits, but maybe lightning quick was the right way to go at the moment.

"Yes," she said. "Yes, I do want the job done at a reasonable price. Actually, what I want is an utterly fantastic job at a bargain basement price."

"You'll have it," he said. He stabbed in a number, barked some commands that were punctuated here and there with curses, flipped his cell phone closed and then told her, "A crew will be here in twenty minutes. Write a list of everything you want them to do. And be specific."

Libby nodded. She could come up with a list for them in less than five seconds, she thought. Number One was *paint everything*. There was no Number Two.

While Libby worked on her list in the office, David walked around the shabby motel grounds once again, scowling, muttering under his breath, telling himself he must really be losing his grip. He'd just done one of the most stupid things in his life when he'd offered to help fix up the damnable place he had every intention of tearing down.

What was the old expression? Putting lipstick on a pig? He shook his head. There wasn't enough lipstick in the world for this dilapidated pigsty.

On the other hand, his crew of painters were on the clock anyway in case of last-minute problems before the Marquis' opening so this little detour across the highway wasn't going to cost him all that much. It wasn't about the money, though. It was more and more about the woman, the luscious little strawberry blond.

She'd already gotten under his skin just enough for him to fashion a lie about who he actually was. He'd introduced himself to her as the architect of the Marquis—an architect, for God's sake—a mere hired hand instead of the Big Deal Boss. That alone was enough to make him question his sanity.

He hadn't actually planned to do that or rehearsed any sort of deception, it had simply sprung forth somehow when she'd offered her soft, warm hand and then inquired, *And you are?* For a split second, while he held her hand in his, he hadn't been quite sure who he was, where he was or what he was doing.

He wasn't a liar, although he'd probably stretched or bent the truth a few times during business negotiations. But in his personal life, what little there was of it, particularly with women, he never lied and he never promised anything he didn't follow through with from the moment he said hello to a woman to the moment he said goodbye. And he'd said a lot of goodbyes in his time.

He'd spent year after year watching female faces and their accompanying body language abruptly change when they heard the name David Halstrom. It was like going from Zorba the Greek to Aristotle Onassis in the blink of an eye, again and again, year after year, woman after woman. Women looked at Zorba with curiosity and pleasure and genuine affection. They looked at Onassis as if they were seeing their own reflections in the window of a bank.

He was thirty-six-years-old now, and he'd been a millionaire since he was twenty-one and a gazillionaire for most of the last decade. But until he'd laid eyes on Libby Jost, with her strawberry-blond hair and her light blue eyes and the nearly perfect curves of her body, David hadn't realized just how much he'd truly yearned to be treated like a normal, everyday guy instead of a damn cash register.

So, what the hell. He'd be an architect for the next few weeks, and then he'd confess, and the fact that he had more money than God would go a long, long way in soothing Libby Jost's hurt feelings at his deception.

In the meantime, he decided he'd better be going before the painters arrived and greeted him by his actual name. He stopped by the shabby little office to tell Libby goodbye and to give her his private number just in case she needed him, and it was only then, when he actually said the words to her, that David realized just how much he wanted her to need him.

The painting crew turned out to be four young men in their twenties or early thirties, all of them in paint-splattered coveralls, and all of them with long hair tied back in ponytails and piercings in one place or another. They looked more like a rock band than a team of professional painters. She hoped David knew what he was doing as she gave them her list, walked them around the place, then waited for the bad news she had begun to expect.

"So," she asked when they'd completed their inspection of the place. "Can you do it? And for how much?"

She held her breath in anticipation of the bad news.

The tallest of the young men shrugged his shoulders and gave a little snort. "Well, it's a challenge, ma'am, no doubt about that. But, sure we can do it. Hell, yes. As for how much, as far as I know right now, you'll just have to pay for the paint. We're all on the clock over at the Marquis, so we get paid one way or another. Over here. Over there. It doesn't matter."

Libby was still holding her breath, waiting for the bottom line.

"I'm guessing seven hundred dollars ought to cover the supplies," he said. "Give or take a few bucks."

Then he pulled a fold-out palette of paint colors from his back pocket. "If you want to choose the main color and the trim right now, ma'am, we can pick it up and get started after lunch."

Libby was still a few beats behind him, still celebrating the seven hundred dollars, give or take, as if she'd just won the lottery. Things were suddenly, terrifically back on track, she thought, after this morning's horrible derailment.

"Ma'am?" He fanned open the color chart in front of her.

"Oh. Sorry." She looked at the chart. "Well, this won't be too hard. I've had these colors in my head for weeks. I want a rich, creamy ivory for the walls. This one. Right here." She pointed to a swatch. "And I want a deep, deep, wonderful green for the doors and the trim. There. That's it exactly. It's perfect."

"Cool," the painter said, then turned to his crew. "We're all set. Mount up, boys. Let's hit the road."

Libby hit the road, too, right after her ever reliable front-desk replacement, Douglas Porter, arrived.

She'd known him since she was two years old, and if her aunt Elizabeth was the mother figure in Libby's life, then Doug was most definitely her stand-in father after all these years. His nearly religious attendance at dozens of school plays and concerts and teacher's meetings, and his presence at every major event in her life more than qualified him for a special kind of parenthood. Plus, it was Doug who'd given her her very first camera on her tenth birthday, then spent hours showing her how to use it properly, not to mention forking over a small fortune for film, filters, lenses and often staggering developing costs.

But he wasn't really her uncle. He'd been the best man at Aunt Elizabeth and Uncle Joe's wedding and after Uncle Joe went missing in Korea over half a century ago, Doug simply stayed around. It was clear to anyone with eyes that he loved her aunt, and it never failed to sadden Libby that the two of them hadn't married.

"Elizabeth's pretty chipper today, Lib," he had announced when he entered the office. "You'll be glad to see that, I know. So what's going on around here? How many guests do we have?"

It had become a running joke between the two of them, about the guests, and she had offered the standard reply. "No more than you can handle, Doug."

She'd paused on her way out the door. "Oh, I'm expecting some painters this afternoon. They know their way around so you won't have to do anything."

"Painters?" His white eyebrows climbed practically up to his scalp. "Why on earth…?"

"No big deal," she said nonchalantly. "I'm just having them do a few touch-ups."

As she closed the office door she could hear him muttering something about throwing good money after bad, silk purses and sows' ears.

Libby was still smiling about that when she parked her car at the nursing home's rehab facility and walked down the long glossy hallway to her aunt's room. She knocked softly, then opened the door, happy to see that the crabby roommate wasn't there at the moment, but not so happy to see the sour expression on Aunt Elizabeth's face.

"Painters, Libby? You've hired painters? What on earth are you thinking, child?"

Libby sighed. "I guess Doug called." She should have figured on that, she thought, as she pulled a chair close to the bed. "I wish he hadn't done that. I wanted to surprise you, Aunt Elizabeth."

"I *am* surprised," she said, rearranging the sheet that covered her. "And not all that pleasantly, my girl. You shouldn't be throwing your money away…"

"Wait. Just wait a minute." Libby held up her hand like a traffic cop. Sometimes it was the only way to stop this woman from going on and on. "I got a very special deal on the labor, so the job really isn't costing much at all. Trust me."

Her aunt narrowed her eyes. "How much?"

"Seven, eight hundred tops."

"I don't believe you," she snapped.

"It's true, Aunt Elizabeth. Cross my heart. I'll even show you the canceled check when I get it."

The elderly woman clucked her tongue. "And I suppose it's already too late to stop this painting nonsense?"

"Yes," Libby said stubbornly.

Her aunt, equally stubborn, glared out the window for a moment before she snapped, "Well, then tell me what colors you picked out. You know very well that I don't like change, Libby, and when your Uncle Joe gets home he'll expect the place to look just as it did when he left for Korea."

After half a century he's not coming home, Libby wanted to scream at the top of her lungs, but she didn't. Aunt Elizabeth was an absolutely sane and reasonable woman, and likely a lot sharper than most folks her age, except for her complete and utter denial of her husband's death.

If you started to argue with her, if you tried to convince her the man was dead, she'd snap, "Well, then. Show me his death certificate." And of course there wasn't one since he'd gone missing in action, so her aunt always won the argument. And that was that.

When Libby was a little girl, she honestly believed her Uncle Joe would be coming home any day. She couldn't recall how old she was when Doug told her that the man had been missing in action since the 1950s. And he wasn't coming home. Ever. *Now, this is just between you and me, sweetie,* he had said.

Over the years, Aunt Elizabeth's friends and acquaintances tolerated this little lapse of sanity, this unreasonableness, or whatever it was. Doug, bless his heart, seemed to accept it completely. Libby did, too, she supposed, after all this time. When the subject arose, they'd all give her aunt the usual sympathetic nod or a brief *tsk-tsk* before quickly moving on to another topic of conversation.

Was she crazy? Perhaps. But the craziness was quite specific and limited to Uncle Joe and his imminent return. Aside from that particular bat in her belfry, Aunt Elizabeth was completely normal.

"Tell me the colors, Libby," her aunt demanded now.

"You're going to love them," she said. "I tried really hard to duplicate the original cream and green of the Haven View. I knew that's what you'd want."

"I must say that if I'd been in the mood to paint, honey, that's precisely what I would've chosen. And now I can't wait to come home and see it."

Libby nodded, feeling both deeply touched and hugely relieved in the same moment. At least her first surprise had ended well. Now there were approximately forty-nine thousand dollars worth of surprises still to come. Heaven help her.

Happily, there were no more surprises and no more ruffled feathers during the remainder of her visit. They had a good time together, and when Aunt Elizabeth's crabby roommate made her return appearance, Libby hugged and kissed her aunt goodbye and returned to her car. She was just fastening her seat belt when her cell phone rang.

David the Bear didn't waste much time, she thought. Hello was hardly out of her mouth when he asked, "Got any plans for this evening? What are you doing for dinner?"

"Hmm. Dinner." She tried with all her might to suppress a grin even though he obviously couldn't see it. And the answer she gave him wasn't all that far from the truth. "I was just now considering picking up a crisp domestic salad with a light Italian dressing and croutons, of course, while on my way home, then pairing it with delicately microwaved macaroni and cheese. Care to join me?"

"I've got a much better idea," he said.

Yes, he did indeed have a better idea, Libby thought when she finally closed her phone. Being chauffeured to a penthouse dinner at the magnificent Marquis most definitely trumped a take-out salad and lowly mac and cheese.

Three

The penthouse elevator door chimed as it swooshed open, and David, who'd been waiting in the marbled vestibule, turned to greet not the strawberry blonde he was expecting, but rather a luscious peach parfait. His heart shifted perceptibly in his chest and his entire body quickened at the sight of her. The woman looked utterly magnificent. If he'd felt merely smitten with Libby Jost before now, right this second he considered himself completely in lust.

She stepped forward into the vestibule, disclosing a delicate and adorable gold-sandaled foot along with a sleek and shapely length of calf. The pale peach fabric clung to her hips and her breasts, to her whole body like a second, shimmering skin. David swallowed hard. Just as he'd suspected, though, it didn't help all that much.

"Welcome to the Marquis," he said, striding forward and claiming her hand the way he wanted to claim every lovely inch of her from her tumbled hair to her golden toes. He couldn't help but think that her work put her on the wrong side of a camera.

"Thank you." She laughed then, a sound that was slightly husky and infinitely sexy. "I know I'm ridiculously overdressed," she said, "but I decided, since this will probably be my only visit here, at least to the penthouse, I might as well go all the way."

David clenched his teeth. He wasn't going to touch that remark with a ten-foot pole. Not even a twenty-foot one.

She blinked, and the color on her smooth cheeks deepened several shades, turning from delicate pink to a deep warm rose. "Fashion-wise, I mean."

Stupid, Libby chided herself. Even without the benefit of wine, she'd managed to put her foot in her mouth immediately upon her arrival. The man—quite gorgeous now and elegant in a black turtleneck and black pleated slacks—must think she's an absolute and unredeemable twit. She wrenched her gaze away from his face, let it stray around the suite and then immediately focused on the southern wall of floor-to-ceiling windows.

"What an incredible view," she exclaimed. "Oh, it's just amazing."

David reached for her hand. "Come have a closer look," he said, leading her into the suite, across a gorgeous oriental carpet that must've been the size of a football field and around burnished leather chairs and glass tables that gleamed richly in the ambient light. It was as if she'd landed smack in the middle of an issue of *Architectural Digest*.

As exquisite as the penthouse's décor was, the view from its enormous window was even better. Or so it seemed to Libby until her roving gaze practically skidded to a halt upon the scruffy landscape of the Haven View just across the highway. She'd never seen the place from so high, and it was not, she had to admit, a very pleasant sight. It was horrible, in fact. It was worse than horrible. The place was pure suburban blight.

The little guest cabins she'd been so thrilled about painting looked more like outhouses from this vantage point, and the glass globes of the lights along the driveway were so dusty and bug-splattered they barely seemed to shine at all. Squinting, she even decided that she could detect some rather significant damage to the shingles of a few cabin roofs, which was something she hadn't even thought to consider in her careful renovation budget.

It all struck her as utterly depressing, every feature, every shingle, every single square inch of the entire bedraggled place. Once again, she feared that her fifty thousand dollars wasn't nearly enough to bring the poor old motel up to speed. Not even a turtle's speed. She must've sighed just then or muttered something under her breath, because David, who was standing close behind her, touched her shoulder ever so gently and asked her what was wrong.

Everything, she thought, before she managed to put her game face back on as best she could, then turned to her host. "Well, the good news, I guess, is that the poor old Haven View will be hidden by leaves for eight or nine months every year from the guests of the Marquis. The bad news is worse than I imagined."

She waved a hand in front of her hoping to rid herself of these brand-new, unbidden feelings of despair. "I really don't even want to talk about it."

There was a small flicker of something close to sympathy or sadness in his expression for just an instant before he said, "Come on. Let's forget about the southern view for now." He clasped her hand in his once again. "Let me show you the really incredible views to the east and the west."

The east view was from a wide, slate-floored terrace with gorgeous wrought-iron furniture where Libby could easily imagine wearing an ivory satin robe with matching slippers while lingering over a late breakfast of croissants, sweet butter and strong Jamaican coffee. Right at that moment she could almost taste it.

"On a fine, clear day," he told her, "you can see the Arch." He pointed. "Right there. You'll have to come back sometime with your camera."

"I'd love to," she said. Oh, boy, would she love to. "I could get some really interesting shots."

A minute or so later, having gone from one gorgeous room to another even more gorgeous room, the promised view to the west was revealed when David pushed a button on a bedside console and a whole wall of drapery silently slithered back. Outside the exposed window, on the highway below, east-bound headlights shone like diamonds while west-bound taillights sparkled like a river of rubies, and she could actually see a bevy of stars twinkling in the dark sky above them all. It momentarily took her breath away.

Oh, how Libby wished she had her camera and a few specific lenses and filters just then to record it all. She wished she had a tripod in order to take a terrific time-lapse exposure of the traffic. Despite David's polite invitation a few minutes earlier, she doubted she'd ever be up here in the penthouse again.

"Does Mr. Halstrom have a place like this in all of his hotels?" she asked.

"More or less," he answered in a tone that struck her as rather brusque. "But when he's not in residence, his suites are all available to guests for the right price."

"Don't even tell me the price," Libby said. "I couldn't stand to hear it considering we try so hard to rent our dinky cabins for sixty-five dollars a day." Sadly, she thought, that economical price was probably far more than the accommodations were worth. Jeez. How long would it be before they might actually be forced to pay people to stay there, just for appearances sake?

"Maybe the new paint job will help," David offered, sounding vaguely unconvinced if not down-right disbelieving.

"Yeah. Maybe." She sighed. And maybe, she thought, maybe there were far more worthy recipients of her unexpected little fortune than the over-the-hill Haven View. Maybe she should reconsider the whole ridiculous endeavor. Like Scarlett O'Hara, she decided to think about that tomorrow.

Libby found herself forcing another smile then as she turned to her oh-so-handsome host. "Didn't you promise me a glass of red wine, David?"

The garnet-colored wine, French and positively ancient by her standards, was far and away the best that Libby had ever drunk. She sipped it cautiously, dreading a repeat performance of the night before, while David showed her the other rooms in this incredible place. The bathrooms alone were worth a hefty admission price.

Dinner arrived almost magically, wheeled into the suite on two shiny silver carts before being placed on the dining room table by two smartly outfitted waiters who gave the impression they were auditioning for a play, or perhaps a silent movie as neither one of them made so much as a sound above the clink of a water glass or the soft thud of a piece of heavy silver on the tabletop.

There were four different entrées to choose from, including a buttery salmon, a gorgeous filet mignon, lamb in an exotic mint sauce and roasted chicken with truffles that Libby ultimately couldn't resist. She was almost tempted to ask for a doggie bag in which to carry home the rejected dishes that the waiters promptly and silently wheeled away.

"Oh, what a terrible waste," she said with a sigh as she watched them turn a corner on their way to the elevator.

"Don't worry," David told her as he prepared to cut into his steak. "When that food gets back to the kitchen, it'll be devoured within a matter of seconds. The chef is working with a small staff prior to the opening while he refines the menu. I had him send up four choices because I didn't know what you might like. Feel perfectly free to be a critic. How's the chicken?"

"To die for," she said, reveling in her very first bite. "And the vegetables actually look edible which doesn't often happen where I come from."

She tried a petite, buttery carrot dusted with parsley and some other herb she couldn't identify, then rolled her eyes in delight. "Who knew a lowly carrot could taste so good? You know, David, your boss must weigh a ton if he eats like this every single day."

"Well, he works out a lot, I'm told," he said before taking another sip of wine and another bite of his filet. "I'd like to hear more about your photography, if you don't mind discussing it."

She didn't mind at all. It was probably her favorite subject and she was quite capable of going on endlessly about it, which she proceeded to do. But every time she politely—and curiously—attempted to change the subject and to inquire about him, David smoothly and affably turned the conversation back to cameras and lenses.

After dinner, they returned to the living room with its glorious window wall, where Libby avoided another painful glance at the shabby motel below. It was nearly midnight when she finally said, "I really should be getting back to Haven View. The man I left in charge, my uncle Doug, is almost eighty years old and really needs his rest."

David's left eyebrow quirked. "And you assume, I suppose, that your uncle has been overrun with demanding guests all the while you've been here?"

Libby had to hand it to him. The guy really did try to suppress his laughter even though he didn't quite succeed. She appreciated his sense of humor despite this particular, rather hurtful and annoying subject matter.

"You never know," she said with a little shrug of her shoulders before she stood up and extended her hand. "It was a truly lovely dinner, David. Thank you."

He stepped forward, smoothly brushing her hand aside as his arms reached out to encircle her. He gathered her close, kissed the top of her head, then her forehead, then the bridge of her nose. "I've wanted to do this all evening, Libby," he said, his breath warm and fragrant as expensive French wine on her face.

Libby felt like whimpering, *"What took you so long?"* But then David's mouth covered hers, and speech was suddenly and completely out of the question. She couldn't even think, but only inhale his wonderful scent and savor the rich remnants of wine on his lips. A tiny moan mounted in her throat, threatening to break loose and inform him just how much she craved his touch.

He leaned back slightly, used his thumb to angle her face up to meet his gaze. Those lovely hazel eyes of his had deepened to a dark and passionate green. "Stay here with me tonight. Don't go back to that dump."

Something clicked in her head, and Libby blinked

hard as her eyes began to focus again. She could feel her mouth flattening to a hard, thin line. Then she straightened up even as she took a step back, out of his arms.

"I don't want to be rude," she said, "especially after that divine dinner, and also because I truly like you, David. I like you enormously. But I won't have my aunt's lifetime endeavor trashed or made fun of. Not by you. Not by anyone." She paused a second, her eyes still locked on his. "I hope that's clear."

He nodded. "Got it," he said. He sounded absolutely sincere if not somewhat taken aback by her rather unexpected challenge. "I won't do it again."

"Good." Libby smiled. "I'm glad you understand." Then she lifted her chin and tapped a finger to her lips. "Now kiss me good-night again. Please."

Women rarely stood up to him, either professionally or privately. It was such a rarity, in fact, that David couldn't remember the last time it had happened. Hell, men rarely stood up to him these days. His little Libby was a tigress in peach silk. He smiled in the darkness at the memory of her fierce, flashing eyes, her stiffened spine and her delicate but formidable chin. More power to her, in fact. She'd had every right to put him in his place after he'd spoken disparagingly of her motel, wreck that it was.

He cursed himself now for deceiving this wonderful woman from the get-go. Had he ever had a more stupid, more self-defeating, almost suicidal idea? He was going to have to make it all right, but at the moment he didn't have a clue how to do it. All he knew was that he didn't want to lose her. Well, hell. He didn't even *have* her yet, but Lord how he wanted her.

He turned over in bed, pummeled the pillow once more with his fist, and eyed the bedside clock. It was two-fifteen. He'd be likely to wake her if he called her right now. With any luck, however, she'd be awake also, just across the highway, tossing and turning and thinking about him. Yeah. He should be so lucky.

Well, maybe he was. She answered her phone on the second ring.

David skipped the usual telephone introductions and niceties and immediately said, "Let's do something fun tomorrow."

A soft, sexy murmur came through the distance. "Like what?" she purred.

"I don't know. Let's just go somewhere, anywhere. We'll just hold hands and wander. We'll be kids on our very first date."

She laughed, and the sound was practically delicious. "I'll have you know," she said, "I sprained my ankle on my very first date."

"No problem. I'll carry you." David smiled in the darkness, imagining her in his arms. "Where should we go?" he asked her. "What about the zoo?"

"Been there."

"The art museum?"

She let out a long sigh. "Been there, too."

"How about the Arch?"

"Done that."

David, at a loss now, said, "Well, pick someplace. Anyplace. It doesn't have to be in St. Louis."

She was quiet a moment and then she said, "I know. Let's go to Hannibal."

"Hannibal?" David scratched his head. "You mean Hannibal, as in Tom Sawyer and Huck Finn?"

"Uh-huh. That's exactly what I mean. I haven't been there since I was a kid, and it's only an hour and a half or so away. I'll even drive if you'd like."

"Wait. I've got a better idea. Can you be ready to go by ten tomorrow morning?"

"Sure. I'm pretty sure I can get all my work out of the way by ten. Definitely by ten-thirty."

"Great. I'll send someone to pick you up then. Sleep well, darlin'. I'll see you at ten-thirty."

Then he closed his phone and, like a contented little boy who'd just had his warm milk and chocolate-chip cookies, David at long last drifted off to sleep.

On her side of the highway, Libby finally slept well, too.

Four

Early the next morning Libby taped a sign to the office door. Closed for renovations. She wasn't kidding herself that half a dozen or more cars would suddenly be turning into the motel's drive in search of accommodations, but the sign made her feel better anyway knowing her aunt Elizabeth would approve of properly informing the public. Libby was sure she could count on Doug to pass along the news when he visited her in the rehab facility.

The crew of young ponytailed painters from the Marquis had returned bright and early. Two of the cabins were already finished with their fresh coats of cream and deep green paint and they didn't look all that bad in Libby's admittedly biased opinion. After admiring them, she called a roofing company to arrange for an inspection of the damage she'd seen from the penthouse the night before. It wouldn't do any good to have brand-new décor, she figured, only to have it ruined by a leaky roof.

What else hadn't she considered? Libby wondered, when she'd budgeted her fifty-thousand-dollar gift? At the moment, she didn't even want to think about all the structural problems she might have breezily over-looked while concentrating on the place's worn and outdated décor. Strange and horrible visions of wood rot and mildew and termites began to tumble around in her brain, threatening yet another headache, some-thing she certainly didn't need this morning.

She looked at her watch and realized she had a little less than half an hour before she'd be swept off to the Marquis once again. Libby sighed, silently acknowledg-ing that her time would be better spent here, going over and adjusting renovation plans, than in Hannibal where she merely intended to have fun with a gorgeous guy.

It had been several years since she'd had the least bit of interest in a man, and now—faced with her fifty-thousand-dollar motel makeover challenge—along came David, who actually made her heart flutter while he gave her the impression that his own heart might be fluttering a little bit, too. How was that for terrible timing?

She showered, dressed and was ready to go without a moment to spare when the hotel's black limousine pulled into the drive. Jeff, the young man who had driven the limo the night before, opened the rear door for her. She thanked him, and then once he was settled up in front behind the wheel, she asked him, "How do you like working at the Marquis?"

"I love it," he said, his chin jutting over his shoulder in her direction. "It's a great place. Well, I guess you already know that."

"I do," Libby responded. "It's a beautiful building. Mr. Halstrom certainly hired the right architect."

"For sure. That Japanese team is tops."

Libby frowned. She had no idea that David was affiliated with an overseas company. He'd never mentioned it, and she had simply assumed he was a one-man operation, and a local one at that. It was probably a naive assumption in this day and age when everything and everyone seemed to operate on a global basis.

And then she wondered if David's permanent residence was in Japan, and, if so, just how soon he would be returning there. But then she decided she didn't want to know the answer to that particular question, at least not right now when she was looking so forward to their day in Hannibal, not to mention the night that might follow it.

Well, a girl could hope, couldn't she? She sank back into the luxurious leather upholstery. She didn't want to think about anything except the day ahead and the pleasure it might bring.

What she'd never anticipated, though, and never would have in a million years, was that David would have a helicopter on the roof of the Marquis, waiting to whisk them north along the Mississippi River.

"I've never been in a helicopter," she said more than a bit nervously as David boosted her inside it.

The rotors overhead were beginning to whirl and roar so he had to shout back. "Well, I've never been to Hannibal, Libby, so I guess that makes us even." He settled himself inside, then held her hand tightly as they lifted off into the bright blue sky. It wasn't much more than a minute or two before the big hotel appeared as just a shiny speck in the distance behind them.

The trip that would normally have taken them an hour and a half by car took them a mere thirty minutes in the air. The river town was busy, apparently preparing for a Huckleberry Finn festival, but since it was a weekday the tourists weren't exactly overrunning the place as they might have on a weekend. By a little past one o'clock, Libby and David had visited Mark Twain's boyhood home, ogled Tom Sawyer's white-washed fence and done a quick, fun trek through the museum, all the while holding hands like a couple of goofy kids. Like Tom and Becky, Libby thought.

For lunch they ordered hot dogs and fries from a street vendor, then carried their goodies down to the riverbank where they sat for an hour talking, watching as the Mighty Mississippi rolled by. As before, it was mostly Libby who talked up a storm while David listened and tended to deflect most of her questions back to her.

"Where were you born?" she asked him.

"Texas," he answered, raising his hand to dab a bit of mustard from a corner of her mouth. "What about you?"

"Here," she said. "Missouri." Then Libby spent a while talking about her parents' deaths, growing up at the Haven View and her aunt Elizabeth and Doug. As far as life stories went, hers wasn't very exotic. It wasn't even very interesting.

"Why did you want to be an architect?" she asked.

His answer was barely more than a shrug, followed by, "Why did you decide to be a photographer?"

Of course, having been asked about her favorite subject, she went into the whole story about her very first camera, her work at the St. Louis newspaper, and on and on.

She snapped pictures all the while—of the wharf, of the riverbank and the river—but hard as she tried, she wasn't able to capture David's face in a single frame. The man had an uncanny knack of turning, bending or lifting his hand at the exact moment she took the shot. She was almost beginning to believe he had some sort of camera phobia, and she so desperately wanted a picture of him, especially since he might be going to Japan at any time and she'd never see him again.

The mere thought of his leaving nearly made her queasy. She excused herself to return to Main Street for a bathroom visit. And then, smart little cookie that she was, she slipped a telephoto lens onto her camera while walking toward town, slowly turned and managed to get some really incredible shots of the man she'd left behind on the riverbank.

The gorgeous autumn day had turned cold late that afternoon, and by the time they climbed out of the helicopter on the roof of the Marquis, Libby was shivering.

"I know just how to warm you up," David said,

punching a number on his phone and telling whoever responded to have the hot tub in the penthouse ready in half an hour.

Then he led her to an elevator whose door swooshed open moments later just a few steps outside the cozy and dark little bar on the mezzanine.

"Two brandies, Tom. The good stuff," he said, holding up two fingers in the direction of the bartender who appeared to be presiding over an empty room.

"Right away, Mr...."

"Thanks," David said, cutting him off as he led Libby to a banquette in the corner where a candle glowed in the center of table.

She scooted into the lush leather seat. David slid in next to her and wrapped his arm around her shoulder. "You'll be warm in just one minute, darlin'. I promise."

She'd already warmed up considerably just from the heat of his body so close to hers. The subsequent brandy, in a huge crystal snifter, was hardly a match for her companion's warmth, she thought. And then Libby cautioned herself not to become too accustomed to the man or his warmth since it probably wouldn't be long before he was warming some other woman on the other side of the planet.

"I had more fun today than I've had in a long, long time," she said, lifting the brandy glass toward him. "Here's to my gracious and most gallant host."

The clink of the crystal when their glasses touched was a bit of music all on its own.

"Here's to Tom and Becky and Huck," he said. "And here's to you, Libby. I don't think I've ever had such a good time. Not even when I was a kid." He put the snifter down, and then his brow furrowed as he gathered in a long, deep breath.

It was one of those moments when a tiny little *uh-oh* sounded inside her head. Furrows and long, deep breaths were rarely, if ever, followed by good news. Furrows and long, deep breaths usually, almost always, meant trouble.

"Libby," he said softly, his eyes locking on to hers. "There's something that I…"

His cell phone let out a sharp little bleep just then. David cursed as he wrenched it from his pocket and very nearly broke it open in order to respond. "What?" he growled. After listening for a minute or so, he pressed a button to put the caller on hold. "I have to take this infernal call, Libby. I'm sorry, darlin'."

"Go ahead." Libby swirled the remaining brandy in her glass. The candlelight turned its color to a dark and lovely honey. "Take your time, David. I truly don't mind."

He kissed her forehead before he slid out of the booth, then walked—well, the man stalked, if truth be told—to the far end of the bar to continue the conversation. From her vantage point, and judging from his body language, it looked as if he were bestowing some very bad news on the person at the other end of the connection.

For the moment, Libby was just thankful it wasn't her.

David felt his mood darkening. Damn. He'd just had one of the best days of his entire life, but then business interrupted in the form of a threatened lawsuit by an irate guest in his London hotel, and his nervous Nellie

of a British attorney felt obliged to alert him, personally, posthaste. David told the hysterical attorney if he
ever called him again, he'd have him chained in the
Tower of London, then drawn and quartered in front
of Buckingham Palace with CNN given the exclusive
rights to broadcast it live.

And now, to make matters worse, he'd be damned
if he could locate something for Libby to wear in the
hot tub. The little complimentary garments should
have been stowed in a drawer in the penthouse spa, but
it appeared as if someone—some soon-to-be former
employee—had decided to stash hotel brochures, post-
cards and stationery there instead.

"It's all right, David," Libby said from her perch on
the edge of the hot tub. "I can wear my bra and panties.
It's not a problem. I've done it before."

The vision of her clad only in scanty silks, see-
through no doubt, beside some big gorilla in a hot tub
didn't do a lot to lighten his current mood. He'd
summon his assistant, Jeff, in a moment, no doubt
ruining another of the man's dinners. But meanwhile
he continued to search like a madman, cursing,
slamming drawers and cabinet doors, and all the while
berating himself for losing the opportunity to confess
to Libby and tell her just who he really was. That, he
well knew, was at the heart of his current furor.

Earlier, downstairs in the darkness of the bar, the
words had been right there on his tongue, and he'd
been ready to get down on his knees if he had to in
order for her to forgive him. He wanted her that much.
He was going to tell her now, even before their time in

the hot tub. What sense was there in prolonging it? Hell. It wasn't as if he were going to confess to her that he was an axe murderer.

She would forgive him, wouldn't she? She had to, otherwise…

Just behind him then, Libby cleared her throat and uttered a whispery little *ta-da*.

He turned to see a vision of absolute delight, Libby clad only in feminine briefs and a snow-white lacey bra. Considering how great she looked when fully clothed, David couldn't even find words to describe her now. She grinned, and then pointed to the bubbling hot tub as she gave a pert little salute.

"Permission to come aboard, sir?"

David sighed inwardly. Whatever he'd intended to confess to her had suddenly flown right out of his head. And he had to admit that, even if he'd remembered, this was not the time to risk a confrontation. He might have been considered a liar under the circumstances, but he wasn't a downright fool.

"Permission granted," he said, quickly shrugging out of his own shirt and jeans, to join her in the warm caress of the water.

Settled chin deep in the wonderfully warm tub, feeling David's lean body right beside hers, Libby's eyes began to drift closed and she nearly fell asleep. How very strange, she thought, to feel so completely at ease with a man she'd only known for a mere two days. It wasn't like her to feel so relaxed with anyone, even after knowing them for months.

"I could stay right here for an entire week," she said, letting go of a soft and wistful sigh. "Maybe even a month."

He chuckled. "I don't know if I'd care to see you turn into a wrinkled, waterlogged prune, darlin'. I have to admit I like you just the way you are."

She turned her head toward him, gazing up at his face where the sexy smile lines had reappeared.

"Do you?"

Her voice was hardly more than a whisper, and even she could hear the longing in her tone. She couldn't help it. She adored this man, and she wanted him with every fiber of her being. If their coming together was fated to be only a brief affair before he went back to Japan, well, then, so be it. *Sayonara* to her dreams of the future. Libby decided to simply live in the present for now. Let the future take care of itself.

Perhaps it was the buoyancy of the water, but David drew her into his arms so effortlessly that Libby felt lighter than a feather. His lips were warm on hers, tender and wonderfully slow and sensuous. The touch of his tongue on hers was tender and exquisite. It seemed, just then, as if they had all the time in the world to explore and discover and make love to each other.

"You're perfect," he whispered. "But I already knew that from the first moment I saw you."

His hand moved to her breast, cupping it, a perfect fit for his smooth wet palm, a perfect distance to her nipple for his thumb to circle and explore. Libby gave a little shudder, and leaned her head back onto the rim of the tub as he covered her neck with languid kisses.

He murmured against her skin. "I've wanted this… I've wanted *you* from the moment I saw you clinging to that silly lamppost like a fallen angel."

"Emphasis on fallen," she said with a little sigh, then blew a puff of air upward to dislodge a damp stray curl from her forehead.

"No." His hand eased from her breast and then smoothed slowly, thrillingly down, over her hip to her inner thigh. "Emphasis on want. I want you, Libby. All of you. Now."

There was a great *whoosh* of water, and then she was high in his arms, clinging to his hard, wet neck as he carried her down a dimly lit hallway and into the bedroom where only the night before she'd watched the traffic flow like a river of jewels out the western window. He put her gently on the bed and left her for a brief moment to open a drawer, tear open a little square package, then returned to gather her into his arms.

"Tell me how to please you," he said, his fingertips drifting up and down her arm, setting off little shock waves of desire all over her. Then his hand strayed to her leg and the shock waves increased. "Anything you want. Anywhere."

Libby pressed closer to the hard length of his body, placing the palm of her hand to his cheek and tracing the now barely visible smile lines with her thumb. "Everything about you pleases me," she said. "I just want you. All of you."

They made slow, sensuous love while the diamond and ruby traffic lights flickered far below. In Libby's experience—which admittedly wasn't vast or all that recent—men tended to go for the gusto, returning to the lady's pleasure only after crossing the finish line alone. David, however, was in no rush at all. His every touch was leisurely, languid and absolutely divine. He seemed to have infinite pleasure in giving her pleasure.

Then it was Libby, when David at last entered her, who revved up the pace considerably, lifting her hips to meet each thrust of his, wanting almost desperately to capture all of him inside her and to keep him there forever. Their soft murmurs only moments earlier quickened to mutual groans of pleasure.

Everything in Libby's body curled tighter and tighter, wound up in itself, as she moved toward climax and then...

And then it felt as if her every cell suddenly let go in wave after wave of pleasure so intense she thought she might either laugh or cry or both. Within seconds, David followed her with a final powerful thrust, his whole hard body shuddering in his release.

They simply lay there then, locked in each other's arms, sated and waiting for their breathing to return to something that resembled normal, if indeed it ever would.

It was nearly nine-thirty before they could rouse themselves from the big bed on the west side of the penthouse. But when David heard a distinct and hungry rumbling coming from the direction of Libby's stomach, he reached for his phone and called downstairs. The chef, of course, had long ago retired from the kitchen, but an eager sous chef—now in line for a rather hefty raise, David decided—was more than happy to prepare his "special" omelette and a vegetable stir-fry.

When he turned to consult Libby on the meal, her eyes glittered like a wolf just spying a lamb.

"Send it up as quickly as you can," David told the sous chef.

They ate, quite ravenously, in bed. Libby wore a Marquis bathrobe, and with her tangled hair and her lips still flushed with his kisses, she reminded him of Venus, come to life right here in the Midwest.

"I should probably be getting back to the Haven View," she said after finishing one of the hotel's signature amaretto and chocolate-chip cookies.

David frowned. "I thought you said you put a sign on the door saying it's closed for the duration."

"I did, but…"

"Well?"

It seemed to dawn on her then that she had no other obligations, at least not at the motel, and there was no one to please for a change but herself. The notion apparently surprised her because she blinked and, for once, since the first time he'd met her, she appeared to be at a loss for words.

But David wasn't.

"Stay with me, Libby."

He brushed aside the silver trays, the empty dishes and the glassware, then drew her once more into his arms. "Stay."

And she did.

Five

When Libby got back to the Haven View at a little after nine the following morning, David's kisses continued to linger on her lips, on her throat, on... Well, everywhere. She felt such a warm and nearly tangible glow inside. It was like a fire that seemed to burn and caress at the same time.

By ten o'clock, however, the fire had fizzled out, most likely because of her tears. The roofing inspector had arrived, looked at all the cabin roofs and then handed her an estimate for forty thousand dollars plus tax.

"Keep in mind," he'd said while shaking his head, "that's just for the roofing, Miss Jost. It doesn't include the new gutters and downspouts this old place badly needs. Otherwise, you're going to see more damage in the future. You can count on it."

After he left, Libby walked inside the apartment behind the office and crumpled on the floor of the shower, letting the hot spray from above blend with her tears. It had been a long, long time since she'd wallowed in self-pity. The last, and probably the only other time she'd given herself permission to break apart, had been when she was ten years old and her cat, Joey, went missing. This morning she felt the way she had when she was ten, as if something so very close to her heart had just been run over or blown to smithereens.

She cried for a long, long time, until she had no more tears to shed, then she dried off, got dressed and went out to the main room of the office where she found Doug wearing his favorite and ancient St. Louis Cardinals sweatshirt while he flipped through a stack of mail. Funny, she thought. If her memory was correct, he'd been wearing a Cardinals T-shirt all those years ago when he'd consoled her about the loss of Joey.

"Morning, honey," he said cheerfully. "Did you have a good time in Hannibal?"

"I had a great time in Hannibal." Libby walked around to the other side of the desk, wrapped her arms around the elderly man's neck and planted a loud kiss on his balding head. "I love you so much, Doug," she said.

"Well, I love you, too, sweetheart." He chuckled. "But what'd I do to deserve such an enthusiastic greeting?"

She flopped onto the ratty floral couch across from the desk. "You were so sweet to me when my little Joey ran away."

Doug scratched his head with the sword-shaped

letter opener he'd been using. "Joey. Just a minute. Now let me think back. Was Joey the gerbil or the cat?"

Oh, jeez. She'd completely forgotten about George the gerbil who'd scampered beneath her bed one day, never to be seen again. Well, now she really was depressed.

"Joey was the cat," she said. "He was black with little white slippers on his feet."

"That's right." Doug's whole face seemed to sadden, every line and wrinkle turning downward. "I'm sorry about that, Lib. I remember. You were so unhappy, honey. I'm just glad I managed to soothe your heart a little bit."

Libby let out a long and weary sigh, thinking her heart could surely use a bit of soothing right now. When she was a little girl, she'd always gone to Doug for his comfort as well as his advice. He was patient and kind and incredibly smart. So why not seek his advice now, she wondered. She wasn't exactly doing a stellar job all on her own. She probably should have consulted him from the very beginning of this fifty-thousand dollar debacle.

"Doug…" she said, then hesitated. No, maybe it wasn't such a great idea. He'd tell Aunt Elizabeth every last detail and then all hell would break loose. Libby chewed on her bottom lip, still tender from last night's kisses.

"What, honey? What's bothering you?" Doug asked. "I know something is."

"Am I that transparent?" she asked.

"You are to me, kiddo. You always have been. Want to tell me what's up?"

Libby crossed her arms over her chest, feeling about

ten years old again and horribly vulnerable. "What's up, huh?" She forced a little half-embarrassed laugh. "Well, let's see. It's such a mess that I hardly know where to begin."

But somehow she began, first with the arrival of the mysterious check for the enormous sum.

Doug stopped her right there. "Wait. Hold it right there, Libby. You're telling me that somebody, some complete stranger, gave you fifty thousand bucks just because he liked your book about dying and dead motels? It was a wonderful book and all, but that's a hell of a lot of money just to say thanks for a good read."

"That's what I thought, too. I thought it was a joke at first. But the money's completely legitimate. The bank had no problem with it at all. There's fifty thousand dollars sitting in my checking account right now just waiting to be spent."

She followed that amazing bit of news by telling Doug of her hopes and dreams of using the money to revitalize the Haven View. She explained her carefully thought-out plans for both interior and exterior repairs, trying to be true to Aunt Elizabeth's original plans and color schemes.

When she got to the part about the painters, however, it was a bit tricky to maneuver around the facts because she wasn't really ready to disclose anything about David or her feelings for him. There was no sense complicating this with the mention of a lover who might not even be here in a week or two.

Finally, Libby concluded her tale with the staggering price of the roof repairs, and then lifted her hands helplessly and said, "I'm still not willing to give up this dream of mine, Doug, but I just don't know how to make fifty thousand dollars go the distance that's required. I just don't know if it's possible. I'd really, really welcome any ideas or suggestions, if you have them. But, please, please don't just tell me I'm crazy for wanting to do this."

Behind the desk, he closed his pale blue eyes a moment and pressed his lips together as if he didn't know what to say or didn't even want to respond at all, which Libby could easily understand. It was her money, after all, and therefore her problem. And she'd certainly made a mess of it so far.

Then Doug cursed gruffly, something he rarely did, before he curled one hand into a fist and pounded the desktop with it.

"Dammit, Libby. I wish you'd come to me, to both of us right off the bat. I know you meant well making it a surprise, but your aunt Elizabeth and I are way too old for surprises, honey. We like to know what's what. We *need* to know. It's pretty important at our age," he muttered. "We really need to be kept inside the loop instead of outside in the dark."

Libby sighed. Doug was absolutely right. She should have informed them. She wished that she had.

"Well, now you know. *What's what* is fifty thousand dollars is burning a big hole in my pocket. And now that you know about it, you can help me do this right, Doug, if it's at all possible." She narrowed her gaze on his face. "Is it possible? Or is it just a silly and impossible dream? Tell me the truth."

He leaned back in his chair, then rubbed his hand slowly across his white-whiskered chin before he spoke. "That's a generous thing you want to do for her, Libby. I think your aunt Elizabeth will be thrilled as all to get-out to see this old dump looking the way it did in the old days. It's been hard on her, watching the place go to seed the way it has over the years."

"Oh, I know," Libby said. "And I so desperately want to change all that. I want to make her really happy."

"I know you do, sweetie." Doug sighed. "But fifty thousand dollars, as grand a sum as it is, just isn't going to cut it. Not with prices like they are today, and not with all the repairs we're in need of around here. Your fifty thousand dollars, honey, is hardly a drop in the bucket." He shook his head so very sadly. "I'm afraid it can't be done, Libby. Not unless you're a magician or that secret admirer of yours plans to add a million or two to his original gift."

Libby dragged in her lower lip and bit down on it, trying with all her might not to give way to another flood of tears. What good would they do?

"Unless…" Doug leaned forward in his chair.

"What? Unless what?"

"Ever heard that old expression, Libby, about there being more than one way to skin a cat?"

She nodded, wondering what in the world he was getting at and why he was smiling all of a sudden when everything seemed so horribly, bitterly bleak. He looked like a damned Cheshire cat, and she wanted to skin *him* at the moment. "What?" she pressed. "What are you thinking?"

"Do you remember the work I did a while back for Father James O'Fallon when he was organizing his halfway house and homeless shelter?"

Again, Libby nodded. She remembered it well. Doug had volunteered his time as an accountant to help the energetic young priest acquire an affordable facility and to properly set up his charitable organization. That had been years ago, but the place—Heaven's Gate—was still doing wonderful work by providing food and shelter and hope to those who lacked all three.

"Just what are you getting at, Doug?"

"I drive into the city to visit that place pretty often, you know. Mostly just to chew the fat with Father James. He's a bigger Cardinals' fan than I am, and that's saying something."

"But what does that have to do with Haven View?" she asked. She had absolutely no idea where he was going with this.

"There's a new program at Heaven's Gate," he said. "It just started a couple months ago. They're training some of their people to work in the trades. Painting, carpentry, plumbing, things like that."

Now a little bulb started to glow above Libby's head as she suddenly saw just where he was going. "All the things we need done here," she said.

Doug nodded. "Yep. We need the work done and I can promise you that Father James needs fifty thousand dollars. What do you think, honey?"

Libby stood up so fast she nearly fell over. "My God! I think you're a genius, Doug. That is just inspired. Can we drive downtown right now and talk to him?"

The elderly man laughed. "I guess with that Closed sign on the door we can leave any time we want, Libby. Let me just give the good father a call."

Across the highway, high above it in the penthouse, David was just getting out of bed at eleven-fifteen. He'd gotten up a few hours earlier to see Libby safely off with Jeff, his reliable chauffeur and assistant and then Jeff had immediately returned to see what else the boss needed done.

"I haven't had time to go through all the Haven View documents yet," David told him while trying to stifle a yawn. "Anything I should know about the situation right now? Anything about it that can't wait a couple of hours?"

Jeff shook his head. "I think it'll keep. I probably shouldn't say this, Mr. Halstrom, but you look like you could use a few more hours of sleep."

He usually maintained a fairly stern demeanor with his employees, but David couldn't help but laugh at the remark. "I'm getting too old for this," he said.

"Well, perhaps it's time to settle down, boss. Or at least to think about it."

The kid rarely, if ever, made personal observations or remarks. A few days ago such comments might've earned him a dark, scathing look and a swift verbal reprimand. Today, however, David felt much too mellow and too downright happy to do anything but say, "Maybe you're right, kid. Maybe you're right."

Now, after a few hours of sleep, he felt somewhat restored, but that little thread of giddiness and gladness was still there inside him. Instead of his habitual Grinch demeanor, he felt almost like a little boy on Christmas morning, and that was some kind of first, he decided, because even when he was a little boy, there wasn't much giddiness or gladness in him. None, if truth be told.

"Libby, Libby," he muttered into the mirror while he shaved. "What the hell are you doing to me?"

After he showered and dressed, he punched her number into his cell phone. She'd written it down for him before leaving, but now he couldn't remember if it was her cell or the front desk at the crummy motel. Either way, there was no answer, which made him feel a little sad and lost for a moment, until feeling sad and lost made him feel like a real jerk.

So, he proceeded to call the Halstrom home office in Corpus Christi. Surely there would be somebody there he could yell at in order to drive this sappiness out of his system.

Once Libby and Doug were downtown, she asked him if he'd mind if they stopped at the newspaper's office for a minute so she could drop off some film for developing. Leave of absence or not, she'd become incredibly spoiled by the paper's freebies. Most newspapers had gone completely digital these days, but the St. Louis paper, out of nostalgia perhaps or pure laziness, still maintained a small, cramped and cobwebby darkroom.

Inside the building, she didn't want to waste time so she tried hard to avoid people she knew—and there

were so many of them—as she made her way to the
northwest corner of the third floor where her good pal,
Hannah Corson, was on duty, looking harried and
hassled as always. Libby plucked several film cans
from her handbag.

"Can you run these for me, Hannah? No rush, but it'd
be wonderful to have the prints in two or three days."

"Sure. No problem." Hannah took the film cans and
promptly stashed them on a shelf in a little metal box
labeled "To Do." "So, it's good to see you, Libby.
How's everything going out at the Weary Traveler?"

Libby couldn't help but laugh. Her coworkers
must've come up with a few hundred alternate names
for the Haven View in the past decade, most of them
rather risqué if not downright X-rated. A few brave
souls had even come out to spend the night in one of
the little cabins, and although they all claimed to have
enjoyed the experience, she noticed nobody ever made
a return engagement.

"Everything's going great," she said, surprised that
she actually meant it.

"How 'bout hanging around and having lunch with
me?"

"Thanks, Hannah, but Doug's waiting for me
downstairs."

"Okay. Well, I'll give you a call when your prints
are ready. Probably day after tomorrow. I'm backed up
here for the Sunday edition. You know how it is. I miss
your nice, crisp black-and-white shots, Libby."

Already at the door on her way out, Libby blew her
a kiss. "Thanks, Hannah. I owe you. Again."

"Yeah, yeah, yeah. Everybody owes me," the woman grumbled. "I really should change my name to Hannah Kodak, I guess."

When she got back to the street, Doug had moved to the driver's seat of her ancient minivan. "Hop in, Libby," he said, starting the engine. "Come on. Shake a leg. We're already ten minutes late."

She hopped in, and immediately reached for the seat belt to yank it across herself and fasten it tight. Doug had always been a very creative driver, and now that he was in his late seventies, he didn't seem to feel the rules of the road applied to him personally. She held her breath as they whizzed three blocks north and then two blocks west to the Heaven's Gate facility.

For all the time Libby had spent at the newspaper's office these past years, she rarely visited the adjacent area to the north. Little wonder, because there wasn't much there except crumbling, boarded-up buildings and vacant lots filled with weeds and every kind of trash imaginable. Ever since finishing her book about down-and-out motels, she'd been hoping to be struck by an idea for another book.

It occurred to her now that there was a strange, haunting, even terrible beauty in all this urban decay. There was a burned-out church on a corner that almost seemed to be begging her for a series of photographs. Libby filed the notion in the back of her brain, hoping that once the repairs were accomplished at the motor court, she'd have time to pursue the concept.

Doug whipped the minivan into a small gravel parking lot, hit the brakes and skidded to a stop, then turned off the engine. "Here we are, Libby, my girl. Let's go. We don't want to keep Father James waiting all afternoon. He's a very busy guy."

As she climbed out of the vehicle, she remembered to check her cell phone for messages. Good grief. There were a half-dozen calls, all of them from David. She didn't know whether to feel flattered or alarmed. Well, emergency or not, he'd simply have to wait until she met with Father James. The fate of the Haven View seemed to be hanging in the balance of this quickly arranged meeting. She couldn't allow anything to distract her.

Not even David.

Six

After their meeting and a brief tour of Heaven's Gate, Father James walked Libby and Doug out to the parking lot. The priest had listened intently to their proposal and seemed to be fascinated by it even though the fine points hadn't been worked out yet. In all honesty, the plan was barely past the light bulb over the head stage, but Libby and Doug had been eager and enthusiastic in their presentation, if not burdened by the details. Obviously the fifty thousand dollars provided Father James with more than a little incentive to take it under consideration.

"I'll present it to my board of directors when we meet early next week," he told them. "And I expect they'll be equally intrigued and enthusiastic."

Libby tried hard to hide her disappointment at the delay. "I don't suppose you could do it any sooner."

He gave her a patient, practically angelic smile, one he must've used a hundred or more times a day in this facility, and then he shook his head. "I'm afraid not."

"That's plenty soon," Doug said. "And remember, both of you, we still have to present this plan to Elizabeth, and Lord only knows—pardon me, Father—how she'll respond. She can be downright cranky and stubborn as all get-out sometimes."

Libby rolled her eyes.

Father James gazed heavenward a moment, then said, "Well, I've been known to get cranky and stubborn myself. If this is meant to be, my friends, it will happen. Perhaps we should simply leave it at that for the time being."

Easier said than done, Libby thought on the drive home. It wasn't going to be so easy for her to put the brakes on her big plan, even if only until next week. Now which one of them was going to make a heartfelt presentation to Aunt Elizabeth, she wondered.

Afternoon westbound traffic was fairly light, so she used her right hand to flip open her cell phone which now registered two additional calls, both of them from David. Libby couldn't help but smile. Persistent fellow, her handsome architect, wasn't he? And, oh my, she thought, how she adored it.

Doug pointed to her phone. "That wouldn't be your new suitor, would it, Libby?"

She nodded.

"I'm looking forward to meeting him."

Libby laughed. "Well, as Father James would say, *All in good time, my dear Doug. All in good time.*"

* * *

As it turned out, Libby didn't have to return David's calls. He was waiting at the Haven View—arms crossed and one hip lodged against his Jag—when she and Doug got back.

Libby's heartbeat immediately picked up speed. How was it possible, she wondered, that this man looked better, more handsome and even more desirable every time she laid eyes on him? At this rate, she would surely go into cardiac arrest at the mere sight of him in a week or so. She could only hope that she caused a similar, significant drumbeat inside his hard-carved chest.

By the time she'd parked the minivan in back of the office, he was standing next to the driver's side door, reaching out to open it.

"Hey," she said, sliding from behind the wheel and practically into his arms. "I was just going to call you."

"So you got my calls?"

She laughed. "I got them all. Yes. They very nearly melted my cell phone."

"I missed you."

Well, jeez, now, in addition to her phone, he was melting her heart. "I'm glad," she said softly. "I missed you, too. Hey, I want you to meet somebody very special to me."

By now, Doug had climbed out of the passenger side of the van and was walking toward them, looking once again like a grinning Cheshire cat.

"Doug, I'd like you to meet David," she said. "David, this is Doug, the very best father in the world."

They shook hands, and Doug immediately said, "I've heard a lot about you, young man. Libby tells me you designed that gorgeous building across the street."

David lowered his head and consulted the pebbles beneath his feet for a moment before he said, "Yes, sir."

"Well, let me congratulate you." Doug angled his head northward. "She's a real beauty."

"Thank you, sir."

"I'll leave you two alone. I never did finish up today's mail in the office so I guess I better get to it." Doug kissed Libby's forehead, then turned to walk away.

"Nice guy," David said softly.

Libby nodded. "Yes, he is."

"I really did miss you today." He reached out to touch the back of his fingertips to her cheek.

There was a slightly yearning quality to his voice that Libby had never heard before, and judging from the expression on his face, he really had missed her.

"Good," she said. "I'm glad you did."

"Come back to the hotel with me," he said, pulling her into his arms and burying his face in her neck. "We can play in the hot tub again, and then see what else the kitchen can come up with for our dinner."

Libby made a little humming sound deep in her throat. "That sounds divine, but…"

He lifted his head. "But what?"

"I just hate to leave Doug alone this evening."

"Is he ill?"

"Oh, no. Nothing like that. The man's healthy as a horse. It's just that we're working on this wonderful idea, and there's so much to discuss."

"What sort of idea?" he asked.

"Well…"

Just then Doug walked around the rear corner of the office, jingling a set of car keys in his hand. "I'm off to see Elizabeth now, Libby. I'll probably stay there and have supper with her while I tell her about today. If you don't need me back here, I'll just go on home afterward, honey."

"Give her my love," Libby said. "And let me know what she says, Doug, will you? As soon as you can."

"Will do." He appeared only a bit stiff and awkward as he angled into the driver's seat of his old Pontiac. "Nice meeting you, David," he said just before turning the key in the ignition.

"Hope to see you again, sir," David responded before he smiled down at Libby. "Looks to me like somebody's a free woman this evening."

The free woman laughed, a luscious sound if ever David had heard one, then took his hand to lead him around the office and into the center of the pebbled drive. The place was deserted. As it should have been, David thought.

Libby made a broad and sweeping gesture with her arm.

"Pick a cabin, my dear. Any cabin," she said. "Or choose a number between one and six."

"What?"

"Choose a cabin, David. We've got the whole place to ourselves." She grinned up at him. "My personal choice would be Three, since it's my lucky number, not to mention the fact that the shower in there still works pretty well."

David decided that his brain was probably operating inefficiently because his bloodstream was shunting its contents below his waist at the moment. She wanted to make love here, in this squalor, rather than in the silk sheets and wall-to-wall splendor of the Marquis across the street? Make love *here?* Was she nuts?

Maybe the better question from David's point of view was could he even perform here under the circumstances, knowing he was making a concerted effort to acquire the crummy Haven View in order to tear it down.

Early this afternoon, after going through the paperwork, he'd sent Jeff, in the guise of a real-estate investor, to pay a visit to Libby's aunt Elizabeth in the rehab facility, where he had offered the woman whatever price she wanted for the place. "Name your price," Jeff had told her mere seconds before the old lady called the front desk to have this shady weasel escorted from her room.

Having struck out with Aunt Elizabeth, David then opted for plan B, and had directed Jeff to prepare a statement for the municipal council, requesting this acreage to be officially designated as blighted, and thus eligible for condemnation and immediate demolition.

The proposal to the municipal council also included the Halstrom's promise to develop the condemned property, its subsequent usage to be determined at a later date. Jeff was probably working on the document right this minute, dotting *i*'s and crossing *t*'s.

David let go of a long sigh. It wasn't that he didn't know he was working at cross purposes with Libby, but suddenly his deception hit him quite physically. He could feel his erection withering at the mere thought of Libby's reaction to this news. She'd hate him for it. And the sad fact was that she'd have every right to hate him.

"I need to make a quick call," he said, reaching for his phone, then flicking it open and hitting Jeff's number. "This will only take me a minute."

She was still smiling when she said, "Well, you better make it fast, mister, or else I reserve the right to choose the cabin."

He tried to smile back, but his face felt nearly frozen. When Jeff picked up the call on the third ring, David said simply, "Stop working on the current project. I'll get back to you about it later. Understand?"

Jeff uttered a surprised, almost strangled yes, then David snapped the phone closed and dropped it back into his pocket.

"Project?" Libby's lovely face was turned up to his, curiosity sparkling in her blue eyes. "Are you working on another hotel, David?"

"Something like that," he said, finally managing to smile. "But at the moment, my love, I'm working on something much more important."

"What?" she asked.

"This."

He gathered her up, held her closely against his chest, and said, "Show me the way to lucky Number Three."

* * *

Libby lingered in the shower, almost too embarrassed to leave the bathroom and face David. Had she ever had a worse idea in her entire life? Why would anyone ask the man responsible for the mirrored and glorious piece of architecture across the highway, the man who'd wined and dined her in its glorious penthouse, to even set foot in this chamber of horrors? What had she been thinking?

The door had opened with a long, drawn-out squeak comparable to a Boris Karloff movie, and then, as they stepped inside, the powerful odor of pine and Lysol had smacked both of them in the face. David, bless his heart, had tried not to cough, but it wasn't possible. Libby herself had had an immediate sneezing fit before running into the bathroom and locking the door.

Now, the fluorescent light over the sink was making an odd, erratic buzzing sound and the toilet, just to the right of the tub, gurgled every once in a while even though she hadn't used it. The plastic shower curtain, with its sand dollars and starfish and various ocean flora, looked so pitiful hanging there that Libby had to keep her eyes closed most of the time she was in the shower.

For one grim and painful moment, she decided that tearing this whole wretched place down was the obvious and only solution. Surely she could make her aunt Elizabeth see that.

But then she knew it was impossible. Aunt Elizabeth, as always, would stand her ground—this ground—her precious turf—the same way she always did when she insisted that Uncle Joe would soon be coming home. Libby couldn't make her change. Lord knew Doug hadn't been able to change her in all their decades together.

When all was said and done, there really wasn't much Libby could do other than go with the flow. And the flow right now, coming down from the shower head, seemed to be welling up in the tub because of a drain that wasn't working properly. She swore under her breath, then yanked the faucets off, hardly caring at the moment if she broke them or not.

She grabbed a towel—thin from years of wear and washing—and did her best to dry off. After raking her fingers through her damp hair, she wrapped the ratty towel around herself and opened the door.

David was sitting on the edge of a twin bed, leaning forward to change channels on the small television, something he probably hadn't done in years.

"Welcome to 1970," Libby said only half in jest. "Do you feel like you're in a time warp? Like you've been transported back several decades?"

"Nope," he answered as he punched off the television, then reached out his arms toward her. "I feel like Prince Charming waiting for his Cinderella."

"David," Libby said softly, hugging her towel tightly around herself. "I'm truly sorry that I insisted on this. I have no idea why it seemed so important to me, but I'm ready to leave, this very minute, if that's what you'd prefer."

He stood, and then took several strides across the gold shag carpet, closing the distance between them. "Actually, I'd prefer to make love to you, Libby darlin'. Here. Now."

She tilted her head up, passed the tip of her tongue across her lips, inviting his kiss. Craving his kiss. "Yes," she said. "Here. And right now."

What did it matter *where* she was, she thought, when David's kisses made her forget *who* she was. She released her grip on the damp towel and let it drop to the floor.

David stepped back. Without even touching her, he ravished her with just his eyes, whose color had deepened to a dark forest green. And his gaze alone caused Libby's stomach to clench with a ravenous hunger, as if she hadn't eaten for weeks. She'd never wanted a man the way she wanted this one. She never even knew, in all her thirty years, that such all-consuming desire was possible.

As he had before, David loved her slowly, exploring every part of her body as if she were the first woman he'd ever encountered, while leading her to discover sensations she'd never felt before.

And as before, it was Libby who, when pushed to the edge by his slow hands, by his warm tongue, by the feel of him so hard and deep inside of her, pulled David with her for the long tumble through magnificent fireworks and bright shooting stars.

Libby let herself drift into sleep, thinking she never wanted this man to leave her. If he did, she just might have to follow him if it meant going to the ends of the earth.

Seven

When Libby offered to fix dinner for him—which translated to popping two cartons of frozen macaroni and cheese into the microwave and seeing what she could come up with for a salad from the contents of the fridge—David politely declined, then offered a far better solution to the problem of dinner.

"Let's go across the street."

Libby laughed. "I thought you'd never ask."

He didn't take her up to the penthouse this time, but rather directly into the Marquis' shining new, state-of-the-art kitchen, where the sous chef who'd fed them so well the previous evening was still on duty.

The young man snapped to his feet the moment they walked in.

"How're y'all?" he said, revealing a wide smile along with a southern accent.

"We're fine," David answered, "and we're famished. Mind if we look around?"

"It's your kitchen. Whatever you find, sir, I'll be more than happy to prepare. Kitchen's are way better for cooking in than for sitting around in."

David took Libby's hand and led her deep into the inner workings of the facility. She'd never been in a restaurant kitchen before, and it was a whole new world for her.

"I'm not a very good cook," she confessed while gazing into a huge stainless-steel refrigerator that was crammed with things she couldn't even identify.

David, close beside her, chuckled. "So I gathered."

"My aunt Elizabeth isn't either." She sighed.

"Maybe it's genetic," David said, his lips sliding into a grin and his eyes nearly twinkling. "What looks good to you? Anything strike your fancy?"

Actually nothing looked good because it wasn't cooked, and there were no pictures to consult for the final product. "You choose for us, David," she said. "As an old mac and cheese girl, I'm more than willing to defer to your expertise."

He called out to the sous chef, naming ingredients and spices and sauces that might have been Martian as far as Libby knew. Then he told him, "We'll be in the bar. You can serve us in there."

As they left the kitchen, Libby saw David slip a bill from his pocket, fold it discretely, then place it on the table in front of the young cook.

"That's really not necessary, Mr....."

David cut him off. "Take it. It's my pleasure."

"Thank you, sir."

She glimpsed a corner of the bill in passing—a whopping hundred dollars—then tried to recall the biggest tip she'd ever bestowed on someone. Last year, she thought, two days before Christmas she'd ordered a pizza and the delivery guy had nearly fainted when she'd given him an extra twenty. She wondered now if he might actually have passed out if she'd given him a hundred.

David's hand was warm on her back as they entered the dimly lit bar. He lifted his other hand to signal the bartender.

"Two Merlots," he said. "The 2004s."

"Yessir."

Libby slid into the same soft leather booth where they'd sat before. It was beginning to feel comfortable. Probably too comfortable, she thought. With any other man she would have been content to enjoy the here and now, never giving a thought to tomorrow or next week, and certainly not worrying about the next year. Her intense feelings for David, however, were making her contemplate the future and that made her feel horribly vulnerable.

He settled beside her, draping his arm around her shoulders, his thigh wedged against hers. "It won't be this quiet here in a little less than two weeks. In fact, it'll be hard to find even a single seat in here."

"Well, that's good, isn't it?"

"Good for the hotel," he said. "But it sure puts a

cramp in our style, Libby. I'm enjoying having the place all to ourselves. What about you?"

"I am, too," she said. "Of course, there's always Cabin Three."

"Not if I can help it," David said, one eyebrow arching just as the bartender approached with a bottle of wine and two glasses.

He aimed the dark bottle perfectly toward David, allowing him to see the label and give a nod of consent before he proceeded to open it, almost magically with a corkscrew and to pour a bit into a glass. David tasted it, then nodded, after which the bartender filled both their glasses.

They'd barely taken their first sip of the rich red wine before the sous chef was sliding a gorgeous salad, edged with fat purple grapes and orange slices, in front of them. He added two salad forks, two stiff linen napkins and a small basket of peppered croutons before he disappeared back into his kitchen.

Libby took another swallow of wine, then set her glass down and said, "Do you know what impresses me the most about this hotel?"

"No," he said. "Tell me."

"The fact that everyone who works here, at least everyone I've seen so far, appears to be ridiculously happy. That's just not normal, David. In my experience, most of the people who work in hotels are crabby if not downright glum."

"Well, I suspect it's because the place hasn't opened yet, and the work schedule is still relatively light. But the Halstrom hotels haven't had many complaints about their staff. They're paid well above the normal scale for hotel workers."

"I wish I could say the same for the Haven View where we all work for free."

Libby picked up her fork to try the salad just as two women appeared in the entrance of the bar. Both of them were absolutely stunning, as if they'd just stepped out from a page of a fashion magazine. The statuesque blonde wore gold bracelets up to her elbows and pencil-thin jeans with leather boots that went all the way to her knees. The brunette beside her sported a long suede skirt, a to-die-for fur jacket and a pair of open-toed pumps with what seemed like six-inch heels.

Libby could hardly take her eyes off of them, but she managed to just in time to see the bartender flick his hand in their direction as if to signal them to leave. At nearly the same moment David began to punch numbers into his cell phone while swearing under his breath.

"Get down here. The bar. Now," he said before snapping the phone closed and breathing one more curse.

"What in the world is going on?" she asked.

He glared at the brass and glass door of the bar as if he were trying to melt it. "Hookers," he said.

"Oh."

She looked again at the two incredibly beautiful women poised in the doorway, then back at David.

"How can you tell?" she asked, her voice barely more than a whisper, as if she wouldn't want the two women to overhear. As far as Libby knew, the only "working girls" she'd ever seen were on television and in the movies.

Before David could answer her question, the sous chef reappeared, balancing a large round tray shoulder high. At the sight of the beauties in the doorway, it was all he could do to keep hold of the tray while still maintaining his own precarious balance. China and silverware clattered madly as he maneuvered the tray to an adjacent table just in the nick of time.

"Looks like the Marquis is officially on the map, sir," he muttered as he set the plates in front of Libby and David. "What can you do, eh? It was just a matter of time."

David's only response was another guttural curse.

"Enjoy your meal," the chef said, taking one last, lingering look at the visitors before disappearing back into his kitchen.

Gazing down at her dinner, Libby didn't have the vaguest idea what it was although it truly did look like a work of art. She was about to ask David what he'd ordered for them when the elevator door chimed and opened, revealing Jeff, her limousine driver, who stomped out to confront the two women.

What he did, actually, was smile broadly as he looped an arm around each of their shoulders, somehow effortlessly turning them away from the bar and toward the main hotel entrance. Only seconds later he and the women were out of sight.

"That was my driver," Libby said, somewhat astonished. "That was Jeff."

"He obviously moonlights as a bouncer, and a damn

good one, too," David responded, sounding at least fifty degrees cooler than he had a few moments ago. "Try your sea bass. It's delicious."

So that's what was on her plate, Libby thought. She picked up her fork and tried a tiny bite, only to discover that it was indeed delicious. Still, she could have done without the brussels sprouts, even though they did look beautiful.

It was over a brandy after dinner that Libby told him about her *absolutely amazing* plan for the motel. All the while David listened, he hoped his face wasn't betraying his feelings, which at that particular moment were bordering on panic and possible murder.

Now— Now—! she wanted to bus in a small army of convicted felons to work across from the Marquis every day. She might as well have said she'd arranged for a chain gang dressed in black and white stripes to pick up trash in front of his hotel. If he hadn't known better, he would've thought she was deliberately trying to drive the Halstrom Corporation out of business, at least here in St. Louis.

"It's a terrific idea, isn't it?" Her face was glowing, only partly from the brandy. "The motel gets a total makeover and Father James's clients get the experience they need. Everybody wins."

Except me, David thought. And he stood to lose millions upon millions, not to mention the deleterious effect on his company's reputation.

"Have you run this past anybody yet?" he asked her. "An attorney? Or someone on the town council?"

She shook her head. "It's still a bit early. Father James's board of directors doesn't meet until next week."

"In my experience," he said, "boards are more than willing to argue a single decision for several meetings, even the insignificant ones."

Libby took another sip of her brandy, then sighed. "And then, of course, there's Aunt Elizabeth who could kill the whole deal with a single 'no.' Doug was supposedly talking to her about it this afternoon, but since I haven't heard from him, I suspect he chickened out."

"Smart guy," David said. "You'll need to increase your insurance coverage to the max, you know, considering who'll be on the motel property. You'll need at least several million in liability coverage, just for openers."

"I hadn't even thought about that."

And that's what David was counting on. The sooner he could toss a monkey wrench into this latest plan of hers, the happier he was going to be.

"Well," he said, "no sense even thinking about any of the details until all your ducks are in a row."

Dead ducks, he dearly hoped.

In the lobby outside the bar David wrapped his arms around her, nuzzled his face into her neck, and then whispered, "So, my place or yours?"

Libby sighed. It had been such a long day, and as much as David was moving into her heart, he was also an incredible distraction at the moment from the things she needed to do as far as the Haven View was concerned. She tilted her head back, and it pained her to see that his smile had already been extinguished in anticipation of her response.

"Come home with me," she said softly. "I'm not guaranteeing you wild jungle sex, but I will fix you a cup of hot chocolate and I promise I won't snore."

"It's a deal," he said. "And in exchange for the hot chocolate, I'll give you the very best back rub of your life."

"Mmm," she moaned softly. "I think I could fall in love with you just for that."

"Good."

Eight

When Libby awoke the next morning, she slipped on a robe—her good cotton eyelet robe as opposed to the ratty flannel one—and wandered out into the office only to discover that David was already dressed and on the phone.

"I'm having breakfast sent over from the Marquis," he said, interrupting his conversation. "I've got the kitchen on the phone right now. Anything special you'd like?"

As someone who was used to deciding between instant oatmeal and cold cereal every morning, Libby thought she'd died and gone to pig heaven.

"Anything?" she asked, just to be sure she wasn't hallucinating or still asleep, dreaming.

David grinned. "Well, anything short of scrambled

ostrich eggs or freshly caught shark steak, I'd say. Just name your pleasure, darlin'."

"Other than you, you mean."

"I'm available," he said.

Now Libby grinned. "Actually, not to disappoint you, but I'm truly starving. Could I have… Let's see. What about a small omelet with hash browns and rye toast? No, wait. Whole-wheat toast with strawberry jam."

He relayed her order into the phone, then asked her, "Bacon or sausages?"

"Bacon." Her mouth was already watering. She hoped she wasn't drooling on the floor.

"Orange juice or pineapple juice?"

"Pineapple," she said, suddenly wondering how long it would take her—once David left town—to get over being so incredibly pampered and rottenly spoiled. Probably forever, she decided.

She walked behind the desk where he sat and bent to kiss the top of his head. He closed his phone, angled his arm around her waist and pulled her closer to him for a moment, burying his face in the folds of her robe.

"I've got a few more calls I need to make, Libby," he said, his breath warm on her hip. "But after that, I'm all yours. We'll do whatever you'd like to do."

"Sounds good to me. I think I'll go take a quick shower before our breakfast comes."

Once in the shower, Libby wondered if it was only yesterday that she'd wept for a solid hour in here while the world, with Haven View at its center, seemed to be falling apart? And then, in a matter of hours, everything had tilted a hundred and eighty degrees and her despair had turned to outright happiness and bright hope for the future. It was like living on a roller coaster.

She shouldn't get too cocky, she told herself. Who knew just what might happen next?

What happened was David got summoned to New York. He'd stayed on the phone while he ate his breakfast, every once in a while throwing her a frustrated glance and mouthing the word *sorry* when he wasn't cursing at whoever was on the other end of the connection.

She honestly didn't mind. It was wonderful to be able to concentrate completely on the best omelet she'd ever had in her entire life. It was as divine as any dessert. She was just chewing the last bit of bacon when David swore once more and stood up, sending the motel's old desk chair rolling backward behind him.

"I've got to leave for New York in—" he consulted his watch "—forty-five damn minutes."

"Oh, David." Libby could feel her mouth turning down at the corners, matching his expression. "On such short notice?"

"It can't be helped. I'm sorry, sweetheart. I'll be back late tonight or early tomorrow morning."

He was already on his way to the door when Libby jumped up to kiss him goodbye in passing.

"I'll be back," he said.

"I'll be here."

Then, in a spray of driveway pebbles and the roar of the Jag, he was gone.

Well, she supposed an architect couldn't do a proper job over the telephone, and it was good that he was so necessary for whatever he'd been summoned for. Libby thought perhaps she'd go to the library today and get some books relating to architecture. It couldn't hurt to be able to discuss it somewhat intelligently with David.

She called Doug then, to see what had transpired last evening during his visit with Aunt Elizabeth.

"I couldn't do it," he said rather mournfully. "We were having such a nice dinner that I just didn't want to spoil it."

"I figured as much," Libby replied.

"What's the rush, honey? Father James's board isn't even going to meet until next week, and I doubt they'll vote on it the very same night. They'll want to think about it for a while. Probably even want to come out and see the place."

She couldn't help but laugh. "You make really good excuses, Doug, for a chicken."

"I admit it."

"Well, you're right, I guess. I don't suppose there's any huge rush, and there's certainly no sense in upsetting Aunt Elizabeth before we absolutely have to."

"Atta girl," he said. "I'm having supper with her again tonight. I'll give her a big hug for you."

After Libby hung up, she glanced outside and saw that her painters had arrived. She was tempted to tell them to take the day off because there would probably be new painters in a week or so, who would be re-painting all the cabins, inside and out, to better learn their craft. Then she decided against it, thinking she might somehow be undermining David's authority, which was the last thing she wanted to do.

With nothing else on her immediate to-do list, she gathered up the breakfast dishes, rinsed them and put them in a box in order to return them to the hotel. Who knew? The chef might be preparing some wonderful experiment for lunch, and she'd arrive just in time to sample it.

Probably not a good idea, she decided, since it wouldn't take long for her to put on twenty or thirty pounds. How in the world could David stay so fit and trim? she wondered. And heaven only knew what Mr. D. E. Halstrom must weigh after indulging for so many years in gourmet meals at his various hotels. The man was probably a blimp.

She left the box of dishes at the front desk of the hotel when no one was looking because she didn't know how to explain why they were in her possession.

After skulking away, she went to the county library, searching through the stacks and the magazine files. It had been a long time since she'd been here, probably since her senior year in high school. She'd forgotten how much she loved this place with its wonderful lighting, the subtle smell of its wooden shelves in the main reading room and the riffling sound of pages turning all around her.

After several hours she learned more about architecture than ever before in her thirty years, from the great Pyramids in Egypt all the way to Louis Sullivan, Frank Lloyd Wright, I. M. Pei and beyond.

Every detail of the occupation fascinated her, not to mention that the research gave her plenty of wonderful ideas for future books of photographs, and a glimpse into David's professional world and a much deeper appreciation of the beautiful glass façade of the Marquis. Libby couldn't wait to discuss it all with him when he returned from New York.

It amazed her, actually, that he seemed so reticent, so truly reluctant to discuss his business. She could hardly say the same about herself, Libby thought. A simple question about cameras or photography in general usually elicited a lengthy, if not too detailed and probably boring, reply from her.

Not so with David. Come to think of it, he had volunteered very little about himself or his profession. Other than telling her he was originally from Texas, which was pretty much a given from his accent, Libby knew almost nothing about him or his family or anything else for that matter.

Well, she thought, slapping closed a heavy coffee-table book on twentieth century midwestern architecture, they were going to have some interesting conversations once he returned from New York. And oh, how she hoped it would be soon because she dreadfully missed him already after just a few hours.

She checked out a few large-print mysteries she thought her aunt Elizabeth might enjoy, then walked out to her car. Much as she hated to admit it, it was a lovely autumn day. With the door open and the late afternoon sun shining on her legs, Libby called the newspaper, punching in the extension for the little darkroom's single phone.

"Is Hannah around?" she asked the man who answered. She didn't recognize his voice.

"Nope. Sorry. She left for the day," he said. "Anything I can help you with?"

"I don't know. Maybe you can. Hannah was going to develop some pictures for me. I was just wondering if she had a chance to do them yet."

"Let me take a look in her secret stash box," he said with a little conspiratorial laugh. "Well, I see two cans of Fuji 400 film here. They yours?"

Libby sighed. "Yes, they're mine. Thanks for your help. I'll give Hannah a call tomorrow."

She'd been hoping the prints would be done and that she could drive downtown, pick them up and then spend a few hours gazing at the furtive long-lens photos she taken of David while he sat on the riverbank in Hannibal.

No such luck.

So Libby returned to the Haven View, where she changed back into her ratty flannel robe and fuzzy slippers and then microwaved some macaroni and cheese. It tasted as horrible as she imagined it would. And the salad she managed to cobble together and douse with bottled dressing wasn't much better.

How could she have become so terribly spoiled in a mere few days? she wondered. This did not bode well at all for her future, whether alone or with a mate.

Maybe when she went back to the library, she thought, she ought to get some cookbooks in order to compete, even minimally, with the gourmet kitchen across the street.

The clunky black telephone on the front desk woke her at eleven o'clock that night. Libby stumbled out of the bedroom to answer it, her immediate thought being that something was wrong with her aunt. When she heard David's voice she didn't know whether to feel enormously relieved or tremendously happy. Both, she decided.

"I miss you," he said. "I had hoped to get back tonight, but that's not happening."

"I miss you, too," Libby said. "How's the Big Apple?"

"Damn lonely without you. I wish you were here."

She couldn't help but smile at that. "Aw, David. I wish I were, too. Hey, you're lucky you're not *here.* I finally had that frozen macaroni and cheese for my dinner this evening, and it was horrid."

"Just call across the street, sweetheart. I'll call the Marquis as soon as we hang up, and tell the kitchen staff to expect it. Order whatever you want, whenever you want it. If you have any problems at all, just call me."

Libby's first instinct was to tell him no because she didn't want to get too terribly used to such a luxury, only to have it disappear when David disappeared. Her actual reply was based more on the thought of, "What kind of idiot would say no to such an offer?"

"Thank you, David," she said. "Although to tell you

the truth, I'd rather have you right this minute than any five-star meal I could imagine."

"I'll be back tomorrow," he said. "Late afternoon, most likely. We'll have dinner and then I plan to make love to you as if the world were going to end in twenty-four hours."

A shiver coursed down her spine. "Is that a threat or a promise?" she asked.

"It's both," he said. "I'll call you just as soon as I get back tomorrow."

Nine

Libby slept in the next morning, something she didn't often do. Since it was Saturday, there were no painters to wake her and the usual morning rattle and clatter of heading-to-work traffic on the highway was merely a low weekend hum.

She thought about calling the Marquis to order breakfast or perhaps brunch. Another omelet sounded so good. She wondered if they had Canadian bacon. Ooh, and melon balls. Libby was practically drooling when she finally decided against it, though. Some-how—she couldn't say exactly why—it seemed to be taking advantage of David's generosity, particularly when he wasn't here to share with her. She knew, when she'd tell him, he'd say that it was foolish, but it was still the way she felt. Had he been with her just then, she'd have ordered double everything.

So, instead of calling the Marquis, she got dressed and drove to her favorite donut shop where she chose a small box of assorted glazed delights to share with Aunt Elizabeth. It was almost impossible not to eat one of them on her way to the rehab facility.

She was glad to see that the crabby roommate wasn't there, but neither was her aunt. Unable to resist the donuts a moment longer, Libby perched on the edge of her aunt's bed and practically inhaled two of them. She was guiltily contemplating a third when the roommate entered, banging her wheelchair against both sides of the door, the dresser and the nightstand before she reached her bed.

"Need some help?" Libby asked as the woman clenched the arms of her wheelchair and began to rise from it.

"Nah. Thanks just the same." She went from chair to bed fairly effortlessly, as if there were nothing terribly wrong with her. "Your aunt's getting her hair done in the little shop downstairs. I don't expect her back for another hour or maybe even more. Those donuts look pretty good."

Libby got up and held the box out for her. "Have one," she said. "They're delicious."

"Thanks. Don't mind if I do."

The woman took three with one quick swoop of her hand, which left one sad little glazed Long John for Aunt Elizabeth. Libby stashed it in the nightstand drawer, then left her aunt a note, saying she'd likely be back tomorrow. With more donuts.

In no huge rush to get home, she took the long way back to Haven View and entered the office just as the phone was ringing. She nearly pole-vaulted over the desk in the hope that the caller would be David. Then, when she heard Doug's voice, she tried her very best not to sound the least bit disappointed.

"Hey, kiddo," he said. "How's my girl?"

"I'm fine," she said.

"I got you a little photo gig, Libby, if you're interested."

As always, this was Doug's way of supplementing her income. If he knew someone who was having a party or some other sort of occasion, he'd convince them that it ought to be memorialized in pictures. Libby usually accepted, more to make Doug happy than to receive the usual few twenties jammed in her hand when she left whatever affair she photographed.

"You'll love this," he said. "They're having a big wingding tomorrow where Elizabeth's staying, and the staff said they'd love some good pictures."

Oh, joy.

"Well, I'd planned to go out there to see her anyway, so I'll just take my camera with me," she said. "What time?"

"It starts at noon, but I don't expect the affair will really get rolling until twelve-thirty or thereabouts."

"Okay. I'll see you there. Or do you want me to pick you up?" she asked.

"Nah. I'm going out there early to help decorate. And, honey, why don't you bring that nice young architect of yours. The more, the merrier."

"He's in New York, Doug. But if he's back tomorrow, I'll ask him. See you there."

Libby hung up, wondering if she had the courage to introduce David to the rest of her wild and wacky geriatric world. At the same time, she wondered about his family, too. Were his parents still alive? Did he have sisters and brothers and a slew of nieces and nephews? Did he have a wonderful dog when he was a little boy? Did he have an ex-wife somewhere? Or children? And, if so, how come he never talked about any of them?

Maybe he just didn't feel comfortable enough with her yet, although she didn't know how that was possible, considering the intimacy they'd shared.

The whole notion of finding out more about his personal life seemed increasingly urgent in light of the fact that he'd probably be leaving St. Louis soon. Then, as she had before, Libby banished that thought from her head. At least as much as she could.

She was going through the mail when she heard a car come to a stop out in front. It wasn't the elegant purr of David's car, but maybe he'd taken a taxi from the airport, she thought, as she went to the office door. No such luck. It wasn't David, and she didn't recognize the man getting out on the driver's side of a white sedan.

"May I help you?" she called. "We're closed right now." She pointed to the sign.

"Sorry. I didn't want to disturb you." He reached into a pocket of his windbreaker and produced a card.

He held it out to her as he walked toward the door. "I'm John Tazwell. I do occasional inspection work for the municipality."

"You're here to inspect the motel?"

"Mostly just to take a look around," he said. "Apparently there have been some complaints about this place."

"Who complained?" she asked sharply.

The man shrugged. "They don't tell me that. They just tell me to go out and have a look at a property. So, here I am."

He was having a look even as he spoke, and to judge from his expression, he wasn't too thrilled with what he saw. She was still miffed that somebody had complained to the local officials rather than to her or to Aunt Elizabeth and Doug. It struck her as extremely rude and underhanded.

"Place looks its age," the inspector said.

Libby couldn't help but laugh. "That's a nice way to say it's fairly downtrodden, I guess. But we're working on that. We really are. It won't be long before everything here looks brand-new."

"New roofs?"

"Yes."

He pointed to the broken lamppost. "Planning to take care of that?"

"Definitely. It's on my list," she said. Actually she ought to bill David for that since he'd frightened her half to death and made her drop the glass.

"You'll need a permit for the roofs." He pointed at all six. "The aldermen voted that in a couple months ago, and most people aren't aware of it."

Libby now counted herself among the clueless. "A permit?"

"It's not complicated, but it needs to be tended to before any work is done, otherwise there's a hefty fine. I know you don't want that. Will there be any plumbing alterations? Showers, tubs, sinks?"

He fired question after question at her, all of which she answered with yes, no or oops.

Finally he closed with, "See that it all gets taken care of. You know, I've always liked this old place. My grandparents stayed here once in the sixties. I can remember visiting them, and using that old swing set." His gaze narrowed as he looked closer at the dilapidated little playground. "Same one, I guess. Imagine that. You're going to replace it, right? I mean, you wouldn't want any little kids to get hurt on that old thing."

By then, Libby could only nod affirmatively. People seemed to be inventing problems and restrictions, simply pulling them out of a hat like big white rabbits in order to torment her at this point.

"Thanks for your time, ma'am. I'll be checking back in about two or three weeks."

Oh, joy, Libby thought.

An hour later she was on her way downtown to pick up her prints from Hannah, who had left a message while Libby was being interrogated by the inspector general. Now how in the world was she going to tell Aunt Elizabeth that the Haven View wasn't up to code in a thousand different ways? She shook her head. Like Scarlett, she'd think about that tomorrow, or maybe even the day after.

As she passed a major shopping mall along the highway, it occurred to her that she really ought to get some new clothes. New man—new clothes. Wasn't there some unwritten rule about that? If not, then there ought to be.

By now, after just a few days and nights, David had pretty much seen her entire wardrobe. Since she hadn't been going out very much in the past year or so, the peach evening dress and various combinations of jeans and tees and sweaters were the sum of it. Maybe she should splurge and get some sexy underwear. Lacy and black. No. Wait. Lacy and red! Would he like that? Probably, she decided, so she planned to stop on her way back home.

Downtown, she parked on the street, fed the meter and then practically raced up the several flights of back stairs to Hannah's dark little domain.

"You're lucky you didn't get here five minutes later," Hannah said. "I was just about to close up and go home."

"Sorry," Libby said, wishing now that she'd used the elevator instead of the stairs. Jeez. She needed to get back in shape.

Hannah made a dismissive signal with her hand. "Don't worry about it. It's not like I have a great date or anything tonight. Truth is I was planning to microwave some popcorn and watch *Gone with the Wind* for the five-hundredth time. Join me, if you want, Libby."

She would have, and quite happily, if she hadn't thought that David would be returning within the next few hours. "Maybe next time, Hannah. I've only seen

Gone with the Wind three hundred times. Clearly, I need to catch up with you."

"Your pictures are over here, Libby. I wasn't snooping or anything, but it was pretty hard not to tell you were in Hannibal. I haven't been there since I was in fourth or fifth grade. Was it fun?"

"It was a blast," Libby said, moving across the little darkroom to the designated shelf. "We really had a great time."

"Who'd you go with? Anybody I know?"

"Oh, just a friend. Not anybody associated with the paper. I'm sure you don't know him."

Libby picked up a few glossy pictures. Tom Sawyer's house, Tom Sawyer's white fence, Tom Sawyer this, Huckleberry Finn that. What she wanted to see was David.

When she reached for the next stack of prints, Hannah said, "Hard to imagine that Halstrom guy in a place like Hannibal, isn't it?"

Libby's hand halted in mid air. "I beg your pardon?" She was sure she hadn't heard correctly. "What did you say?"

"Halstrom. You know. His new hotel is only right across the highway from your place. The great and grandiose Marquis. The mirrored monster." Hannah's arms were crossed and her expression seemed to indicate that Libby might be going deaf or blind, if she wasn't both already.

"I know what it is, Hannah. I just don't know what you're talking about. What does it have to do with Hannibal?"

Libby, of course, knew what it had to do with Hannibal as far as she was concerned. It had to do with David. But there was no way her friend could know that. Was there? She tried hard to recall if Hannah had ever expressed any interest in architecture, but as far as she remembered the woman's only interests were photography and old movies.

Hannah reached out and pulled a photo from the stack. She pointed to the man on the riverbank. "Him," she said.

Libby looked closer. Oh, it was such a good likeness. She'd managed to capture that aura of *I'm in charge here* that so often surrounded him, and there was even a hint, just the slightest, of those adorable smile lines. For a moment, she almost forgot that Hannah was standing next to her, staring at the same photo.

"Him," she said again, stabbing her index finger at the image.

"I see him," Libby responded irritably. "For heaven's sake. I'm the one who took the picture."

"Well, what was he doing in Hannibal?"

Libby rolled her eyes. What a stupid question. "He was sightseeing, of course. What else do visitors do there?"

Hannah snorted. "D. E. Halstrom was sightseeing in Hannibal, Missouri? I mean, it's a neat little place, but it's not exactly on the A list for travelers. What? Has he been to the Eiffel Tower and the Taj Mahal and the Pyramids too many times?"

"I think you're confused," Libby said.

"Well, somebody is." She jabbed her finger again.

"This is the Halstrom hotel guy. The one who's worth billions."

"His name is David."

"Yeah, I know. David Edward Halstrom."

For a second, Libby felt as if she were in a time warp or a science-fiction movie. Everything she knew suddenly seemed to have lost its basis in reality. Her whole head felt like a dark cavern, and her memory seemed like nothing but a blank slate.

Hannah was staring at her. "Hey, are you okay?" she asked. "Do you need to sit down? How about a glass of water? You look like you're about to pass out, Libby."

"That's David Halstrom?" Libby asked. There was a slight tremor in her hand as she pointed to the picture.

"Jeez." Hannah slapped her own forehead. "What have I been saying all this time?"

Libby didn't respond as she gathered up all the photographs and jammed them into her handbag. Finally, she managed to take a deep breath and thank Hannah for developing them.

"I hate to rush," she said then, "but I've really got to get back to the motel. Doug's been there alone all afternoon." It was a lie, of course, but she didn't know what else to say.

"No problem. Hey, I'll walk out with you. Just let me get the lights."

While Hannah busied herself extinguishing bulb after bulb, Libby practically ran for the exit and disappeared down the stairs.

Ten

David looked at his watch for the twentieth time in the past few minutes, and the answer it gave him was the same each time. It's later, you idiot, and she's still not here.

He'd called the Haven View line repeatedly this afternoon on his way back from New York, and each time he listened to unanswered ringing followed by the tape of Libby's slightly-sultry voice saying, "Please leave a message," he'd felt abandoned somehow. Abandoned? It was a ridiculous notion, actually. Almost bizarre. Even when his own father died when David was eighteen and still really a kid, he hadn't felt abandoned. He'd grieved, and then had simply gotten on with what he needed to do.

It barely made sense to him that his usual tightly controlled emotions were suddenly so flimsy and so on edge. Most of the meetings in New York had been dismal and non-productive because he—the boss—wasn't able to fully concentrate on matters at hand. Frankly, he hadn't been able to concentrate at all.

"So, the property is available, David, and highly likely at a relatively good price if we decide to move quickly. I believe speed is of the essence with this one. What do you think?"

"Which property?"

His vice-president in charge of acquisitions swallowed hard and then had tried to disguise a rather long and impatient sigh. "Um. The building on the Upper East Side. The one pictured there up on the screen."

David had blinked at the enormous image of the twenty-story tan brick building right before his eyes, and wondered how long he'd been looking at it without even seeing it. What did he think? Good lord. He wished he knew.

"It depends. What's your ballpark estimate for renovations?" he asked.

The silence in the conference room had been almost palpable then, and he knew those figures had already been thoroughly discussed while he was off in his own little mental wonderland.

Idiot.

So, he'd stood up then, rather brusquely and announced that he had a raging headache. Any decision on this particular project would simply have to wait for further discussion when his schedule permitted. Then he'd stalked out of the room more like a king than the joker he truly was at the moment.

Was this what it felt like to be in love? He shook his head and nearly laughed out loud because it seemed such a juvenile question for a thirty-five-year-old man to be asking himself. He had more than his share of experience in loving, but never before in the falling part of it. Was he falling in love with Libby Jost?

If that was the case, David wasn't sure he cared for it one bit. His temperament, he was fairly sure at his age, wasn't well suited to such emotional ups and downs and that went double where his business ventures were concerned. They'd no doubt lose the Upper East Side property that was the subject of today's meeting because of his damn love-fueled daydreaming and inattention. It was pretty obvious that this "being in love" business could get him in a world of financial trouble faster than he could blink an eye.

On the other hand, he thought, what choice did he have?

He couldn't answer that question at the moment because all he wanted was Libby. Today. Tomorrow. Forever. He sighed. He felt like a fish with a hook firmly implanted in his guts. In his heart, more specifically.

And then he heard the crunch of gravel as her minivan turned into the motel driveway. His internal hook gave a sharp, almost painful little twitch.

White-hot anger, Libby discovered, caused a person to drive much faster than usual. White-hot anger coupled with the knowledge that she'd been horribly deceived caused her to drive even faster, so it wasn't much of a surprise to see the red lights flashing behind her as she traveled west on the highway.

She had pulled over, rolled down her window and handed over her driver's license with barely a peep, fearing that in her current mood she might do or say something that would land her in jail for the next five or six years.

After she took the ticket and resumed her drive home, she thought maybe she shouldn't have been so compliant. Five or six years in jail didn't sound so bad, actually, at that particular moment. In prison, she'd have no motel problems. She'd probably meet some interesting new people in her cell block. She'd lose weight from the not-so-tasty food. And, if given access to her camera and equipment, she could get some great pictures from "inside" and perhaps even put them together in a book.

Best of all, she wouldn't have to see David "The Architect" Halstrom again. Ever.

The instant his identity had registered on her in the newspaper's darkroom, Libby thought she was going to be sick, and she'd done everything she could to get away from Hannah as quickly as her feet would carry her.

How could he have done that to her? *Why* would he have done that to her? She struggled to think of a reason, but couldn't even come close. It just didn't make sense. Why would any man worth what he was worth try to pass himself off as a mere hired hand? He might just as well have told her he was the reservations clerk at the Marquis, or the head chef, or even the elevator inspector.

She didn't like being lied to. She hated it, in fact.

What made it even worse was that he'd lied to her while he was making love to her. Libby didn't know if she could ever forgive that.

How dare he? Her every thought ended with that question. How dare he? And it was what she was thinking when she turned into the Haven View drive. Her heart tripped an extra little beat, and she swallowed hard to still it.

How dare he be here, leaning against his Jag, smiling her way as if everything were fine and dandy? She wanted to step on the accelerator, aim her van in deadly fashion and pin the bastard to his sleek green vehicle. Prison for that? No problem.

Instead she drove the minivan to the rear of the office, where she jammed it into the parking gear, grabbed the keys from the ignition and hoped to scramble into the office's back door and promptly lock it without being accosted by the wretched lizard who was lounging out in front.

No such luck.

She reached to lock the driver's door, but he already had it open a few inches.

"I thought you'd never get home," he said. "I came here straight from the airport."

How could he look so happy? Libby wondered. The man was living a lie while he was acting as innocent as a newborn babe, and—she couldn't help noticing—looking as gorgeous as a cover model. She wondered how many other women he'd deceived.

But what a weird deception, to pass oneself off as relatively poor, at least compared to the man you really were. Was he crazy? Libby felt her eyes widen in fright, and just as the question occurred to her, David took hold of her hand and almost yanked her out of the van.

"I couldn't think about anything or anyone but you, Libby, the whole time I was in New York." His green eyes almost flashed with urgency. "And then when it took you forever to get back here…"

Before he'd even finished his sentence, he was wrapping both his arms around her and drawing her against him. Libby's heart was torn between the hard warmth she'd come to yearn for and the coldness of the lies she'd just discovered. Her hands pushed against his chest even as her head tilted to receive his kiss.

"Libby, oh, Libby," he whispered just as his mouth took possession of hers.

For one long and lovely moment she didn't even have to pretend that she detested this man. She gave herself up completely to the warmth and the wonderfully familiar taste of his kiss. Once again the little electric shocks coursed through her veins and her heart battered against her ribs like a wild bird in a cage. David's arms held her so tightly that she didn't even have to stand on her own. For that long and lovely moment all was right with the world, and Libby wished that she could turn the clock back a few days, even a few hours.

Then hard facts and reality crashed back into her consciousness with a vengeance.

She pulled away from his kiss. "Stop it. Let me go."

David looked at her as if he didn't understand a single word she'd said.

"I said let me go." She flattened her hands against his chest and pushed with all her might.

"Libby, what's wrong?" he asked.

"Let. Me. Go."

He withdrew his arms, and Libby promptly took a step back, at the same time taking a deep breath.

"Now I'd be very grateful if you'd leave, David. Please get off my property."

Once more he looked at her as if her words made no sense to him at all, as if she were speaking Swahili or some ancient, dead language. As if screaming would aid his comprehension, she did just that.

"I said just go. Leave me alone."

Now David took a step back, as if he needed to see her from a different perspective. "I don't understand this at all. Why the hell are you so angry?"

"I don't want to talk about it now." She couldn't talk about it now, she knew, or she'd burst into tears like a fool. She slammed the door of the van, clutched her handbag to her chest and turned toward the office's back door. "Please, just go."

"Libby…"

"Goodbye."

"Libby. Darlin'."

She whirled around to face him. "Don't you *darlin'* me, David Halstrom. Don't you *anything* me ever again. Ever."

Then Libby marched inside, slammed the door in his face and locked it.

In the Marquis underground parking lot, David slammed the door of the Jaguar so hard that its echo was like resounding thunder in the huge concrete cavern. He took the elevator up to the lobby, then strode to the express elevator in order to reach the penthouse, greatly relieved that nobody stopped him for any reason because in his current mood he might have been capable of great bodily harm if not outright cold-blooded murder.

He stared at his reflection in the polished brass interior of the elevator, barely recognizing his own face. There was more than anger in his expression. There was a kind of pain that he'd never seen before. He'd never felt it before, either. And, by God, he never wanted to feel it again.

Once inside the penthouse, he poured himself a stiff drink and took it to the southern window, from which he glared down at the Haven View Motor Court. A part of him devoutly wished he'd never laid eyes on the shabby little place, that the Marquis' penthouse had been designed with a northern exposure, and that he'd never looked toward the south. Not once.

It wasn't true, though. And his heart skipped a significant beat just to remind him. The fact was that he had not only met Libby Jost, but he had fallen head over heels in love with her in what must have been world-record time. David raised his glass toward the shoddy motel.

"Here's to you, Libby, darlin'. Now that you know who I really am, what do you intend to do about it?"

He didn't have a clue how she'd found out, but it had been bound to happen from the second he'd introduced himself to her as an architect. What kind of fool was he, thinking he'd find "regular love" wearing a disguise?

He really couldn't blame Libby one bit for being so angry, as would he if it had happened in reverse. But it wasn't the worst lie that had ever been told. Hell. What if he'd actually been an architect who tried to pass himself off as David Halstrom? Surely that would have been a larger crime and would have angered her even more.

He drained his glass, refilled it, then sat on a leather couch staring south, wondering what to do next. For the first time in his life, David didn't have a clue.

Eleven

The very last thing Libby wanted to do that afternoon was take photographs of the festivities at her aunt Elizabeth's rehab facility. She'd rather do a dozen birthday parties for three-year-olds with amateur clowns, ugly cupcakes and demanding mothers. Actually, she'd rather take a long walk off a short pier.

She'd hardly slept a wink the night before, tossing and turning, getting up for a cup of warm milk, then tossing and turning some more. Finally, at four o'clock in the morning she'd gotten up and put on her ratty blue sweats and running shoes, intending to jog away her problems and anxieties. It didn't work.

Things just got worse when she sat down on a curb and put her head in her hands, intending to work herself up into a good, cleansing cry. Patrol Officer

Tom McKenzie had pulled up in his big white cruiser. He was a really nice guy who made it a point to drive through the Haven View a few times each week.

"Is that you, Libby?" he called out the window.

She lifted her head. "It's me, Tom. Sort of." She gave a wave of her hand. "I'm fine. You don't have to stop."

"You sure?"

No, she wasn't sure at all, but she responded, "Yes. I'm just catching my breath. It's been a long time since I've jogged and I really need to get back in shape. Thanks for stopping, though."

"Well, okay then."

After he drove away, his taillights slowly disappearing down the narrow suburban lane, Libby's wish to drown in tears of self-pity seemed to disappear as well.

The worst part of it was that she couldn't quite decide why she was so angry at David and so wounded by his lie. It made her feel like a fool, actually, to have shared a bed with one of the most successful men in the country, not to mention one of the richest, and not to have known who he was.

She wondered if he did this with all the women he met—introduce himself as somebody else to see if he could get away with it? To have a grand laugh at his victim? Or perhaps, she thought, he did it to avoid being taken advantage of by gold diggers. It made perfect sense in a way, but Libby wasn't yet willing to afford him any motives for his behavior other than perversely criminal ones.

Libby showered and dressed for the big wingding, as Doug called it. Since she'd unofficially be working with her camera, she decided it was fine to dress casually in bleached jeans and a navy turtleneck. Instead of her trusty Nikon and regular film this time, she took her digital SLR which would enable her to send the pictures immediately to the rehab staff.

The party was in full swing when she arrived a few minutes after one o'clock, and Libby put her camera to work immediately in what turned out to be a candid photographer's heaven.

The main assembly room was decorated with silly pumpkins, goofy ghosts made from bedsheets and fanciful scarecrows, all of it topped with twisted strands of autumn-colored crepe paper in red, yellow and brown. The long refreshment table was festooned with real leaves and piles of corn cobs and gourds.

In one corner of the large room was a three-piece band, the musicians—not a one of them under seventy—doing their best to play songs from the 1930s and 1940s for the few brave souls willing to risk further injury on the tiny dance-floor space.

Catty-corner from there, a group of women sat with their knitting and embroidery, little smiles on their faces that seemed to indicate more than a few secrets were shared and gossip exchanged. A bingo game was going full throttle in another corner of the room. Libby managed to get a wonderful shot of a woman's flushed and excited face the exact moment that she yelled "Bingo!"

She was burning film like crazy and really getting into the people and the setting when a warm hand curled around her upper arm and a familiar voice said,

"Your aunt Elizabeth is wondering when you're going to take a picture of her."

Libby almost couldn't breath when she looked up into David's face with its cordial and oh-so-sexy smile. It took a moment for her brain to clear enough for it to register on her that he, of all people, didn't belong here.

"What are you doing here?" she asked him.

"I've been having a cup of hot spiced apple cider and a very nice chat with your aunt Elizabeth," he said. "She's been telling me about your Uncle Joe."

Libby could feel her stomach tie itself into a tight knot. Here we go again, she thought. "He's dead," she said, her tone absolutely flat. "He's been dead for the last six decades."

"I gathered that, Libby," he said softly.

She blinked up at him. "You did?"

"Your friend Doug clued me in, right after I apologized to him for letting him believe I was an architect."

"Oh."

Libby couldn't think of anything else to say. This was all moving way too fast for her. Suddenly it seemed as if David Halstrom, the sleazy liar, was on the inside with her treasured family and she was on the outside staring in.

"I don't want to keep any more secrets from you, Libby," he continued. "The truth is that I came here to talk to your aunt about buying her motel."

"No. You can't," she snapped without even thinking. Well, what was there to think about? "We have plans for it. Well, I have plans. It just isn't for sale."

His voice was low and calm as he replied, "It's not

yours, Libby. As much as you love the place, it still belongs to your aunt. Any decision about selling it is hers, and hers alone."

Argumentative as she felt just then, Libby knew she couldn't argue with that. It was indeed her aunt Elizabeth's place, free and clear. There hadn't even been any debt on the Haven View for the past quarter of a century. In its heyday, the motel had done well enough to pay for itself entirely.

"I know who it belongs to," she said, looking around the big room now. "Where is she? I haven't seen my aunt or Doug yet this afternoon, and I really want to get some pictures of them."

"She's over there." David angled his head toward a set-up of tables and chairs on the far side of the room. "But she sent me over here for one specific purpose. I had to promise, which included crossing my heart and hoping to die and sticking a needle in my eye, that I'd get you out on the dance floor."

Libby lifted her chin and gave a sharp little snort. "Not on your life, Mister."

No sooner were the words out of her mouth, though, than the little three-piece band began playing Glenn Miller's "Moonlight Serenade," one of her favorite songs of all time. When she was a little girl, no more than seven or eight years old, she'd listened to Aunt Elizabeth's old 78 rpm version until she practically wore out the grooves on the brittle old record. Funny. She hadn't thought about that in years, and she wondered if that old record was still around the motel somewhere.

Just then David wrapped his arm around her waist,

and almost before she knew it she was on the little corner dance floor and in his embrace. It was the very last place Libby wanted to be, but there was no denying that it felt wonderful—exquisite!—to be back in his arms, her body pressed tightly against his.

He stood back for a moment in order to gently lift the strap of her camera over her head, then he leaned toward the nearby upright piano, where he set it down, telling the piano player, "Keep an eye on this, will you?"

The old gentleman winked and nodded without even missing a beat in the tune.

David gathered her back in his arms. "Don't fight this," he whispered against her ear. "You'll disappoint your aunt."

Libby snorted again, but this time even she recognized that it was half-hearted and utterly useless. Why, oh, why did his taut, trim body feel so good so close to hers? And why did it set off spectacular Fourth of July fireworks all through her?

"I'm still angry with you," she muttered against his shoulder. "Really angry."

"That's okay." A warm little chuckle sounded just under his breath. "As long as you can be angry and dance at the same time, darlin'."

Apparently she could. Perhaps it was because David turned out to be a divine dancer who communicated every step he wanted her to take by some magic telepathy that went from his hand on her spine directly to her brain and her limbs. They moved on the little dance floor so well, so perfectly in step and in tune, that Libby found herself wishing she were wearing her peach gown rather than her ratty everyday jeans. As long as she felt like Ginger Rogers with Fred Astaire, she dearly wished she looked the part, as well.

She hadn't realized that all the other couples had left the floor to watch them until the music stopped and a spattering of applause coupled with some frail whistles sounded all around them. David graciously acknowledged the cheers, grinning and bowing slightly in their direction. Libby could only blush and hold more tightly to David's hand in the hope that she didn't throw up or pass out as the applause increased and somebody yelled "Encore! Encore!" It didn't take more than a few seconds for an entire chorus to join in.

Dammit. She wasn't meant to be in the spotlight. Her business was behind the lights, taking pictures of those on whom the bright lights shone. Naturally, David was accustomed to all that clamor and adulation, she thought, but she wasn't and she didn't like it one bit. She hated it, in fact.

"So, are you up for one more spin around the dance floor, Libby?" he asked her.

"I'm outta here," Libby announced abruptly.

She wrenched her hand from his, grabbed her camera off the back of the piano and then shouldered her way through the gawkers in the direction of the nearby refreshment table where she hoped that she would find something a bit more bracing there than apple cider.

Just as she was ladling some of the golden liquid into a paper cup, David's voice sounded behind her, but this time there was a slight touch of Bogart in it.

"There's a guy in the kitchen who'll spike that for you for two bucks. Follow me, sweetheart."

Libby had to force herself not to laugh, and as wonderful and medicinal as the kitchen brew sounded to her just then, she declined. Pointing to the camera once more slung from her neck, she said, "Thanks, anyway. I still have a lot of work to do around here this afternoon."

All the merriment seemed to drain from his face in a single instant, and he gazed at her quite soberly. "We need to talk, Libby. Now. Later. Have dinner with me tonight, will you? Let me explain…"

She shook her head adamantly. "I don't think so, David."

Why did he have to be so persistent? It wasn't as if she was the only woman in the world. For heaven's sake, the man probably had a little black book the size of the St. Louis telephone directory with every female listed in it just aching for him to call.

"What are you afraid of?" he challenged her, his green eyes almost penetrating hers with a fierce light.

Libby stiffened. "I'm not afraid of anything."

"Then prove it. Have dinner with me. Please. Give me a chance to explain, Libby. Then, if you still believe I'm lower than the underside of a worm, I'll never bother you again." He raised his right hand. "I promise."

She drained the rest of her cider, then turned back to the table to refill her cup, wondering just how he thought he was going to explain away his deception in any way that she would find acceptable or forgivable. She doubted very much that he could, but admitted to herself that it really wouldn't be fair not to give him the opportunity. For all she knew, he'd probably just dig himself deeper into her enmity.

It wasn't easy pretending that her hand wasn't shaking while she refilled her cup, but her spine was stiff enough and her mind was made up.

Libby turned back to face him. "All right, David. I guess it's only fair to give you a chance to explain. I'll have dinner with you and I'll listen to whatever you think you need to say, but not—absolutely not—in your penthouse at the Marquis."

She didn't bother to add that the memories of that exquisite place and their equally exquisite lovemaking there would haunt her for the rest of her life.

A flicker of relief passed across his expression. "Fair enough," he said. "They've just put the finishing touches on the main dining room, so we'll christen it."

She pictured a great ship getting whacked by a bottle of champagne. With her luck, it was probably the Titanic.

"Eight o'clock?" he asked.

"Eight's fine," she said coolly, already imagining herself back at the Haven View by eleven at the latest and this man already turning into a memory, firmly consigned to her past.

Twelve

After the festivities at the rehab facility, and after Aunt Elizabeth had stubbornly refused to discuss any of her conversation with David Halstrom—other than "Isn't he a nice young man? And so successful! And quite taken with you, Libby, I must say!"—Doug had followed Libby back to the motel, where he made himself comfortable behind the desk and flipped through the latest mail.

Libby didn't really feel like talking. It was four-thirty in the afternoon. She had a headache trying to firmly lodge behind her eyebrows, not to mention a heartache deep in her chest. The mere thought that this evening would be her last with David, even if it was by her very own choice, weighed heavily on her thoughts.

"You know, honey," Doug began as he pulled his

reading glasses down his nose, "This old place served a purpose fifty years ago, in more ways than one, but you've got to admit the old Haven View is way past its prime."

"Yes, I know, but we've got plans to fix that," Libby said. "Father James's board of directors is going to meet in two days, and…"

"And will probably reject the entire idea," Doug said. "They're a pretty conservative group, as I understand, and not inclined to do things that haven't been done before. You need to be aware of that. It was a wonderful idea for this old place, but it might not happen."

"It's such a great opportunity for them," she said.

"They might not see it that way, honey."

He leaned back in his chair now, crossed his arms over his chest and put his feet up on the desk. Libby could tell he had more to say, and somehow she wasn't looking forward to it.

"Your aunt Elizabeth isn't getting any younger, you know, sweetheart," he said. "And, though it might come as a complete surprise to you, neither am I."

Oh, don't, Libby wanted to say. Stop right now, my dearest Doug. I don't want to have this conversation.

"I know that's not easy to hear, honey," he said as if reading her thoughts. "But it's true. It needs to be said."

She felt like a child again, and a somewhat frightened child, too. All she could manage to do was sigh rather loudly.

"Libby, this afternoon David Halstrom presented your aunt with a very sweet offer."

Libby snorted, feeling less like a frightened child now than a betrayed lover. "I'll bet he did."

"This property is worth a pretty penny, you know," Doug continued, "and he offered her all of that and more. In cash. No strung out payments over the years. Just cash. Up front."

Petulantly, she wanted to reply "So?" But she didn't. She just stared across the little office, using her teeth to worry a cuticle on her thumb while waiting for Doug to continue, to drop the other shoe.

"She's considering it," he said.

"Well, that's good, I guess."

His gaze zeroed in on hers. "It is good, honey. I hope she'll have the sense to accept it. And I'm hoping, if she asks for your advice, that you'll encourage her to go ahead with the deal. Or if you can't find it in you to encourage her, then I hope you'll just keep quiet."

Libby wasn't ready to give up all that easily. "But what about all the plans for this place? What about all that money sitting in my bank account, just waiting to go to work around here?"

He rocked back and forth for a moment in the tipped-back chair, then he pressed his fingertips together, and held them almost prayerfully beneath his chin. "If this place is what you want, honey... If this is your heart's desire, then there's no way your aunt will sell it out from under you. All I can tell you is..." He paused for a long, deliberate sigh. "Be very careful what you wish for, Libby, sweetheart. Just be very, very careful."

He didn't give her a chance to respond. Doug heaved forward in the chair, levered himself up and stretched his arms over his head. "Well, this has been a long day, kiddo. I'm going to take myself back to my place for a well-deserved bit of shut-eye."

Libby stood up and met him at the door. She wrapped her arms around him. "Did anybody ever tell you that you're the very best father in the whole world?"

His pressed his lips to the top of her head. "I think somebody just did," he said.

Libby stood in front of the full-length mirror on the closet door a few hours later, making last minute adjustments to the peach-colored dress. She'd already given up on her hair, letting it fall over her shoulders in whatever curls and corkscrews it desired.

She told herself she wasn't dressing for David so much as for the inauguration of the Marquis' dining room, but in the end even she didn't believe that. She was dressing for David, all right. If this was going to be their last evening together, then she damn well wanted him to know what he was losing.

Well, not that he had her to begin with.

Then she heard the crackle of tires on the driveway outside, and mere seconds after that there was a brisk knock on the office door. Ready or not, Libby thought, here we go. After taking a deep breath and one final glance in the mirror, she gathered up her handbag and wrap and headed for the door.

It was Jeff who greeted her. "Good evening, Miss Jost."

Libby stepped through the door and pulled it closed behind her. "Good evening, Jeff."

She couldn't help but wonder if he'd been part of the deception from the very beginning. Still, if he was on David Halstrom's payroll, what choice did the poor guy have? She decided to bite her tongue rather than pepper him with questions that his company loyalty probably wouldn't allow him to answer anyway. She'd simply add that to all the questions she'd stored up for his boss.

He drove the limo out of the pebbled lot of the Haven View, then headed north, across the highway overpass and then turned just a bit west to the entrance of the Marquis, where all the lights were burning bright, as if the place were already full of guests and doing brisk business.

And there stood David, at the front door, looking as if he'd just hired himself to be head doorman. All he lacked was the proper hat, not to mention a patient and helpful attitude.

At the sight of him, Libby wanted to lock the limo doors and order Jeff to step on the gas and get her out of there. Suddenly she didn't want to listen to David Halstrom and his litany of excuses as to why he'd lied to her. She was actually afraid that she might forgive him.

And then what? A few more dazzling nights in his bed and then goodbye? Libby was wishing she'd never met the man when he opened the limo's rear door and extended his hand to her.

She dragged in a deep breath and silently vowed that, no matter what he said, even if it included a deprived childhood, regular beatings and lost puppies and kittens, she would not—absolutely not—forgive him for deceiving her.

* * *

David wasn't accustomed to talking about his private life. He'd been interviewed over the years by the best reporters from all the major newspapers and business magazines, and yet he'd managed to maintain a veil over his life outside of the company.

He wanted to push that veil aside this evening with Libby. He wanted to be honest and forthcoming, to tell her everything about himself from his earliest memories. More than anything else, he wanted her to forgive him.

He'd had the small kitchen crew set up one of the banquettes in the main dining room, so when he saw that Libby had chosen to wear her wonderful peach gown, he was glad he'd chosen the elegant room for their meal.

"This room is gorgeous, David," Libby said as she settled into the banquette.

"Thanks. My design team has been together now for six or seven years, and they've really learned how to put a room together in very little time."

Her head tilted sideways and her lips crooked into an odd little grin. "Am I speaking to David the architect now, or to the real David Halstrom? I'm just curious."

He couldn't help but laugh. "It's funny, you know. There was a time when I was a kid that I really did want to be an architect. I probably had the world's biggest Lego collection. Now I try to have as much input as they'll allow for each one of my hotels."

Now her head tilted the opposite way and David hoped that what he was seeing in her eyes was genuine interest rather than mere politeness.

But, hell, even politeness was a start. At this point, he'd take whatever she was willing to give him and be extremely grateful for it.

Five minutes into their conversation Libby knew she was a goner, and she hated to admit that the sole reason was the tiny little tremor on David's upper lip. If only he'd tried to brazen it out by insisting that the lie he'd told her was small and insignificant, and what difference did it make anyway when all things were considered? Then she would've been able to keep her righteous indignation and her anger stoked for at least another hour or so.

Funny, she thought. The gorgeous décor of the restaurant had no effect on her whatsoever. Sure, there was more crystal dripping from the ceiling than she'd ever seen before in one room in her life and there was enough velvet on the chairs and banquette seats to cover half the city, but she really couldn't focus on anything beyond David's worried face and rather nervous gestures.

"I had the chef prepare the chicken you enjoyed so much the other night," he said when their plates appeared. "I hope you don't mind the repeat performance."

"Mind? I could eat this every night. Thank you."

Okay. So he was thoughtful. She'd give him a few points for that, she decided. He'd even remembered what she had for dinner that night, which most men couldn't do if you bet them a thousand dollars.

When the waiter stood beside their table and expertly uncorked a bottle of wine, then poured a small bit into her host's glass for him to sample, damned if there wasn't a slight tremor in David's hand as he lifted his glass. If Libby was seeking a visible sign of victory, she decided she had it right in front of her, right then and there. Not the outright wail of contrition she wanted perhaps, but it would do.

Of course, that didn't necessarily mean she was going to take up their relationship where it had left off the day before. She had hardly forgotten that her dinner companion was a millionaire many times over, and that he could have his pick of women all over the globe, if not the entire galaxy. Libby had never been known as a shy and retiring little violet, but in this particular case it didn't seem so very odd to wonder, *Why me?*

"You could still be an architect if you wanted to," she said in reference to his earlier statement. "You'd only have to go back to school for a few years."

He sipped his wine, his eyes never leaving hers, then he put down the glass and folded his hands atop the table. "More than just a few years, darlin'. My mother died when I was a baby, and I was barely eighteen when my father died and I had to leave school to take over his business. I had maybe three or four days of college."

"I'm so sorry about your parents, David. I lost both of mine when I was just a baby," she said. "But considering how successful you are, that was obviously all the formal education you needed."

He shook his head. "I've been lucky, to be perfectly honest. More than anything, I've been in the right place at the right time."

The crystals in the dining room fixtures glittered in his eyes as he laughed softly. "But you have to promise not to repeat that, or I'd have to kill you."

Libby sketched a cross over the bodice of her dress. "I promise. My lips are sealed."

"Actually, I've spent the past fifteen years trying to make up for the formal education I missed out on. I've been taking correspondence courses in just about every subject I can find, from anthropology to zoology, and I try to read as much as I can. I've probably enjoyed it more than I would have when I was eighteen. I know I've profited more from it."

Libby was hugely impressed, although she tried not to let it show in her expression. Much as she yearned to find some really horrible, truly hateful qualities in David Halstrom to make it easy for her to reject him, she was becoming more and more impressed with the man. This wasn't at all what she'd planned.

And the more he talked about his past, the more she respected him for not walking away from the family business after his father died, even though it signaled an end to his college days and to his youth. She thought he and her aunt Elizabeth had a lot in common. They were tough hangers on, the both of them. Of course, that still didn't explain or excuse his lie.

When the waiter cleared away their dinner plates and filled their coffee cups, Libby decided it was time to ask since it was obvious by now that he wasn't going to volunteer. As she stirred a teaspoon of sugar into the dark brew, she tilted her head toward David and said, "Did it bother you at all that I truly believed you were the architect who designed this beautiful building?"

He didn't hesitate for a second before he answered. "Yes. It bothered me tremendously. Much more than you can imagine. I regretted the lie the instant it passed my lips."

"Then, why…?"

"Libby, you were my lamppost angel. I didn't want to lose you just a few hours after I'd finally found you. I didn't want to see your sweet mouth making fake smiles and your lovely eyes turn hard and calculating when you discovered who I really was."

In a strange way, it made absolute sense to her. "I take it that happens a lot."

David sighed. "It happens all the time. Like clockwork. And I just couldn't let it happen with you."

She frowned. "That's not much of a compliment to my sterling character, David. You just naturally assumed I was a gold digger like all the others."

"Only because I didn't know you," he protested.

"And now that you do know me?"

"Libby, darlin', if I had to meet you all over again…" He paused to reach for her hand, then held it tightly in both of his as he continued. "I'd get down on my knees and beg my lamppost angel to marry me even before I asked your name."

Her heart did that weird swan dive again. Had she heard him right? Was that some Texas expression she'd never heard before? Or was it—Good Lord!—was it an actual proposal?

How could it be? They hadn't even known each

other a week yet. Then she reminded herself that it had taken her all of about twenty-four hours to fall madly in love with him. Was it possible that the same thing had happened to him? That Cupid had struck them both with a single arrow?

Her hand was still nestled warmly in his as she swallowed hard and decided to ask him exactly what he meant when young Jeff rushed into the quiet dining room. His eyes were huge and full of barely contained panic.

"There's a problem across the highway," he said. "A fire. I've already called 911."

Thirteen

As they raced from the restaurant to the hotel's front door, David used his cell phone to order the limo to the main entrance. It arrived, tires squealing around the corner of the building, only seconds after they had reached the front door.

David ordered the driver out of the vehicle, then jumped into the front seat himself, while Jeff and Libby nearly dove into the backseat. She could already see smoke rising across the highway and a faint but distinct orange glow beneath it.

"Hurry, David. Please," she said.

He hurried. In fact, he pushed the accelerator to the floor and barely braked for the two stop signs between the Marquis and the Haven View. In the backseat, Libby was holding on tight as David swung the big limo into the graveled parking lot and skidded to a stop only feet from the door of the office.

"Oh, my God."

The words left her lips almost like a desperate prayer as she saw the fire leaping from cabin Number Six at the far end of the motel compound. The little cabin was already engulfed in flames.

"Where's the fire department?" Jeff said, the panic obvious in his voice. "I called them. They should be here."

David said nothing. He was out of the limo nearly the second it stopped, looking around as if memorizing the entire situation. "Libby, where's the nearest hose?" he shouted over the roof of the vehicle. "Where?"

Her mind went absolutely blank for a moment. She barely knew where she was herself, only that her whole world seemed to be going up in flames right now.

"Libby," he shouted again. "The hose? A hookup? Tell me where they are."

As she jumped out of the limo, she snapped back to the present and its obvious danger. "Over there." She pointed to the third little cabin. "The hose is hooked up already, I think. It's wound around a holder on the west side wall."

David was running toward the cabin almost before she finished speaking. In the distance now, Libby could hear the high whine of sirens. Why couldn't they get here faster?

She felt paralyzed again, watching the flames eat away at the wood siding of cabin Number Six. There was a slight breeze coming from the west, nudging the flames eastward, toward the next cabin in line. Sparks were already coming down like red rain on the rooftop of Number Five.

Oh, God. Was this how her aunt's lifetime endeavor would end? In flames and ashes? Without her even here for one final chance to see the place, to take it all in as she bid it goodbye? That was a tragedy all by itself.

Then, at last, Libby's professional instincts kicked in. Maybe she didn't know how to put out fires, but she sure as hell knew how to photograph them. She'd been doing it for a decade at the newspaper. She turned to race to the office, where she grabbed her camera, which thankfully had fresh batteries.

If it was all going to end tonight, if this was the last gasp of the Haven View, then Libby would bear witness to its sad and final moments. She aimed her camera and started snapping pictures as soon as she stepped out the office door.

The breeze was blowing harder now out of the west, sending not only bright sparks, but flaming pieces of debris—clapboard and roof tiles—toward the cabin next to it. It wouldn't be long before it caught fire, too.

That's when she caught sight of David. He was standing between the two little buildings, hosing down the adjacent side of Cabin Five and trying to aim water toward its roof. He seemed totally unaware that sparks were landing on him as he attempted to keep the fire from spreading.

"David!" she screamed. She let go of the camera with one hand to wave him toward her. "Get out of there! It's way too dangerous!"

He looked in her direction for a second, but he didn't seem to hear her.

"Get out of there!" she yelled again.

The fire trucks sounded closer now, their flashing lights coloring the view to the east. Hurry, Libby urged them silently. Oh, please, please hurry.

She turned back toward the fiery sight, aiming her camera just in time to capture the collapse of Cabin Six's walls. As they fell in upon themselves, sparks and debris and fierce flames seemed to explode into the night air.

"David!" she screamed again.

Finally, through the black smoke and the falling debris, she saw him drop the hose and race out of the dangerous space between the two cabins, batting at his sleeves and his hair as if he, too, were about to ignite.

Cabin Five's roof went up in flames then just as the big trucks pulled into the drive. The ground shook beneath Libby's feet as the fire engines roared closer. It felt like an earthquake. She took a few shaky steps backward onto the playground gravel and lowered herself to the ground before her trembling legs gave out completely.

From there, she took a few more pictures, but the angle was horrible and because her hands were shaking now, too, she decided to stop being a photographer and simply sit there feeling and no doubt looking like a half-dazed victim.

Jeff came over to sit beside her. She had no idea where he'd been, but in the light cast by the fire she could see that he had soot on his face and his clothes looked damp and rumpled, quite different from his usual well-pressed appearance.

"I'm so sorry about this," he said.

Libby leaned in his direction to gently nudge his shoulder with hers. "Thanks, Jeff. It could've been a lot worse, I guess. At least nobody was hurt."

"Thank God for that," the young man said, his hands propping up his chin as he stared straight ahead at the firemen who were now aiming hoses at the slowly diminishing flames. "You know, just between us, Miss Jost, I didn't think the Haven View was such a horrible place."

He spoke as if the place was already gone, Libby thought. It made her want to weep.

Then he added, "At least I didn't think it was the eyesore that the boss considered it."

"Thanks," she murmured.

So David considered it an eyesore. It shouldn't have surprised her in the least, but Libby still felt betrayed somehow. Her feelings were hurt, as if the old motor court were a close relative whose honor she was obliged to defend. In fact, it was her dear aunt Elizabeth whose honor was involved in this, and Libby would defend her aunt to the ends of the earth, if it came to that.

The thought crossed her mind then that maybe— just maybe—David had arranged for this fire, either through his lap dog, Jeff, or some other underling on his staff. A whispered instruction. Some cash handed over. A few sloshes of accelerant. A match or two. Who would know? And, more important, who would care except Aunt Elizabeth, Doug and Libby?

Maybe his daredevil drive from the Marquis and his

manly and heroic stance with the hose between the two cabins was simply for show. And maybe, just maybe, Libby thought, she was letting her fears and frustrations run away with her.

Then, as she was trying to rein in her worst suspicions, David appeared as if out of nowhere and lowered himself on the ground beside her. The three of them—Jeff, Libby and David—watched in silence as the flames went out, one by one by one.

Half an hour later the air was sodden and acrid. There were no more flames or smoke, but the firemen loitered around Cabins Five and Six just to make certain their work was done.

Libby still sat on the edge of the playground flanked by David and Jeff. Now that there was no longer a canopy of smoke to block the view of the sky, she noticed all the bright stars shining overhead. It struck her as incredibly sad that something so horrible could happen on a night that was otherwise lovely.

Her interrupted dinner in the gorgeous Marquis dining room seemed so long ago she could barely remember it. She did, however, recall David's words and she wondered now if they were merely meant to distract her from what was happening here, across the highway.

She looked to her right. The lights from the fire trucks played across David's face while his gaze was still locked on the devastation on the other side of the driveway. Oh, how she prayed he had nothing to do with the fire. If he did…

A heavily clothed and booted fireman approached them.

"I'm Captain Burford," he said. "I'm looking for the owner of this place."

Libby pushed up from the ground, clutching her peach-colored shawl around her shoulders. "That would be me, I suppose." She extended her hand. "I'm Libby Jost. My aunt is the legal owner, but she's currently in a hospital facility."

"We've got the fire put out for the most part," he said. "It's standard procedure to watch for a while, just to make sure there aren't any flare-ups."

Libby nodded.

"Were you here when it started?" he asked.

She shook her head, wondering if she looked guilty somehow. "No. I wasn't here. I was across the street, across the highway, having dinner." She was about to volunteer David as a witness when the fireman continued.

"Okay. At this point in time, we're relatively certain it was a faulty electrical switch in that last cabin rather than arson. But our inspector will be back in the morning just to have a good look around and to make a final determination."

"Okay," Libby said. So they really were considering arson, she thought. Or maybe they always considered it until they made a final evaluation of a fire.

She cast a quick glance down at David, still sitting on the ground, and didn't see the slightest bit of panic or even concern in his expression. But what did that mean? She already knew the man was a good actor, having convinced her that he was an architect rather than a mega-millionaire.

The fireman was writing something on a clipboard when he said, "I'm going to have to red flag this whole place in the meantime. That means it can't be open for business. Understand?"

"Yes." She nodded again, deciding it would be useless to tell him it hadn't been open for business anyway.

"All right then." He tore off the top copy of whatever form he was filling out and handed it to her. "You don't have to stick around if you don't want to. We've got it under control. But I hope you'll be here tomorrow when the inspector arrives sometime around nine."

Libby took the paper, noticing that her hands had begun to shake once more. "I'll be here," she told the fireman in the same tone she might have responded, "Yes, sir."

She sat back down between the two possible perps.

"All done?" David asked quietly.

"Yes. At least, I think so."

"Then come back to the hotel with me. You don't want to spend the night here, Libby."

No, she didn't. The thought of it alone made her almost panicky.

"Thank you, David," she said.

What choice did she have?

Fourteen

By the time the elevator reached the penthouse, Libby looked half drowned from the spray of the hoses and seemed almost asleep on her feet, so David picked her up and carried her to the beige and pale blue bedroom, the one he'd always considered the most feminine in the suite.

The room had no south-facing window, either. The last thing she needed right now, he decided, was to gaze out at the destruction across the highway.

"Let's get you out of this damp dress, darlin', and then I'll find you something else to wear."

She stood beside the bed like an exhausted child while he unhooked and unzipped the peach dress that now smelled like smoke and ashes instead of lovely perfume. He dipped his head to kiss the cool skin just above her collarbone, and heard a soft little murmur rise up in her throat.

Longing, unlike any he'd ever felt before in his life, ripped through his body like a hot and powerful tide. Nearly overwhelmed by the strength of the emotion, David took a step back and swallowed hard. For a moment he had to force his brain to regroup, not to mention force his bloodstream to remain within bounds.

Good God, how he wanted her. With any other woman, he might have figured "what the hell" and pursued his desire right then and there with little or no regard for her current emotions or delicate state of mind. He wouldn't do that to Libby. He couldn't do it to her. He cared far too deeply for her well-being.

He sighed deeply and turned away to give himself a minute to recover while he went to find something for her to wear. Luckily, there was an ivory silk kimono on a hook in the adjacent bathroom. In the mirror there, David caught a glimpse of himself, the first since he'd left the site of the fire.

Like Libby, he looked as if he'd been through a fiery wringer, too. There were dark streaks of soot on his forehead and cheeks and neck and there were more than a few burnt holes in his shirt. Even the hair on his head appeared to be singed in a couple of places. Once Libby was comfortably asleep, he planned to take a long, hot shower before falling into bed himself.

Back in the bedroom, he found Libby still standing at the side of the bed, staring into space. "Put this on, sweetheart, while I fix you a nightcap."

"Thanks," she said, her voice sounding almost as

listless and worn out as the rest of her. Her eyes glistened but he couldn't tell if she was crying or if it was just irritation from all the smoke.

He picked up the peach dress she'd tossed aside and left in search of some hundred-proof medicine.

In the living room, he poured himself half an inch of brandy, then carried the snifter to the south-facing window. A patrol car was parked in the motel driveway, no doubt stationed there to make sure no flames erupted during what was left of this long night. It seemed odd not seeing the last two little cabins. He almost missed them now that they weren't there.

David thought how the fire would've delighted him last week. Good God, he would've stood here watching, actually cheering on the flames as they coursed through the shabby little place, cabin by cabin. He would've laughed out loud as each wall collapsed, sending fireworks into the night sky. The spectacle would've felt like a victory, another measure of his success.

But that was before Libby. A little smile curved upward at the edges of his mouth. His life now seemed divided into B.L. and A.L. Before Libby and After Libby.

He walked back to refill his snifter and to fix one for Libby. He'd put her dress down over the back of a nearby chair, and his first thought upon seeing it again was to call Jeff to arrange to have the garment cleaned. His second thought was that he would let the poor kid sleep, and maybe even give him a day off tomorrow, or—he looked at his watch—today, actually.

Imagine that, he thought, while he poured several fingers of brandy into Libby's snifter. He seemed to be turning into a nice guy, one who actually cared about other people's feelings. David hoped nobody found out about it. That would definitely be bad for business.

When Libby woke up, she had no idea where she was, but she somehow knew where she was supposed to be at nine o'clock. At the Haven View, with the fire investigator. Unfortunately, the bright blue digital clock on the night table informed her it was way past nine. It was, in fact, just a bit past eleven.

She groaned as she levered up in the bed. She wasn't sure what she was wearing, either, but she knew the silky garment wasn't hers. Good grief. Drawing in a deep breath of frustration, Libby realized that her hair smelled like smoke. Then vivid memories from the night before rekindled in her brain.

There was a quick little knock on the door then. She heard David's voice inquire softly, "Libby?"

"I'm awake," she answered and watched the bedroom door as it opened and David stepped inside.

She was surprised to see him wearing a beautifully fitted gray business suit, complete with matching tie. He appeared fairly well rested, too, which made Libby instantly consider pulling the bedcovers over her head.

"How do you feel this morning?" he asked as he settled on the edge of the mattress.

"Better," she said. "But I'm also feeling rather guilty for sleeping through the meeting with the fire inspector. I wonder if I can call and reschedule it."

"You don't have to. I went as your representative."

"Really?" Libby didn't know whether to be grateful

or suspicious, nor was she sure whether David was helping or hindering. "What did the inspector have to say?"

"Well, first of all, your uncle Doug was there."

She sank back against the pillows. "I should've gotten up this morning to call him and tell him the news. Oh, God. It must've been just awful for him to drive in there and see…"

"It was," David said. "But he's a pretty philosophical guy. He didn't seem to consider it the worst tragedy in the world. Mostly he was just happy and relieved that nobody was hurt."

"Yeah. Me, too," she said softly.

"The inspector will send you a copy of his report, Libby. In a week to ten days, he figured. He spent about an hour going through the place, the burned cabins as well as the other structures. The guy was very thorough."

"And…?" She was holding her breath now, she realized, not that she was expecting David to even mention the word arson, but still…

"And I'd say he's about ninety-nine percent sure that the culprit was the old wiring in the sixth cabin. There wasn't any hint of accelerants or anything remotely suspicious, so the guy ruled out arson right from the beginning. Doug seemed pretty satisfied that his conclusion was correct. He told him that there'd been a fire at one of the cabin outlets a couple of years ago."

"I had no idea," she said.

"Yeah, I know. Doug told me later that they didn't want to worry you."

"Well, we'll just have to update the wiring, I

guess." She tried to sound optimistic. "How difficult could that be?"

David merely shrugged in response. "You aren't going to like hearing this, darlin', but the inspector red-flagged the whole place for the time being."

"What does that mean?"

"Basically, it means zero business activity and zero residence there until another inspection."

Libby moaned as she reached back for a big soft pillow to plop over her head. After a moment or so, she lifted one corner of it in order to look at David and ask, "Is there any other horrible news I need to know about?"

"Nope. That's it for the time being, kiddo," he said, chuckling softly as he reached out to pat her leg. "The good news, though, is that I've got the hot tub going for you, and your breakfast ought to be here in about ten or fifteen minutes."

All things considered, that really did sound like good news to Libby, at least the best she'd heard so far this morning. She'd have plenty of time, she decided, to groan and mope after her body was clean and her stomach was full.

David watched as Libby promptly sank all the way to her adorable chin in the hot tub. If he could've been granted any wish just then, it would've been to repeat this sight, day after day after day, for the next seventy-five years.

He handed her the huge, icy glass of orange juice and then used his thumb to gently erase a little streak of soot on her forehead and another small spot on her cheek.

"No more playing fireman for you, my girl," he said.

"Right back at you," she replied, grinning up at him over the rim of her goblet.

Considering the recent upheaval in her world and that of her loved ones, he was amazed that she could smile at all. After his father had died when he was just eighteen, David couldn't recall smiling for another decade or more.

He'd asked her to marry him the night before, a moment that had caught him completely by surprise. It was as if someone else had been using his mouth to form the words. But right now he knew that he'd meant every word of the proposal. It didn't matter a bit that he'd only known her for five or six days. He should only be so lucky to have this beautiful, brave woman at his side for the rest of his life.

Unfortunately, the object of his unexpected proposal didn't seem to have heard it, or if she had, then didn't seem to remember a single word of it. But, really, who could blame her after the trauma that had followed his question the night before. And right now, David, for all his executive finesse and verbal skills, didn't have the slightest idea how to ask her again.

For all his bravery in business, he felt like a complete coward in his personal life.

"David," she said, her blue eyes widening and gazing up at him through the faint steam of the tub. "Do you, by any chance, know if Doug has said anything to my aunt Elizabeth yet?"

He nodded. "As far as I know, he was planning to visit her this morning and fill her in on everything that happened last night at the Haven View." He knew a bit more than that, but he didn't volunteer it at the moment.

She sighed and sank a few inches deeper into the tub, up to her earlobes now. "She's going to be really upset. Poor thing. That motel is her entire life. And she's going to need a place to stay once they've released her from the center, which could be any day now."

"Well…"

"Well, what?" she asked, cocking her head to the side and narrowing her eyes. "Why am I getting the feeling there's something else you aren't telling me?"

"Well…"

David wasn't accustomed to such back and forth conversations, a bit like the flurry of a table tennis game with nothing getting accomplished. Usually, he said what was on his mind from the get-go. He decided he might as well do that now.

"I offered your aunt a suite here at the Marquis, Libby. For however long she needs it." He looked at his watch. "I expect Doug is telling her about it right now."

She merely stared at him then, for a long, long moment. To David, it seemed like an hour or more under the Spanish Inquisition. He couldn't tell from her expression whether he was about to be thanked or slapped, and he felt baffled enough at the moment not to even know the distinction.

Libby took a long and leisurely drink of her orange juice before she finally deigned to put him out of his misery.

"That was incredibly kind and generous of you," she said. "Thank you, David. Thank you so very much."

He let his breath out slowly, then gestured around himself with both hands. "This is a hotel, Libby. A very large hotel, in fact. There's plenty of room for your aunt and for Doug, too, if and when he decides to join her here."

Water sloshed off her shoulders as she suddenly pushed upward in the marble tub. She set her empty juice glass down on the edge. "Are you kidding me, David? That was one of the options you gave him? Or her?"

"Yes," he said. "Yes, I did." David didn't know why she seemed so startled by this particular offer. "I just assumed they'd been together, the two of them, for a very long time and they wouldn't want to separate now."

Libby was blinking as if she had water in her eyes. "They *have* been together," she said. "But they've never *lived* together. At least not in the three decades I've been around."

It was all he could do not to laugh. "Well, darlin', maybe it's high time they started. I'm sure you know the old expression about it never being too late."

"Hey. I have no problem if they were to live together. I've even suggested it over the years, so it's absolutely fine with me," she said. Then she sighed as she raised her gaze heavenward. "I'm just not too sure about the ghost of Uncle Joe."

"I see what you mean," he said. "I almost believed the guy was alive when your aunt mentioned him to me at the rehab place. She doesn't really believe it, does she?"

Libby shrugged. "Maybe he'll decide to stick around to haunt the Haven View rather than move across the street."

"Well, then. I guess we'll just have to wait and see what happens, won't we?"

Watching Libby sink down once again into the warm water of the tub, David couldn't help but think that "wait and see" wasn't exactly his style. But since he was currently enrolled in Patience 101, he decided he'd just have to…well…wait and see.

Fifteen

Libby barely had time to dry off from her long and relaxing breakfast time in the hot tub when her cell phone signaled for her from somewhere in the depths of her handbag. Still clutching the towel around her, she extracted the phone and answered it.

It was Doug on the other end of the line, practically shouting. "Libby, honey, I've got some great news. The doctors have sprung Elizabeth. We'll be out of here as soon as we can gather up all her clothes and other things."

Libby could feel her mouth fall open as her jaw dropped at least several inches. It was wonderful news, indeed. She just hadn't been expecting it for a few more days. A bit light-headed all of a sudden, perhaps even waterlogged and way too stuffed with scrambled eggs, sausages and toast, she lowered herself onto the edge of the bed.

"But… But where are you planning to take her?" she finally managed to ask.

Doug chuckled. "Well, you know how stubborn she is. I told her about the fire, of course, and then I gave her a choice. I told her it was either my place or the Marquis. And since she's no fool after all these years, and knows all too well that my place is usually a foot deep in dust and half-read books and magazines, she very wisely chose the Marquis."

Libby remembered that David said he'd offered a suite for one or both of them, or all three if Joe's ghost planned to accompany them. For some reason, though, it just hadn't occurred to her that they'd actually be taking advantage of it. And so soon!

"We'll be driving up to the front door of the Marquis just as soon as Elizabeth can get all her junk organized and packed," he said.

It was at this point in the conversation that Libby realized she didn't have anything to wear except the towel that was around her now, or the skimpy little kimono she'd slept in the night before. It was always nice to greet family, especially the elderly, in proper clothes.

"Where are you right now, Libby?" he asked her.

"I'm at the Marquis," she answered. *Virtually naked.*

"Oh, that's perfect. Well, keep an eye out for us, my girl. We should be there…" He sighed. "Eventually."

After she broke the connection, Libby called out to David in the hope of finding her dress from the night before.

"I had it sent to the laundry," he told her. He laughed softly as his warm gaze moved from her chin to her toes. "I wouldn't mind seeing you in only a towel for the next few weeks, I must say."

"Well, I don't think my aunt Elizabeth will say the same, and she'll be here in an hour or so. I need my clothes, David."

As usual, the task fell to Jeff, who was given a list of items to retrieve from the Haven View. He was back in half an hour and Libby was grateful to be wearing something other than a towel, in this case her usual uniform of jeans and a black turtleneck.

While David locked himself away to attend to business, she took the elevator downstairs to wait for her aunt's arrival. Now that the grand opening was just a few days away, it seemed as if the big hotel had suddenly come to life. The lobby was brightly lit and crowded, and there were actual guests checking in. The place truly seemed like a hotel now rather than merely David's private playground.

She walked out the wide front doors into the sunshine to watch taxis and expensive, luxurious private cars come up the long and suddenly busy drive. Whatever had possessed her, Libby wondered now, to imagine that anyone would choose a stay at the Haven View, even a free one, over this magnificent place. If sentimentality had ever clouded anyone's vision, it was certainly true in her case.

There was still a chance, of course, that Father James's board of directors would vote in favor of the old motel as a training center for Heaven's Gate clients, but Libby seriously doubted that the municipal fathers would ever endorse such an operation. Nor would David ever approve of the location of such a facility directly across from the Marquis.

And maybe, after all, he was right.

It was time, she decided, to revamp her plans for that magic fifty thousand dollars. She was starting a mental list of options when she saw Doug's car turn into the Marquis' drive.

Jeff ushered them painlessly through the hotel's registration process, then accompanied them to the beautiful suite on the twentieth floor. There were two lovely bedrooms, two baths, a luxurious sitting room and—wonder of wonders—a small, well-equipped kitchen. It was probably no accident that the windows faced north, and Libby was oh-so-grateful that her aunt didn't have to look out and see the devastation of the motel.

Before he left, Jeff handed Libby the room-service menu.

"They'll bring lunch up as soon as you're all ready to order," he said. "The bill's already been taken care of."

"Thank you, Jeff. For everything," Libby said.

He grinned. "Don't thank me, Ms. Jost. It's all Mr. Halstrom's doing. I just carry out his orders. Besides, it's me who should be thanking you because the boss has been a lot easier to get along with ever since he met you. I hope you'll stick around for a long, long time."

Their lunch arrived in less than half an hour after Libby called in with their order, and the waiter laid it all out beautifully on the table next to the small kitchen. When Libby tried to tip him, the young man refused.

"It's against the boss's orders," he told her. "Enjoy your lunch."

Her aunt Elizabeth, joyous as a kid at the prospect of something other than institutional food, had ordered a fresh-fruit plate as well as a small steak with a baked potato. Libby was astonished to see her practically clean both plates. If she was upset about the fire at the motel, it certainly didn't show in her appetite.

When she had finally finished her meal, Libby refilled her coffee cup and said, "We need to talk about the Haven View, Aunt Elizabeth. Now, if you're ready, but definitely soon."

"Doug and I have already discussed it to death, Libby. Pass me the cream, will you, sweetie?"

Libby looked at Doug then. His neutral expression spoke loud and clear. Don't talk to me. Talk to her, it said.

She tried again. "Well, have you reached any decisions? Or maybe I can help you clarify your options."

Her aunt put down the spoon with which she'd been stirring her coffee. "I don't want you to be upset by this, Libby, but my mind is fairly well made up. I'm going to sell the place just as soon as the paperwork can be put together."

"Sell?" Libby repeated the word as if she didn't understand its meaning.

"Pass me a packet of sugar, sweetie, will you? I thought you might be upset which is why I didn't want to say anything right away, not while we're all enjoying being back together again."

Her aunt ripped open the small packet Libby had put in front of her, and then, just as she was stirring the coffee again, there was a knock on the suite's door.

"I'll get that," Doug said, rising from his chair. "I expect they've come for the empty plates."

Libby sat silently, not wanting to launch into a family discussion in front of a waiter. She was irritated, to put it mildly, that her aunt had seemingly done this sale behind her back. Not that it wasn't her property to keep or sell or burn to the ground if she wanted, but still, Libby felt left out of the process.

"I knew your feelings would be hurt," Aunt Elizabeth whispered as she leaned toward her. "But Doug thought it best if we didn't waste any time under the circumstances."

"What circumstances?" Libby's whisper was more like a hiss, and then she said something she never thought would actually come out of her mouth. "What about Uncle Joe?"

"Oh, honey." Her aunt reached out to pat her hand. "Now I know that you, Libby, of all people, didn't believe a single word of that tall tale of mine."

"But…" No other words were available in Libby's brain just then. She wondered how her aunt could look so composed and calm while her own head was threatening to explode.

"It was just my way of coping, sweetheart," Aunt Elizabeth said almost matter of factly. "And I suppose it was a way of keeping your Uncle Joe alive in some fashion. At least it seemed that way at first."

"But…"

"The more people thought I was nuts, the more they left me alone." Her aunt took a sip of coffee. "Oh, it didn't start out that way. I really did believe my sweet Joe would come home. But after a decade, even I knew he was gone forever. Even so, I kept up my little charade because it helped protect the Haven View. There wasn't a single person at City Hall all those years who'd dare start proceedings against *that poor looney old woman.*"

"I wish you'd told me," Libby said when she finally found her voice.

"Well, honey, you were such a smart little girl, and I guess I more or less assumed that you knew since you never asked."

Just then Doug came back with an enormous grin on his face. "Look who's here!" he exclaimed just as David stepped into sight right behind him.

David. In his expensive looking three-piece suit, Italian shoes and an award-winning smile. Everything seemed to fall into place for Libby at the sight of him. The man had been working and plotting and making deals behind her back the whole time he'd been making love to her. She didn't have a doubt in the whole world.

And now the snake passing for a man actually had the nerve to bend down to kiss the top of her elderly aunt's head.

"How's the suite, Elizabeth?" he asked. "There's a larger one available, if this one doesn't give you enough space. All you have to do is whistle, as the saying goes. We can make a change in just two or three hours."

Aunt Elizabeth laughed. "After my previous accommodations, David, this is pure paradise on earth. Please sit down. Join us for coffee, won't you?"

"Thank you," he said.

He pulled out a chair and sat.

Libby couldn't take it one second longer. Her head was about to explode. The moment David's back end hit the chair, she was up on her feet.

"Well," she said, with a perky nod toward her aunt, "I'll check back with you two later. There are a few things I need to tend to this afternoon."

She made a quick retreat, and was nearly to the suite's door when she heard David excuse himself. Once outside the door, she knew there was no way she could get to the elevator before he caught up with her, so she turned toward the nearby fire-escape stairs.

"Libby," he called just as the heavy door was closing behind her.

Damn. Taking the stairs two at a time as if the brand new hotel truly were on fire, she made it down almost two whole flights before David caught up with her.

"Libby." He caught her arm.

Knowing it was useless, she shrieked at him anyway, "Let me go, David."

"Why are you running away from me?"

"I'm not running away. Just let go of me."

"Not until you tell me why. This is crazy, Libby. Why are you doing this?"

"Because, David, you went behind my back and you stole the Haven View from my aunt. Did you think I wouldn't find out?"

He merely stared at her then while he shook his head. "Find out? I assumed you knew. I assumed she told you about our discussions."

"Well, I didn't know. She didn't tell me anything. I just found out a few minutes ago."

Libby was so angry, it was all she could do not to slash out a foot at his shin. "So you gave her…what?…in return for her prime acreage? A midsized hotel suite, some free all-you-can-eat room service and maybe a couple dollars on the side? Was that the deal?"

"Is that what she told you?" he asked.

"No. It's just what I'm guessing a sleazy, conniving real-estate shark would do."

David took a step back, looking at her with a kind of dazed disbelief. "Your aunt hasn't signed the papers yet, Libby, but my offer for the place was three-and-a-half-million dollars, and yes, I did tell Elizabeth and Doug they're welcome to stay here at the hotel however long they like, even if it's years, but that wasn't in any way a part of the deal."

And now it was Libby who took a step back as she blinked up into his face. "Three-and-a-half million? You paid too much, David," she said. "Way too much. That acreage is expensive, but it's only worth two million, tops."

His voice was considerably lower than before and much calmer now, while his green eyes had stopped flashing, having turned back to the deep and sensuous autumn glow that she adored. "Yes, I know exactly what it's worth, darlin'," he said. "Trust me, Libby. It's my business, and I do know that."

"Well, I just don't understand this at all," she said, shaking her head. "I know I'm probably way too protective of my aunt Elizabeth, who doesn't seem to need me even one little bit right now, and at the same time I'm deliriously in love with you, David, and yet I'm so angry with you, I could just…" Her voice sputtered out.

He chuckled. "Well, the love part is good, anyway. We'll have to work on the angry part, though. Come here."

He reached out and drew her into his arms, hard against his body, as he sighed deeply. "I love you, too, Libby, darlin'. I don't know how it happened, or why it happened, but I know I'm yours forever, if you'll have me."

Libby almost laughed as she remembered her confusion about his earlier proposal or non-proposal.

"Just for clarification, David," she said now, pressing her cheek to the warmth of his chest, "would that be a proposal of marriage?"

"Yep. That would indeed be a proposal of marriage. Unless, of course, you'd prefer following in your aunt Elizabeth's footsteps." He stroked her hair. "I just know I want to be with you for the next fifty or sixty years."

"Is that all?"

"Well, it'll do for a start, darlin'."

Sixteen

The next few days seemed to go by in a blur for Libby. She fell asleep in David's arms each night after making delicious love and woke each morning close beside his warm body. But other than those two lovely daily details, there was so much going on at the Marquis that Libby often didn't know whether she was coming or going.

The crowd for the grand opening was enormous, just about filling every suite and room. A two-hour wait for seating in the main restaurant was common. The bar was crowded from the moment it opened each day until it closed for the night. Libby saw more celebrities, both local and Hollywood types, in a few days than she'd seen in the previous thirty years of her life. If she'd been a paparazzi, she would've thought she'd died and gone to celebrity heaven.

"Is it always like this?" she asked David while snuggling close to him in bed.

"Seems like the openings get bigger and more extravagant with each new hotel," he said, a distinct note of weariness in his voice. "But that seems to be what people want these days."

She sighed, angling her face in order to kiss his chin. "I just want you."

"When this is all wrapped up, sweetheart, we'll get away someplace quiet," he told her. "A honeymoon, if you want."

"Oh, that would be lovely."

And it was during those busy, bustling few days that Aunt Elizabeth and Doug's presence at the hotel turned out to be a blessing in disguise. Doug spent a great deal of his time in the lobby, thoroughly enjoying the frenetic activity and people watching and cheerfully volunteering information about local attractions whenever he overheard a guest ask a question.

He was so helpful, in fact, that when David heard about it, he arranged for an information table to be set up in a corner of the lobby, where Doug sat each day, happily fielding questions, making suggestions and handing out tourist brochures. The man had turned into a concierge extraordinaire. Every time Libby caught a glimpse of him, he looked like he was having the time of his life.

Not to be outdone, Aunt Elizabeth—no stranger to the guest business—somehow got hold of a stack of, "How was your visit at the Marquis?" cards, which she thrust into the hands of guests who were checking out or waiting in a restaurant line and insisted they fill out the cards on the spot. She carried extra pens—provided by her sources in housekeeping—in her handbag just for this purpose. "Be honest," she warned them. "Your opinion counts and it means a great deal to us here at the Marquis."

Who was going to deny an eighty-year-old woman on crutches?

Whenever she could get a few minutes of David's time, she went over her notes with him. He was utterly and amazingly patient with her, much to Libby's relief.

"Of course I'm patient," he said in reply to her thanks. "Damned if she isn't finding major flaws in the operation, Libby. There were numerous complaints about the timely delivery of luggage to the rooms during opening week. Aunt Elizabeth's got an idea for color coding the bags from the front desk that will probably cut the delivery time in half. The woman's incredible."

"Well, she's been in this business for a long, long time. You should put her on the payroll," Libby said jokingly. "Doug, too."

"By God, I think I will."

"David! I wasn't serious."

"Well, I am."

Libby really only had one problem left. The magic fifty thousand dollars was still sitting in her savings account, and with the Haven View out of the running as a beneficiary, she needed to come up with another way to use the wonderful gift.

David wasn't much help. "There are countless organizations that could make good use the money, Libby. You don't have to choose just one, you know. You could spread it around."

"That just seems so impersonal," she said, shaking her head. "I'd really like this to be special, David. I'd like it to be much more than merely handing over a check."

It was on the day that she accompanied Aunt Elizabeth and Doug to the lawyer's office to sign the papers for the sale of Haven View that Libby finally found the perfect way to use that magical money.

David had arrived earlier at the law firm to conduct some other business unrelated to the motel's sale. The transaction for Haven View went smoothly enough. Libby hadn't slept well the night before, worrying that her aunt might be overcome with sadness and regret at the last minute and perhaps change her mind.

Rather than sadness, though, Aunt Elizabeth seemed hugely relieved to sign the property and all of its attendant problems over to David. She very nearly glowed when she signed the documents and looked younger than she had in the last ten or so years.

"If that's it," she said, using her cane to rise quite regally from her chair, "I'd like to get back to the Marquis where Doug and I have a great deal of work to do."

There were hugs and hearty handshakes all around, then after they were gone, the attorney leaned back in his chair and asked David if he had any immediate plans for the Haven View property. "I'm inquiring because I have a party who's very interested in that acreage," he said. "Not that he'll match the price you just paid for it, but his funds are ample and he's willing to talk, if you are."

"Well, I…"

Libby interrupted. "David, may I speak to you in private for a moment?"

The attorney, as if he'd heard this exact question or some form of it a thousand times before, immediately excused himself to get some more coffee.

"Don't sell it, David," Libby said the moment he closed the door. "Please, don't sell it."

"Honey, I never intended to. At least not for a long time."

She sighed and sank back in her chair. "Oh, thank heavens."

David reached for her hand and brought it to his lips. "You have a plan, don't you? I can see it glistening in your eyes."

She did, indeed, have a plan.

With a sizeable contribution from David, in addition to her own fifty thousand dollars, the Haven View Children's Park was born.

Libby and her camera spent the next month overseeing every detail of the little wonderland, beginning with the destruction of the poor old worn-out cabins. She kept the lampposts, though. If her aunt wasn't sentimental about the motel, at least Libby felt compelled to keep the lamppost where David had first "accosted" her. Besides, they gave the little park a lovely light after dusk.

It was so lovely, in fact, that Aunt Elizabeth and Doug decided to take their wedding vows there the first week of November, accompanied by a few of their old friends, with Libby and David as maid of honor and best man. It was a beautiful ceremony conducted by Doug's friend, Father James, and when Libby wasn't officiating as maid of honor, she was snapping pictures left and right.

David had offered the newlyweds the company plane and a suite in one of his hotels anywhere in the world for a honeymoon, but they both claimed to be far too busy at the Marquis to take any time off.

"I think we should have our wedding here, too," David said as people drifted away after the ceremony to attend a wedding reception at the Marquis. "This place is truly family."

"Fine with me," Libby said, her teeth chattering as the temperature dropped. She unbuttoned his tuxedo jacket and stepped into his wonderful warmth, planning to stay forever.

* * * * *

THE TYCOON'S
SECRET

BY
KASEY MICHAELS

...els is a *USA TODAY* bestselling author of ...han one hundred books. She has won a Romance Writers of America RITA® Award and a *Romantic Times BOOKreviews* Career Achievement Award for her historical romances set in the Regency era.

Dear Reader,

Did you ever wonder what you would do if something
you wanted very much just fell in your lap as an
anonymous gift? Would you keep it? Or, once you finally
had what you thought you needed so much, would you
look around and see that others need so much more, and
begin to wonder if maybe you could manage without
this "something" you had wanted so badly?

That's the dilemma facing Paige Halliday when a
messenger brings her a letter that leads her to something
she really wants, even needs. Does she keep it? Or does
she pass it on to someone who needs it more?

For Paige, this is a fairly easy decision, in keeping with
the way she lives her life. Her *real* problems begin when
she realises that it's the *messenger* she doesn't want to
give away.

But that messenger, ridiculously wealthy, unbelievably
handsome Sam Balfour, now has some problems of his
own, and they all seem to revolve around Paige Halliday
and the way the look, taste and feel of her seem to haunt
his every waking moment.

Our anonymous "gift-giver" had *no* idea what he was
starting when he put these two together. Or did he?

I hope you enjoy *The Tycoon's Secret* as much as I
enjoyed playing the "what if" game with Paige and
Sam.

All the best!

Kasey Michaels

To everyone who pays it forward

One

The honor of your presence is required
At an undisclosed location,
December Twenty-fourth of this year,
At eight o'clock in the evening,
for a black-tie affair,
At which time an explanation
Concerning your anonymous gift
will be offered.
Enclosed are all pertinent travel
arrangements for both you and
One guest of your choosing.

Sam Balfour spared a last disinterested look at the words on the invitation and then lightly tossed it and a dozen others onto the large mahogany desktop.

S. Edward Balfour IV sat back in the burgundy leather chair that was two sizes too big for him now that the years had begun to shrink him, tented his fingers atop a generous belly and looked across the desk at his nephew. "You're making a point with that gesture, aren't you, son? Do I get three guesses now as to what that point might be?"

"No need for guessing. Let's just let these serve in lieu of a November progress report, why don't we? I'm sorry, *Santa,* but our fellow man is living down to my expectations again this year, rather than up to yours. Three good-hearted givers and fifteen bottom-feeding takers. I just got word that the last one, the youth counselor in Florida, took off for Vegas within three days of getting a cash gift. I warned you about cash gifts. Three, Uncle Ned, three out of eighteen. That's a new low."

"All right, I suppose I'll agree to accept that deviation from the usual monthly report. But please let me remind you, Sam, that the gift is always given with an accompanying note that instructs the recipient to do what he or she feels best."

"Right. And for most of them, what they feel *best* is to keep their good fortune to themselves, and the hell with everyone and everything else. Kind of like the guy who grabs his bread from the middle of the loaf—and then leaves the bag open so that the rest of the slices get stale. Hey, as long as I've got mine, who cares about anyone else, right?"

"And here I was going to add that I was wondering if that *new low,* as you call it, disappoints or delights you, Sam. But that would be only a rhetorical question, wouldn't it, son?"

"It doesn't matter what I think, Uncle Ned. That's not the point," Sam said, not liking the defensive tone of his own voice. "You've been doing this for nearly ten years now, and each year the numbers get worse. What's it going to take to convince you that people aren't what you'd like to believe them to be? By and large, we're a bunch of grasping, self-serving bastards, some of us putting a good face on for the world, sure, but all of us are really out for number one, and nobody else."

"And some of us may even be cynics," Uncle Ned said, his tone more amused than accusing as he sat forward in his chair once again. "I agree, Sam, that the responses to this year's gifts have been fairly disappointing. When I began this, more than half of the recipients took their gifts and turned them into something good, something that served others rather than merely themselves."

"Yeah, I know—considering the greater good over the individual benefit. Terrific in theory, lousy in practice."

"Not entirely. You said there were three."

Sam felt sorry for his uncle and employer. "Look, you gave it your best shot, Uncle Ned. But let's just send the three who passed the test their million bucks, have them sign their confidentiality agreements and put this project to rest, okay? No party this year. It's senseless. Unless you want to invite all the others as well and watch their faces as Bruce explains the rules and only three of them get checks."

"You'd enjoy that, wouldn't you?"

Sam shrugged. "Maybe. No. No, I don't think so. I mean, what's the point? As far as I'm concerned, the ones who react the way most of them do are the normal ones. Only an idiot gives away what he can keep. You know—don't look a gift horse in the mouth? You gave, they took. Why should any of them do anything differently?"

"Oh, Sam. You're breaking an old man's heart here. You really are."

Sam half sat on one corner of the large desk. "I'm only saying what I believe. Besides, Uncle Ned, I've shown you the articles in the newspapers. That dame, that Leticia Trent, she isn't giving up. Word is getting out on what you're doing."

"Yes, yes, I know. The reclusive billionaire Santa Claus who gives out unexpected gifts so he can watch what the lucky recipients do with them and then awards the generous with one million tax-free dollars in their Christmas stockings. It's rather shocking, how on the money she is with her stories. But it's only rumors so far, remember, no more than speculation. I'm not worried. I'm rather flattered, in fact, to be seen as some modern-day Kris Kringle." He patted his stomach. "I'm even working on the bowlful-of-jelly belly."

Then his uncle sobered. "This is what Maureen wanted, Sam. This is what she and I did those last few years before she was taken from me. This is her legacy. I'm not going to stop, not until the world has run out of good people, and I don't think it ever will."

"I understand. I'm sorry I brought it up," Sam said, reluctantly giving up the fight. Aunt Maureen had been bedridden for the last five years of her life, and the generous project had been her idea. She and Uncle Ned would scour the newspapers, the Internet, every day, looking for possible worthy recipients of unexpected gifts, be it the gift of money or something else of particular interest to the individual selected.

If the person kept what was given, used it selfishly, that person was out of the running for the larger gift at the Christmas Eve gathering. The initial gift would have been earned, as Maureen saw it, but no additional gift would be coming to these people.

Sam privately thought that Maureen and Uncle Ned were playing God with other people's lives, but he had always kept that opinion to himself. It was watching his uncle's generous heart being bruised year after year that made Sam want to see an end to the project.

Sam also knew his uncle's arguments for keeping the project going.

Uncle Ned had sworn that the searching, the

choosing, the anticipation, the joy when people they'd chosen had done such magnificent things with their gifts, had kept his beloved wife alive long past the predictions of her doctors.

Now maybe the project was doing the same for her husband, a thought that, when he admitted it to himself, scared the hell out of Sam. Because if Sam didn't believe in the goodness of man all that much, what he really hated was the *reclusive billionaire* part, as his uncle had been hiding from the world since the day Maureen died.

"Sam?"

"Yes, sir," Sam said, picking up the invitations that would not be sent this year, intending to toss them in the trash.

"You might want to hang on to one of those." His uncle opened the top center drawer and pulled out a dark green file folder. Sam knew the drill. Green, for *giving*. "I've selected one more recipient for you."

"You don't give up, do you?" Sam reluctantly took the folder. "Even if this one works out, Uncle Ned, you'd still only be four for nineteen. You wouldn't consider that a good return on your investment if these people were stocks or bonds."

"But that's the point, Sam. People can't be toted up on a balance sheet. People can't be assigned to the profit or loss columns of a ledger. I wish you understood that. You worry me, son. Your poor opinion of people in general worries me, as you've no good reason to hold such low opinions. Anyone would think you grew up in a hovel, downtrodden and oppressed in every way, rather than here, which I would think even you would say is the lap of luxury."

Sam smiled. "I know. I almost developed a speech impediment, trying to talk with that entire set of silver flatware in my mouth."

Uncle Ned tipped his head to one side and smiled at his nephew. "Did you ever consider that it might be the company you keep that's colored your judgment, inside and outside of your business dealings with some of the less than munificent of corporate leaders? Not that they aren't all beautiful women."

"They are that, and always in it for what they can get out of it—or out of me. Thankfully, they're also disposable and interchangeable, rather like the corporate leaders. But we'll leave psychoanalyzing my inappropriate response to being born with a silver spoon in my mouth for another time, okay?" Sam said, holding up the folder. "I'll take this to Bruce and get him started."

"No, Sam, you won't. There's been a change of plans. This one you'll handle yourself."

"Me? Uncle Ned, come on. I handle the paperwork, the gifts, the funds transfers. I take care of the invitations—all three of them this year. I arrange for the damn million-dollar checks and the Christmas Eve party. Bruce takes care of everything else, the meeting, the greeting, the hosting and most especially the delivering of the initial gifts and the follow-up. Not my job, not my table, you know?"

"You'll do what I tell you to do, Sam," his uncle said, his tone the one that had, in earlier years, been the terror of several boardrooms. "This one's local. You won't have to travel or lose any time from your busy schedule of running my companies and sleeping with any pretty woman with a pulse. Although that redhead last month would have tempted a rock."

Sam looked at his uncle in astonishment. "Pardon me? What was that? You're keeping tabs on *me* as well as your recipients? Wonderful. You'll have to excuse me now, so I can go find Bruce and break his nose for him."

"Leave Bruce alone. He only does what I tell him. Depressingly well in your case. I had to warn him not to bring me any more, shall I say, *interesting* photographs of you and your interchangeable and disposable young ladies. Frankly, I'm surprised they don't all have constant chest colds, the way they dress. You're my sole heir, Sam, my brother's child. I love you. But I don't like what I'm seeing. You're turning cold and perhaps even hard. You may well be on your way to being a *user,* and will end up a lonely, disillusioned old man."

"And here I thought you liked me," Sam complained, trying to deflect his uncle with humor. "I'm your namesake, remember? Raised at your knee, taught everything you know? I never realized I was such a sad disappointment to you."

"Don't fight me on this, Sam, because you won't win. You've known nothing but the cutthroat world of business, and you're very good at it. Well, and your ladies. According to Bruce, and those photographs that have been burned into my retinas, you're more than very good with them. In fact, I believe Bruce's last communication to me before I told him to stop included the words *he could give seminars*."

"Well, thank you, Bruce." Sam grinned. "I'd still like to break his nose. After that, I may ask him for a few eight-by-tens."

"Smiling and being funny won't get you out of this, Sam. Humor me. Let me try to show you what Maureen showed me. I've sidelined Bruce and his camera."

"You're actually serious, aren't you?"

"Deadly serious. Beginning to end, Sam, *you* will handle this prospective millionaire. *You* will bring me all the reports. I don't know what will happen, although I've chosen this person very particularly and will admit that my hopes are high. I want to see if you'll have your bad opinion of your fellow humans reinforced, or if you'll begin to see what Maureen taught me to see—that the good in this world outnumbers the bad."

"But never outnumbers the greedy," Sam said under his breath on his way back to his own suite of offices in the immense Philadelphia mainline mansion.

He tossed the green folder on his desk, refusing to look at it, and went to lunch. He was pretty sure he was having *blonde* today….

While holding a phone to her ear, Paige Halliday frantically rummaged through a sheaf of notes on a desk piled six inches high with sliding stacks of papers.

"No, Claire, I'm sure I'm right. I just can't find my darn notes! *Ten* lords a-leaping. Not twelve. Twelve is… Damn, what's twelve, Claire? Oh, God, maybe you're right and I'm wrong. Where am I going to find a dozen lords a-leaping? I didn't think I could find ten. Are you sure? No, wait, I found my list, I've got it in front of me right now. It's twelve *drummers drumming*. Ten leaping lords. You got those? *Please* say you've got those. Yes, I'll hold."

Paige slumped against a corner of the desk, wondering why she'd so blithely said *sure, no problem* when her client had asked for a display of the Twelve Days of Christmas at the last minute, making the display a part of their mall-wide after-Christmas sales.

What were they planning? On the fifth day after Christmas my true love gave to me five golden rings—marked seventy percent below the normal sale price? On the ninth day after Christmas my true love gave to me—nine ladies dancing through the home goods department in search of January white sale bargains?

And all of the displays would be life-size, no less,

because the mall atrium was huge, and a smaller display would be dwarfed.

"Dwarfed," she grumbled to herself. "Dwarfs I've got in stock. It's the freaking eight maids a-milking that are going to kill me… Hello? Claire? No good on the lords a-leaping, huh? Okay, then how about— damn, Claire, someone's at the service door. Probably another delivery. I'll call you back, okay? Don't forget the four calling birds. No, I don't know what calling birds *look like*. What normal person *would* know that? Just wing it—ha! Get it? *Wing it*. Oh, hell. There goes the doorbell again. I'll call you back—gotta go."

Paige put down the cordless phone and jammed her hands against the sides of her head as the person at the delivery door had stopped leaning on the doorbell in exchange for banging on the door. Not that anything could muss her short pixie cut cap of black hair, but she hoped the pressure of her fingers against her temples might push her aching brain back into place.

She counted to three, dropped her hands to her sides and took a deep breath, letting it out slowly.

In the land of Paige Halliday, owner and operator of Holidays by Halliday, October was frantic and November was nuts. December was October and November put together, and then squared. The fact that the Christmas season brought her more than sixty percent of her yearly gross usually was enough to keep her moving, keep her functioning at the highest level.

But that didn't mean anything kept her *sane* between the day after Thanksgiving and December twenty-fourth, as the turkeys and cornucopias came down and the Santas and angels went up.

"Keep your shirt on out there, I'm coming as fast as I can!" she called out as she hastily worked her way between mounds of ribbon rolls and plastic crates filled with oversize Christmas balls piled everywhere she could find space for them. She sucked in her breath and her already-flat belly to edge between a grinning eight-foot-high snowman and a reindeer whose nose was *supposed* to be both red and electrified, but wasn't, and into the back room.

The knock came again, and she might have been a little bit careless as she pushed at the stack of corrugated boxes filled with loose silver glitter—loose because, after the reindeer fiasco, she'd already opened one box to check the contents. "Be right there—*damn!*"

She opened the door while picking bits of silver glitter from the tip of her tongue before closing her eyes and shaking her head, sending glitter showering from her hair, her face, her shoulders. She'd caught the box before it fell, but the contents had *sprinkled* on her a bit.

"There, that's better. Sorry about the delay in answering. So? How may I help you?" she asked, not really looking at the man who stood in the alleyway.

"That would depend," the man said, and the amusement in his decidedly sexy voice had Paige blinking the last of the glitter from her eyelashes and concentrating her attention on her visitor.

Well, would you look at that. Even the man's eyes smiled. Whew boy. Why did all the good ones show up when I look like an escapee from an institution for the terminally idiotic?

"That would depend on what?" she asked, once more brushing at the glitter on her shoulders. Silver dandruff. Wonderful.

"Are you Paige Halliday?"

"If I say no, will you come back in an hour, when I'm decent?" she asked him, wondering if his teeth were capped. If not, his children should go down on bended knees to thank him for such beautiful straight teeth. "Do you have a delivery for me? If there's a God, it's the pink artificial tree from Beekman's Supply. Green trees I've got in that garage behind you. White ones. Pink? Not so much."

"I'm sorry, no. No pink tree. It's starting to rain. May I come in?"

"I don't know…um…" She squinted at him. *Nice tie*. "Do I know you?"

"No, Ms. Halliday, you don't. Do I need a note of introduction from my mother?"

Paige felt her cheeks growing hot. "No, no, of course not. It's just…it's just that you don't look like a deliveryman, er, person."

"That's…very comforting, thank you."

Great. Now she was a master of understatement, of the obvious. The guy sure didn't look like a delivery…person. He looked like that perfectly mussed haircut had cost more than the down payment on her condo, his dark suit twice the value of her delivery vans. Tall, slim, handsome, he looked like money should ooze from his pores when lesser people can only sweat.

Still, Paige didn't know the man. "If you could tell me why you're here? I mean, if you're here to talk about decorating your home or business for the holidays, I'm open Monday through Friday. I even have a door on the main street, so you didn't have to come all the way around here into the alley."

"Nobody answered my knock on the front door. And it's after business hours," he said. "But I saw lights on inside, so I thought I'd take a chance. I'm harmless, Ms. Halliday, I promise. In fact, I'm the bearer of good news. And it's raining harder now."

"Oh, all right, all right, come on in," Paige said, backing away from the door. "Careful of that leaning tower of boxes over there. I don't think silver glitter would go too well with that suit."

"I agree. It looks much better on you."

"Uh…thanks." She turned to lead the way back into her workroom/office. "What's your name, anyway?"

She watched as he went nose-to-nose with the reindeer as he maneuvered his way toward the doorway. "Bru—that is, that reindeer is a real bruiser, isn't he? I'm Sam," he said, clearing the doorway.

Paige had caught the hesitation, the quick recovery. Still, she stuck out her hand. "Nice to meet you, Bru-sam."

He took it, his grip comfortably firm, his contact just a split second longer than maybe it should have been. His eyes, now that she was closer to him, were a lovely warm brown. And they were still smiling. "Just Sam, please. I tend to stammer when in the presence of a woman as beautiful as you, Ms. Halliday."

Paige was visibly deflated. "Oh, great. You're selling insurance, aren't you? Look, I'm perfectly happy with the coverage I've got, and I told the guy that when he called last week, okay?"

"I'm not selling insurance, Ms. Halliday," Sam said as he reached into his suit jacket's inside pocket and withdrew an expensive cream-colored envelope. "I'm here to give you something."

"Sure you are," Paige said, brushing at the silver sprinkles on her shoulder yet again. "Why, you're about the fifth person this week to stop by in the rain, just to *give* me something." She leaned back against the high worktable, wishing she had worn something classier than black jeans and an old Christmas-green angora sweater to work today.

"Is that so? Lucky you."

She had a feeling she wasn't making a great first impression. Especially since she couldn't seem to *shut up*. "Okay, look, Sam. I'm sorry, I really am. I'm not usually such a grouch, but I have these maids a-milking to find, not to mention the calling birds and the leaping lords, and I only have a couple more days to do that, let alone get them ready for prime time. You're not seeing me at my best."

Sam nodded, just as if he understood what she'd just said—and she barely understood what she was saying. "This is quite an operation you have here, Ms. Halliday," he said, looking around the room that should have been twice as big to fit in what she'd found a way to fit into it. "I think this is what is called controlled chaos."

"Only if the person saying that is being really, *really* polite. I'm hoping to expand into the empty building next door, after the holidays, but for now it's a bit of a squeeze in here. The rest of the year isn't this bad or this hectic."

She looked around the room, seeing it with his eyes, the eyes of an outsider, looking in. The tall topiary trees for either side of the Heckman's front door. The red and white striped pole with the Welcome Santa sign on it. Not to mention the seven swans a-swimming she'd already located.

Most especially not to mention that two of those swans looked like they were getting *way* too friendly with each other.

"Would you like to go next door to the cafe for a cup of coffee?" Paige asked brightly, trying to redirect Sam whatever-his-last-name-was away from the pseudocopulating fowl. "It can get kind of claustrophobic in here, and Joann's coffee is really good."

And maybe the sexy smell of your cologne will get lost in the other smells, and I wouldn't feel so much like jumping your bones.

But she didn't think it would be such a good idea to say that. It wasn't even a good idea to *think* that.

"A cup of coffee sounds very tempting, Ms. Halliday, but I'm afraid I have a dinner engagement in an hour, across town. I'm only here as a favor to a friend. So, if you wouldn't mind, I'd like to just hand you this envelope and be on my way. The letter inside, I understand, is self-explanatory."

"Oh." Paige stared nervously at the envelope but didn't attempt to take it from him. "All right. Um… thank you?"

"Not me, Ms. Halliday," he said, and suddenly the man didn't look quite as amused. "Believe me, I have nothing to do with this. Although delighted to meet you, I'm just the messenger."

"You don't look like a delivery guy or a messenger," she told him honestly. Was he flirting with her now? She was pretty sure he was, at least a little bit. Okay. What was good for the goose was good enough for the six geese a-laying, or something like that. She blinked several times, doing her best to look adorably flustered, as they said in romance novels. "So, no, Sam, I don't think I believe you."

He was staring at her now. Positively *staring* at her. Maybe she looked good in silver glitter? Who knew, it might be a whole new look for her.

"You should believe me, Ms. Halliday, because I'm telling you nothing but the truth. I'm the messenger. My... A client of mine felt he needed someone he could trust to take care of this matter for him. So I may be a messenger, yes, but I'm a very well-paid messenger."

Paige quickly shoved her hands behind her back as she panicked. "You're a lawyer, Sam? The person who sent you here is one of your clients, is that it? You did say a *client,* right? That's a summons, or something? I'm being sued?"

"Absolutely, not. Look, just take this and—"

"Not yet, no, thank you. Is this about the Gobble-Gobble for Dollars contest display in Bailey's Super-Shop? Hey, nobody got hurt, you know. It wasn't *that* big of a turkey, which is why it all happened in the first place. And it was only a blow-up plastic thing. How bad could that hurt? The kid shouldn't have been trying to ride it, right? Who tries to ride a turkey? And where the hell was his mother? She has to be equally culpable. That's the word, right? Culpable?"

"Gobble-Gobble contest? Turkey riding? I think you might lead a very interesting life, Ms. Halliday. I'm not a lawyer, no. But please do consider me sworn to secrecy as far as my client goes, even though I'm not a priest, either. No, definitely not a priest..."

He was looking her that way again. Why? She wasn't that *interesting*. Was she?

He stepped closer to her. "Hold still. One of those silver sparkles is very close to your eye. We need to get rid of it."

"We do?" Paige held her breath as he cupped her chin in his hand and used the index finger of his other hand to lightly stroke the skin beneath her right eye. He was so close to her, so intent on what he was doing. She could see little reddish flecks in his warm brown pupils. The slight laugh crinkles around the outside of his eyes.

She felt herself almost falling toward him.

Okay, so her body wasn't moving.

Her mind, however, had already jumped into bed with him and was ripping off his clothes with her teeth.

He continued to stroke her skin, out and over her cheek. His fingers trailed down her face, followed the line of her chin.

If either of them had a knife, there was enough tension in the air to give even a freshly sharpened blade a run for its money.

Paige swallowed and heard the sound of that swallow in her ears.

She was so…suave.

Sam smiled. Yes, all the way up to and including his eyes. "There, all done. You're safe now. For the moment, at least," he said as he stepped back, his neat double entendres circling fast and furious around her slightly muzzy head.

"Huh? Oh. Right. Er…thanks?"

"You're very welcome, but the pleasure was all mine." He lightly tapped the envelope just between her breasts, once, twice, and then held it there until she grabbed it from his hand. "It has been interesting, Ms. Halliday. Meeting you, that is. It's time for you to read your letter. But I think we must find a way to do this again sometime soon. For now, I'll find my own way out."

Paige quickly looked down at the envelope and at the way her name had been written on it in a dark, bold, definitely masculine script. "Uh-huh," she said, mentally saying goodbye to the handsome man who had to be the best-looking and best-dressed messenger in history, and hello to, well, she wouldn't know that until she opened the envelope, would she?

"Sam? Don't forget to watch out for the top box of glitter. Oh, and the door will lock automatically behind you."

Once she heard the heavy door close, she pulled a stool from beneath the worktable and eased herself onto it, so that her shaking legs didn't have to worry about supporting her.

What the hell had just happened?

Who *was* that masked man?

Most importantly—was she nuts? A stranger comes knocking on your door, and you open it, you let him in, you let him…touch you. You let yourself think about how *else* he might be able to touch you?

You even consider giving him detailed *directions* on where and how to touch you?

He had said they must find a way do this again. Soon, he'd said. She hoped he could find that way soon. She'd even be willing to offer to help him look.

"Well, this isn't good. I've really got to get out more. I'm beginning to have sexual fantasies, or something," Paige said out loud, fanning herself with the envelope until she remembered that, yes, she was holding an envelope.

She laid it on the worktable. It looked harmless enough. It wasn't going to jump up and bite her, for crying out loud.

She stared at the envelope until she thought she might be ready to read what was inside it, and then she picked it up, sliding loose the glued flap. Sam had told her to read the letter, so she'd read the letter.

Inside was one sheet of paper, typed. Unsigned.

Ms. Halliday, this communication is to inform you that a benefactor who wishes to remain anonymous has become aware of your continued outstanding good work with the Lark Summit Orphanage and wishes to reward your laudable volunteer spirit with a small token of appreciation.

Please contact the Sales Manager at Maintown Motors at your earliest convenience. What awaits you there is yours, to do with what you wish.

Be assured it is true, Ms. Halliday, that to give is more blessed than to receive.

"That's it? That's all? Give what? Receive what? That's *it?*" Paige turned the letter over, to find that, yes, that was indeed *it*. Just those few words. No other explanation.

The phone beside her rang, and Paige jumped, her mind immediately leaping to the idea that Sam was calling her, to explain the letter to her. She picked it up and pressed Talk.

"Sam? What does— Oh, hi, Claire. No, no, I wasn't expecting anyone else. Not really. You're kidding! You found the calling birds? That's wonderful." She slid off the stool, still looking at the letter, wishing for more words to appear, or to at least understand the few that were written there.

None did, so she put down the sheet of paper, the typed side facedown. She had more important things to think about right now. "Gee…that really is great. So, um, inquiring minds want to know, Claire—what *do* calling birds look like?"

Two

"I missed you at the dinner table, Sam," S. Edward Balfour said as he settled himself into his favorite chair in Sam's sprawling apartment in the west wing of Balfour Hall.

Sam never sat in that chair himself. It was his apartment but that was Uncle Ned's chair. It would always be Uncle Ned's chair, even after the old man was gone. "I'm sorry, Uncle Ned," Sam said now, closing the file he'd been looking at and placing it on the coffee table in front of him. "Time must have gotten away from me."

Too late, he realized that the file was still the same manila folder Uncle Ned had given him last week. The green one.

And Uncle Ned had noticed. Indicating the folder with a tip of his chin, he asked, "What have you got there? And why were you frowning when I walked in here?"

Sam picked up the short, fat glass he'd half filled with single malt an hour earlier and had yet to finish. "This? Nothing. Still a work in progress. I'll have the written report for you soon. So what did I miss? Please don't tell me Mrs. Clarkson made her famous spaghetti and meatballs. Except that I think she did, if that stain on the front of your shirt can be taken as a clue."

His uncle looked down at his shirtfront, which was curved over his belly, and laughed. "Soon I'll be forced to wear a bib, eh? As long as I kick off before I get to the adult diapers stage, I guess I can handle that. Yes, spaghetti and meatballs. It is Tuesday, you know, unless you've forgotten that, as well?"

"No," Sam said, smiling, "I hadn't forgotten." His uncle had very particular tastes, not to mention very limited tastes, which fit well with Mrs. Clarkson's obvious talent but equally limited repertoire of menus. In other words, if it's Tuesday, it must be spaghetti. "What brings you up here, Uncle Ned? Did you want to talk to me about something?"

His uncle's smile told Sam that he might as well forget trying to divert him, because there was no fooling the old man. There never had been—not in business and most definitely not in their personal lives. "Tell me about the girl."

At last, Sam took a swallow of the single malt. "Did you really call Bruce off, or am I just going to be telling you something you already know?"

"Bruce is on his way to Hawaii, for a well-deserved vacation. Your *face* is telling me at least some of what I know. I found another winner, didn't I?"

Sam slowly put down the glass and opened the folder. "I'm not as good with the camera as Bruce— I did get him to give me a couple of eight-by-tens, by the way, before I had him destroy every other photograph and negative while I watched. He loaned me his camera and telephoto lens, but I still felt like a voyeur. Anyway, here you go, minus the typed report," he said, pulling out a stack of photographs and lining the first few up across the front of the coffee table.

S. Edward levered himself up and out of the chair and walked over to the coffee table even as he pulled a pair of drugstore reading glasses from his shirt pocket. The man was worth two-point-six billion dollars as of the last quarterly report, but he liked drugstore glasses, so that's what he wore. He purchased them by the gross and had pairs shoved into drawers in every room in the mansion—a billionaire's idea of convenience *and* economy.

"Tell me what I'm looking at, Sam, please."

"You're just rubbing it in, aren't you, Uncle Ned? All right, I'll play your game." Sam pointed to the first photograph. "Our Ms. Halliday, arriving at the car dealership bright and early last Saturday morning, the day after I delivered the envelope. I had a feeling she's one of those bright and chipper in the morning types, so I was outside her condo early, hiding across the street in Mrs. Clarkson's car. The Mercedes doesn't quite blend with Ms. Halliday's neighborhood."

He moved his fingertip to the next photo and the next. "Ms. Halliday's mouth dropped open wide enough to see her tonsils while looking at the deluxe van with Holidays by Halliday painted on the sides…. Ms. Halliday stroking her company logo with something pretty close to awe…. It was almost embarrassing to watch her, as a matter of fact. As if I was invading her privacy as she gazed at her beloved. Well, you know what I mean."

"I have vague memories of what a loverlike look is, yes. Pity. Bruce would have gotten some nice close-ups of her face. He snaps a lot of film—click-click-click, you know? Then he gives me only the best shots. You're more the aim-carefully-and-shoot-once type, I think."

"Is that a comment on how I handle a camera or on me?"

"Ah-ah, touchy, touchy, Sam. Cut off her head on that one, didn't you? Maureen used to do that. We had to identify most of her photos by the shoes we were wearing at the time," Uncle Ned commented, inspecting the photograph. "But I suppose you did as well as you could. Your talents simply lie elsewhere, so don't worry about it. Go on. There are more, aren't there?"

"Thanks for overlooking my lousy camera skills, and yes, there are more shots," Sam said with absolutely no inflection in his tone before he handed his uncle the remainder of the photographs. "What you're looking at are shots of what happened after she was done crawling inside the van, sitting in the driver's seat—honking the horn a few times. She got out, stared at the damn thing for what had to be five full minutes. I think she might have been crying, but I'm not sure. Could have been the sun was reflecting off the van and getting into her eyes."

"How sweet. Pretty girl, isn't she? Maureen would think she had very nice posture. And then?" Uncle Ned asked, his eyes twinkling above the reading glasses as he shuffled to the next photograph.

"You know how to twist a knife, Uncle, I'll give you that one. And then she handed the keys back to the sales manager."

Uncle Ned looked up from the photographs, his grin as wide as his chubby cheeks would allow. "Did she now? Wonderful! And then what happened?"

"Right. Wonderful. And then I just sat there like a two-bit private eye waiting for someone's straying husband to slip back out of the by-the-hour motel he'd entered an hour earlier, camera at the ready and wondering why my uncle hates me."

"Poor, poor Sam. You lead such a hard life.

Continue. Ms. Halliday, as I see here, eventually re-appeared? Tell me—what's that she's driving?"

"Her old van," Sam said, barely able to unclench his teeth. What the hell was the matter with him? Why was he so angry with Paige Halliday for being a good person? Being a good person didn't make her any less bed-able, did it?

Uncle Ned was still looking at the photograph. "Ah, all right. Her *old* van, literally. So, the dealer-ship is going to deliver her new van?"

"Just keep looking through the photographs, will you? Or do you like shoving those bamboo strips up under my fingernails?"

"Touchy tonight, aren't you? Have some more scotch." Uncle Ned flipped through the remaining photographs, holding on to the last one. "You know, Sam, if I were the type to gloat, I'd be gloating right now. As it is, I'm just too happy to see that the or-phanage has a nice new van. But it's not the same one Ms. Halliday was looking at, is it? This one is longer and has windows. Talk to me, Sam."

"I got the details from your friend, the sales manager. Who, by the way, tried to hit me up for the cost of repainting the original van. Ms. Halliday, as you've probably figured out, traded the closed van you bought for her for a fifteen-passenger number she then donated to the orphanage. That includes an extended warranty, so said the manager, that she talked him into kicking in at no extra charge. As she explained to the sales manager, the kids often go on field trips and some other trips, and their current van is in the shop more than it's in running condition."

"Which very nearly describes the condition of Ms. Halliday's van, I would imagine?"

"If it doesn't, it should. The thing has to be ten years old." Sam got to his feet. He'd been turning over an idea in his head ever since he saw the orphanage kids riding off the grounds inside their new van. "So go ahead, crow all you want. You won, Uncle Ned. You found another winner. Another truly unselfish person is wandering around wide-eyed and gullible in the land of the grasping and greedy. Someone who actually believes it is more blessed to give than to receive. Now, it's *my* turn."

Uncle Ned was still looking at the photographs of the orphanage children. "Your turn? Your turn for what?"

For the first time in three days, Sam smiled with real humor. "I always arrange for the Christmas Eve party at some downtown hotel, correct? This year? This year, I have other plans. The party is going to be here, Uncle Ned, right in this house. And, if she isn't too busy sprinkling herself with fairy dust and separating copulating swans, I think I've found just the decorator to help me out."

"Here?" Uncle Ned paled, visibly paled. "But... but I'm not up to that, Sam. No, we can't do that.

We…uh…we haven't had guests at Balfour Hall for a long time."

"I know that, too," Sam said gently, aware that the last time more than he and Uncle Ned and the staff had been in the huge house had been the afternoon of Maureen's funeral. It was more than time to begin filling up the rooms again.

And there were so many of them.

Hell, a man could fly a kite just in the ornate banquet hall in the house Sam's great-great-grandfather had designed to be a miniature of the famed Biltmore House. Sam had been very impressed with the room as a child but mostly because of its great echo, not the hand carved stained oak paneling or the baronial-sized dining table.

And he had one distinct memory, at the age of seven, of taking a running start and sliding down that highly polished tabletop, doing fine until he crashed into a five-foot-high solid silver candelabra and ended up in the emergency room, getting a dozen stitches in the top of his head.

Who said rich kids never had any fun? It was rich adults who didn't get to slide down tables very often….

Sam shook off the past to concentrate on the present. "I think it's time we opened up the place. We haven't had so much as a Christmas tree in five years. I remember how the house and grounds looked during the holidays while I was growing up. And I've checked. Most of the decorations are still on the grounds."

"I should know better than to piss you off, shouldn't I?" Uncle Ned said wearily, collapsing into his chair once more. "No. I'm sorry, Sam. I can't do it. Not yet. The answer is no. I'm not ready."

"I didn't ask you if you were ready, Uncle Ned. I'm telling you what I'm doing. You do remember that you've already deeded your half of this beautiful monstrosity to me three years ago, for tax purposes? So, my house, my decision."

Sam knew he sounded hard, unfeeling, but he'd been giving his idea a lot of thought, and this wasn't some twisted way to see more of the frustratingly *nice* Paige Halliday. Not *all* of it, anyway. It was time his uncle returned to the world.

"Good thing I didn't gift you with my back teeth, or I'd be chewing with my gums right about now."

"Very funny. You don't have to come to the party, Uncle Ned. You've never done that before, in any case, either you or Aunt Maureen. I just want to have it here. If you think you *can* do it, that would be good, too."

"Which is what you're hoping for. You're a little transparent, Sam. In fact, I think I can see straight through you at the moment, all the way to your motives. Let me guess. You, not Bruce, will play host this year to the do-gooders, as you so cynically call them?"

"I will, although I'd prefer that you took on the role of host. And I don't mind being transparent, if it makes you realize how important it is to me that you... Well, it's just time, Uncle Ned, that's all. I worry about you.

Aunt Maureen would kick your butt if she knew how you've pulled back from the world."

"Leave your aunt out of this, if you don't mind. Even if you're right." Uncle Ned took a deep breath. "So all this for me, and the fact that Paige Halliday is quite a remarkably pretty young woman has nothing to do with any of this?"

"She doesn't," Sam said, feeling his jaw growing tight. "I can promise you that."

"So you say. This idea of yours is all due to some crazy scheme to get me up off my ass and back into the world?"

"I already said it did," Sam said, beginning to relax again.

"I know you did. And I believe you—about me, that is. But not about the girl. What I also don't believe is that the pretty little girl in those photographs deserves what you have planned for her. *I* didn't bargain for that. She's not in your league, Sam. She doesn't know the rules."

"You make me sound like some sleazy playboy out to collect another notch on his bedpost," Sam protested as he reached for his glass of scotch.

"No, I don't think you're sleazy," Uncle Ned said, smiling wanly. "And I don't think you're a playboy. You work too hard to be called a playboy. As for collecting those notches? You tell me, Sam. You're thirty-six. Why are you still acting like you're twenty-one and bedding women who just became legal, or something? Have you conquered so much in business that you need to keep searching for other conquests? Is it the chase that thrills you more than the capture?"

Sam drained the last of his single malt, not even tasting it. "How many sleepless nights have you spent trying to figure me out, Uncle Ned? Why do I do what I do? I don't know, Uncle Ned. I don't know."

"It wasn't because you had an unhappy childhood. Your parents loved you and they loved each other. Until the day my brother died, your mother looked at him with stars in her eyes. You're not emotionally scarred, you don't belong on a shrink's couch—at least I don't think you do. So why all the women, Sam, why the constant parade moving in and out of your life? Why don't you like women?"

"Hey, you saw the photographs. I'm extremely fond of women," Sam said, his smile crooked.

"All right. Let's talk about that. They might amuse you, for a while. But none of them lasts more than a few weeks, before you're off on the hunt again. Maybe that's the real question, Sam. You said your women are interchangeable and disposable. Obviously none of them is touching you in any way. So that's the question you need to ask yourself, son. What *are* you looking for?"

"Right now, a way out of this conversation," Sam said honestly. "If I promise again not to take aim at your little do-gooder, will you agree to my plan to have the dinner at Balfour Hall? Because the bottom line here, Uncle Ned, is that I don't want to upset you."

"Upset me? Now I'm fragile? I don't like that. All right, have your damn way, have the dinner here. Decorate the place, if that's what will make you happy." Uncle Ned got to his feet and handed the stack of photographs back to Sam. "But don't make promises unless you're sure you can keep them."

"No problem, Uncle Ned," Sam told his uncle as the man walked to the doorway. "She's not my type."

Uncle Ned stopped at the door and turned to look at Sam. "Apparently, no woman is. At thirty-six, Sam, if I were you, I'd start to worry about that. Seventy-five and alone comes soon enough. If you have nothing, no happiness to either hold or to look back on, I can imagine that seventy-five could be a pretty miserable experience."

Sam had no answer for that, so he merely nodded and waited for his uncle to leave before he moved to gather up the photographs and put them, and the green file, somewhere that he didn't have to look at them again for a while.

The photograph of Paige Halliday looking adoringly at her company logo painted on the side of the van seemed to stick to Sam's fingers. She was a beautiful woman, he had to admit that. Different.

When she'd opened the service door, spitting silver glitter, he'd thought her comical, uncaring or unaware of her beauty and extremely natural.

When she'd taken him into her workroom and stood beneath the harsh work lights, the glitter in her midnight-black hair, dusting the shoulders of the fuzzy green sweater that matched her eyes, sparkling against her creamy white skin, had made her look like some sort of Christmas spirit. A slightly naughty Christmas angel.

He wished he could get that image out of his head...but until he could, he was going to stick very close to Paige Halliday, to figure out *why* that image was still haunting him.

And one more thing...he probably was going to have to take at least a cursory look at the idea that, while he thought himself happy, even content with the way his life was going, his uncle seemed to think he should be miserable.

At ten o'clock on Wednesday morning, Paige Halliday stood in the alleyway behind Holidays by Halliday, a large blue plastic tarp spread out on the macadam, a painter's mask held to her nose and mouth as she carefully sprayed imitation snow onto a short, squat, too-pink-to-be-passable Christmas tree.

The idea was to tone down the pink, and she thought it was working. Well, it would be working, if the wind would just die down for a few minutes. As it was, she was getting a lot of the fake snow on herself and not the artificial tree. Good thing she'd taken the time to pull on the white coveralls her friend Bennie had given her last year, when she helped him paint his office down the street.

She bent down, keenly eyeing the bottom branches. Yes, that one needed another squirt, definitely. A little squirt here…another one just over there. One more quick shot on the lowest branch on this side of the tree. *Perfect*. Ah, the eye of the artist; it was a beautiful thing. She was the Michelangelo of pink Christmas trees…the da Vinci of artificial snow…the Picasso of—

"Is that offer of coffee still open?"

Paige stood up and turned around, all in one motion. The only thing she forgot to do was to take her finger off the spray can button. "Ohmigod, ohmigod!" she yelped when she saw what she'd done and who she'd done it to.

She tossed the can and face mask to the ground and all but leapt at Sam to keep him from trying to brush the puffy white artificial snow from his million-dollar suit. "No, no, don't do that! We have to let it dry. It'll brush right off once it's dry, I promise. I mean, I think it will. That's what it says on the directions, anyway. I'll pay for the dry cleaning. I'm *so* sorry—but you really shouldn't sneak up on people like that."

Sam held his hands up at his sides, like she was holding a gun on him or something. "You're right. This is entirely my own fault. What was I thinking?"

She blinked up at him, trying to gauge his smile

and tone. "Are you being sarcastic? Well, of course you are. And you're right. Who expects to be attacked by a spray can?"

"Not me, obviously. I wasn't sure it was you, at first. Who's Bennie?"

Paige was trying not to notice that the zigzag spray of puffy white on Sam's suit jacket pretty much looked like the Z mark of Zorro. But she wasn't sure he would appreciate the joke if she pointed that out. "I'm sorry? Bennie?"

"Yes, Bennie. Of Bennie's Bug Bombs. It's printed on the back of your...whatever it is you're wearing."

"Oh, Bennie. Right. Bennie gave me the coveralls. They're called coveralls. He's an exterminator, business and residential. But you've probably already guessed that." She tilted her head to one side. "Why are you here?"

"You had offered me a cup of coffee, remember?"

"I remember," Paige said, avoiding his eyes. His smiling eyes. His too-sexy-to-be-real eyes. "But that was Friday. Today's Wednesday. I didn't think you'd remembered. Hold still, this stuff dries fast. I'm pretty sure I can brush it off now."

"Thank you, I think I can manage. And you might not need the warning, because you're unarmed now, but there's someone standing behind you."

Paige frowned and then turned around to see one of her assistants standing behind her. "Oh, Paul, good. Hey, do you think you can put this tree back in the storage garage? It doesn't go out until to-morrow. Be careful, the bottom branches might still be damp in places."

"I'll be careful," the too-thin blond youth said. He was already holding both her mask and the spray can. "You've got some snow on your head."

"Of course I do. Why should my life be easy?" Paige muttered under her breath, quickly ruffling her short hair, hoping to dislodge whatever snow had landed there. "Thanks, Paul."

"Shall I meet you at the café?"

God, he's still here. Most men would have made a run for it by now. At least the sane ones.

"Sure!" Paige said brightly as she turned to him again. Too brightly. Nothing like advertising your desperation. "Sounds like a plan, Sam. Just give me five minutes to get out of these coveralls, and I'll meet you there. Go ahead and order. I take mine black. And I'd love a glazed donut, if Joann has any left. She probably doesn't. I already bought a half dozen this morning for my gang."

Without waiting for Sam's answer, Paige ducked into the building, already frantically stripping off the coveralls. "Mary Sue?" she called to her assistant, a chubby redheaded matron with the look of a weary soccer mom. "Where are you? Mary Sue—*help*. I've got to look drop-dead gorgeous, professional yet approachable and maybe even reasonably adorable, and I've only got five minutes."

Three

Sam had taken a booth with a view of the front door stuck in the middle of two plate glass windows.

He saw Paige Halliday sort of skid to a halt from a full run, take a breath and then slowly walk the rest of the way to the door. She looked so elegant, sleek, tall and slim, her unusual short cap of black hair a definite turn-on, as were her deep-green eyes, long, swanlike neck and a tightly sculpted chin line.

Paige Halliday could be a top fashion model. It was difficult to believe she was also such a klutz. He was really looking forward to getting to know her better. Much better.

She opened the door, paused at the entrance and cast her eyes around the café, spotting him.

He lifted his hand slightly and waved to her.

Her answering smile threw a figurative uppercut to his solar plexus, and he got to his feet, waiting until she'd slid onto the facing banquette seat. "Black, just as you ordered," he said as he sat down again. "But they're out of glazed, so I ordered us each a slice of apple pie. I'm told it's the best apple pie this side of the Delaware. I have no idea what's on the other side of the Delaware, do you?"

"Last I looked, New Jersey." She took a sip of coffee, and then smiled. "But not *the* Delaware, as in the river. Joann meant Delaware Avenue. Her brother owns a café on the other side of Delaware, and the apple pie is from his recipe. So, technically…"

"Got it," Sam said, smiling. "I saw that you solved the problem of the pink Christmas tree."

"Look, about that," Paige said, folding her hands on the tabletop. "I really will pay to have your suit cleaned. How is it? Did the snow all turn to powder and brush off?"

"It's fine, the suit's fine." He'd left the jacket in the car to deal with later. "Don't worry about it. It was my fault for coming up behind you like that. Ms. Halliday, I would like to talk to you about—"

"Paige. Please call me Paige. I call you Sam. Of course, that's because I don't know your last name."

"Balfour. The full name is Sam Balfour. And why are you suddenly looking at me like that?"

"Because I know that name from somewhere. Balfour, Balfour." She leaned against the faded imitation leather back of the booth and stared at him. "Oh, wait a minute. Now I remember. Laurie. Laura Reed. You remember the name, Sam?"

Sam rifled through his mental filing cabinet and came up with a folder marked *Mistakes*. And there was Laura Reed's name, pretty close to the top of the list. "I might," he said carefully.

"You might? That's it? You *might?* She thought you were getting serious," Paige said, sitting forward once more, and picking up her fork. Although instead of using it to break off a piece of pie, she pointed it toward him, accusingly. "Choosing china patterns serious, as a matter of fact. She was my roommate our last year in college, and we still keep in touch once in a while. She's married now and expecting her second child."

Sam coughed into his fist. At least Paige and Laura weren't related. That could have been worse, even if this was still pretty bad. "That's nice. That she's married, I mean. It was a few years ago, Paige, but I don't remember ever leading Laura on, doing anything to make her think I might be serious."

"You took her to London with you for three days. Wined her, dined her in this castle you rented for the duration. I can see where she probably overreacted, read too much into the whole thing. The private jet, the intimate dinners, the diamond earrings? Shame on her for thinking she wasn't just a quick fling for you."

Sam searched for something to say and came up empty, which probably didn't matter, because clearly Paige wasn't finished.

"And then, when you only saw her one more time once you got back to Philly before dropping off the radar, not showing up for another two weeks or so, when she saw you coming out of a restaurant while pretty much chewing off the face of some willing blonde, I suppose she overreacted again?"

Sam closed his eyes, the memory of what had happened that night more than five years ago suddenly fresh in his mind. "I didn't press charges," he said quietly. And then he smiled. "It was a hell of a shiner, you know. Your friend packs a pretty strong punch."

"You think this is *funny?* Laura was heartbroken."

"Really," Sam said, beginning to relax, which was probably smarter than allowing himself to get angry. He remembered a lot about the beautiful, ambitious Laura Reed. She'd known the drill. She was chasing him to catch him, his name, his money. She'd gambled, and she'd lost. But she'd known the rules going in. That was Sam's policy; he only played with the ones who knew the rules.

The problem was, once in a while his judgment was a little off, and he came up against a sore loser. "And how long did poor, devastated Laura remain heartbroken?"

"She was married six months later. Chad's father owns his own investment bank, in Dallas, something to do with oil and gas," Paige said quietly and then looked at him accusingly. "But that's not the point. The point is, I *know* you. I know who and what you are, and you're nobody's messenger boy. So maybe you'd better tell me who sent you and why you came back."

Her eyes had gone a darker green, Sam noticed. Pretty, intriguing, but probably not good news for him. "As Bob Dylan said so well in one of his songs, 'you're gonna have to serve somebody,' Paige."

"I suppose that's true. I'll give you that one," she said, finally cutting into the pie with the side of her fork. Clearly the woman's appetite didn't suffer when she was confused or upset. "So tell me who you serve, Sam."

"Sorry, I can't do that. Why don't you tell me what was in that envelope?"

Her grin was so full of evil delight that he had to suck in a breath or else laugh out loud. "Sorry, I can't do that," she repeated right back at him. And then she lost her smile as she looked at him with narrowed eyelids. "You really don't know what was in that envelope?"

"Not until you tell me, no." It was either lie or involve his uncle, something he wouldn't do. Not now, when he was liking more and more the idea of grabbing that uncle by the lapels and pulling him back into life. At the moment, getting Paige Halliday into his bed was in the column Sam had marked *bonus*.

"Ah, but I'm not *going* to tell you," Paige said around a mouthful of pie. "Mmm, it's still a little warm. I forgot Joann was baking this morning. Quick, taste your pie."

He did as she said. "They're right," he said after he'd chewed and swallowed. "Best apple pie this side of Delaware. Why won't you tell me? Don't tell me my client is into something illegal."

Paige coughed into her fist and quickly reached for her cup of coffee. "Why…why would you say that?"

"No reason," Sam said, concentrating on his pie. "But, to be truthful, the least I can do is to assure you that my client is very upstanding. In his own way." Then he watched for her reaction.

"What's his way? No, don't. Never mind. I know who you are now, and I doubt that any client of yours is laundering money through me or something."

"How would he be laundering money?"

She rolled her eyes. "Well, I certainly don't know how. I don't even know what laundering money means, at least not exactly. Look, Sam, thanks for the pie, really. But you're not talking and I'm not talking and I've still got to spray paint five hula hoops gold before five o'clock, so I've got to go."

Sam reached across the table to lay his hand on top of hers as she braced her palms on the tabletop, getting ready to slide out of the booth. "Don't go. Not yet. And don't worry, please. My client is the most honest man I know. Whatever his business with you,

I can promise you that it was entirely aboveboard, all right? But that's not why I'm here."

Paige subsided onto the imitation-leather cushion, but still looked ready to bolt. "It isn't?"

"No, it's not," Sam said, looking deeply into her eyes, his hand still on hers. "I'm going to be perfectly honest here, because I think that's what you'd want. I came back for you."

She pointedly extracted her hand from beneath his. "I'm not Laura."

"Good. I know where to find Lauras when I want them."

"That's really tacky," Paige said, shaking her head. "Not to mention insufferably arrogant, even if it's true."

"I know. I'm sorry, Paige. Let's just say I don't need my past misdeeds tossed in my face, all right? Especially when all you know is one side of the story."

"That's where you'd be wrong, Sam. I know both sides. Laura was out for the main chance, and you were more than happy to string her along so you could get what you wanted. Neither of you would have been up for saint of the year, and maybe you both got what you deserved. It's really none of my business. It's simply a life, and a lifestyle, that doesn't appeal to me. So thank you very much, I'm glad I bothered to wash the fake snow out of my hair, I'm almost flattered, it's nice to know that thirty isn't too over-the-hill to be hit on by handsome guys—but no, thanks. Now, once again, if you'll excuse me."

"I want to hire you to decorate my house and grounds for a small but elegant dinner party I'll be hosting Christmas Eve," Sam said quickly. "I'm also considering a large open house for New Year's Day, for friends and business associates, although that plan is still somewhat liquid."

"Really." Her tone told him she didn't believe him.

"Yes, Paige, really. It's been a long time since Balfour Hall has been dressed up for the holidays. As a bachelor, I haven't really thought about decorating the old homestead. I'm usually in the islands over the holidays."

"But not this year?"

"No, not this year. It turns out that I'm needed here. At any rate, most of the decorations have been in the family for generations, but it would take a more talented eye than mine, or anyone's on my domestic staff, to display everything to its best advantage. And then there are the trees—live, please, and at least five of them. And the live greens to decorate the staircases, the fireplaces. There are eight fireplaces in the downstairs, public areas of the house. I have some photographs of how it all looked years ago, and I hope you can re-create my childhood memories."

"I'm pretty sure I've seen pictures of Balfour Hall somewhere. It's huge. Photographs *would* help…"

Ah, she was weakening! Hit 'em where they live; that had always worked in business and in Sam's personal life. Diamonds for one, exotic locales for another—and, it would seem, Christmas decorations for one Ms. Paige Halliday. And Sam gets what he wants, just like he always does. Life was good…as long as Uncle Ned stopped making him feel like something was wrong with that life.

"I've got plenty of photographs. And then there's the exterior, of course. No blow-up Santas on the lawn, if you please. I'm thinking more of potted greenery and some discreet lighting. I know you're already busy with your pink trees and maids a-milking, but I believe I can make it worth your while to agree to the job. What do you say to fifty thousand dollars pure profit, in addition to any costs?"

"I'd say you're certifiable," Paige told him, sounding slightly breathless. "I'd…I'd have to hire an entire crew to take over all my current clients and then more for your job, as I'd have to spread my experienced people between the two. Even then, I'd be working at the house almost constantly if you want the decorations in place by even the middle of December. You should have contacted a designer months ago, Sam. A year ago!"

"My sincere apologies. And the extra crew costs would also, naturally, fall to me. Would you say that would run about another ten thousand?"

"Fifteen, easy. I don't cut hourly wages just because the people are only there as temporary Christmas help." She held up her hands. "No. Stop that. Stop throwing five-figure numbers around like that. You're not impressing me."

"Of course I am," Sam said, grinning. "Let's not play around anymore, Paige, all right? You're a businesswoman. You've probably already figured your profit and how you'll word the notice you'll put in the newspaper's want ads."

Her grin was self-deprecating. "Oh, I'm way ahead of you, Mr. Balfour. You forgot the phone calls I'd be placing to all the local magazines and newspapers, hoping for a photo spread. Visions of a national magazine four-page photomontage are already dancing in my head. My business would double."

"I could make a few calls, arrange that for you."

"God, you're smug. It's all that money, isn't it? You're just used to getting your own way."

"Wealth has its perks, I won't deny that. So, how am I doing? Convinced yet?"

She didn't say anything else for a few tense moments, moments during which they both, he was sure, readjusted the conversation to where all of this verbal foreplay was *really* heading.

When she finally spoke again, he knew they were both on the same page.

"I don't have a price, Sam," she warned him tightly.

"We all have a price, Ms. Halliday. It just isn't always money."

And then he went for the jugular. He had a feeling that his Ms. Halliday—he was already thinking of her as *his*—longed to be more creative than her commercial clients allowed her to be. A canvas like Balfour Hall would give her the perfect palette for some serious creativity. Nobody spends years and years in a design school for the chance to one day spray paint pink Christmas trees.

"Did I tell you that one of the trees I most remember from my youth wasn't a tree at all? Let me see if I can describe it for you. It was in the shape of a tree, yes, but it was made entirely out of enormous red poinsettia plants arranged in decreasing circles, to form a tree. There's a rather immense oriel window in the library, and the tree was always positioned in front of it. Incredibly striking, especially if there was snow on the grounds outside the window. That tree must have been fifteen feet high and half again as wide—or I was still quite small. Would you know how to re-create something like that?"

Paige nodded, not saying anything. She was, he was sure, already mentally figuring out how to build a poinsettia tree. He could almost hear the gears turning inside that pretty head.

"The banquet hall—sorry, but that is what we call it—will prove a bit of a challenge. It's three stories in the center of the house, behind the great foyer. Paneling, exposed beams, what you'd call an English gothic architecture, I suppose. My father used to joke that you could roast sinners on a spit in the fireplace. It's that huge, and I think he was right. That's where

I'd like to have the dinner party—in the banquet hall, not the fireplace. It will be a real challenge to make such an expansive space seem intimate. Maybe you're not up to that large of a project?"

She reacted to his last statement as if he'd physically slapped her. Her head went back, her chin went up and those fascinating green eyes narrowed once more. "Oh, please, don't dangle goodies and then try reverse psychology on me, Sam. *Mister* Balfour. You know damn well no designer would ever turn down a job like the one you're waving in front of me right now. If you let me invite photographers, the publicity could set Holidays by Halliday up for life, and you know that, too. I just don't know *why* you're doing the dangling."

Did she really want him to say the words? *Because I want to have sex with you. I want us to enjoy each other.* No, he didn't think so. She wasn't ready for that, not yet. Hinting, yes, but not anything quite so blunt.

"Do you really need to know? Or do you interrogate all your potential clients as to their reasons for hiring you?"

That seemed to stop her. She opened her mouth to say something and then seemed to reconsider. "No, I suppose not. Maybe I'm overreacting, or even flattering myself. I wish I didn't.... You made a much better first impression when I didn't know who you were, you know?"

"I understand. Give me Laura's address in Dallas. I'll send her flowers."

"Oh, yeah, that'd go over real big with Chad. Look, let's start over, okay?" She held out her right hand. "Hi, I'm Paige Halliday. I understand you're interested in hiring the services of Holidays by Halliday. How may I help you?"

Sam took her hand, and raised it to his lips and then held it there as he looked at her, as he lightly stroked across her knuckles with his thumb. "We could start with you coming to see my home. I could take you there, after we've had dinner tonight."

Once again, she withdrew her hand. "Oh, how smooth," she said sarcastically. "And now I know for sure, don't I? I want this job, Sam. Only an idiot would turn it down, but the price just went up. Fifty-five thousand, independent of paying for all materials and my crews," she said flatly. "And I have a feeling I'm going to earn every penny. You can pick me up next door at six. That should give me enough time to spray the hula hoops and hunt up a chastity belt."

He was barely on his feet when she was gone from the booth and on her way out of the café, waving to a gum-chewing blonde behind the counter as she went.

She'd certainly drawn the battle lines, thrown down the gauntlet or whatever else he could think of that might sound reasonable if he was standing in the middle of the Balfour banquet hall.

Sam gestured to the same blonde, to ask for the check and a refill on his coffee, and then sat in the booth, slowly finishing his slice of pie. It really was good apple pie.

His pursuit of Paige Halliday was turning into a very expensive project—he'd almost lost her over the Laura Reed debacle—but he also had a feeling that Paige Halliday would be worth every penny she'd earn.

For her decoration of Balfour Hall, that is. That's where she'd earn her money.

He'd think of convincing her to go to bed with him as a special Christmas present to himself....

"The van's all loaded with the last of it," Mary Sue said, leaning half into the minuscule office Paige had carved out in one corner of the workroom. "And you're sure you don't want to go along to drive us all crazy, positioning everything precisely?"

"Positive," Paige said, hitting the return key on her computer. "It's only a matter of assembling everything according to the plan. I trust you implicitly, Mary Sue, and it's mostly your design anyway. Did you remember the eggs? Six of them, for the geese a-laying. They're in the box on top of the worktable."

"Got 'em," her assistant said, peering toward the computer. "Whatcha doin'?"

"Nothing," Paige said as she turned in her desk chair, blocking the computer screen with her body.

"Were you able to make the deadline for the ad? I want it to run clear through the weekend."

"Also done. We'll be fine, honey. There's always a bunch of people looking to pick up some part-time holiday work," Mary Sue said, leaning to her left, again to try to see the computer screen. "That him? I was going to go next door to grab a cup of coffee and, you know, sneak a peek at him. All very discreet, and with him never even noticing me. But the darn phone wouldn't stop ringing. Move over. Let me see. Will he ruin me for all other men?"

Paige swiveled back to the computer screen and the photograph that had come up of Samuel Edward Balfour V. He was wearing a tuxedo and escorting a tall, willowy blonde down a flight of marble steps into what was probably a ballroom. "That's him," she admitted. "The picture might be a couple of years old, but he hasn't really changed much. Maybe he's a little harder around the edges now, but it looks good on him."

"And *this* is what you're telling me did everything but come right out and say he wants to jump your bones? Rich, handsome *and* eager? How long do you plan to hold out, hon? Five minutes? Ten? I'll talk to Paul and the others. We could start a pool."

"I didn't say he *definitely* wants to jump my bones, Mary Sue. It's only a theory. I think Sam Balfour sees all women as potential conquests," Paige protested, turning back to her assistant, whose smile was pretty much bordering on the lascivious. "And stop that. You look like a wolf eyeing up a tasty sheep."

"But I do love a juicy lamb chop. Okay, okay, don't frown, you'll get wrinkles and our sugar daddy might change his mind and take his business elsewhere. And you did so say he wants to jump your bones. Maybe not in those exact words, but that's what you meant."

"I don't know what I meant," Paige admitted honestly. "He throws around money like it's water— very expensive water. Except that, for him, he's using pocket change."

"A whole *lot* of pocket change. You must have really made a big-time impression on him, Paige. He doesn't look like the type who has to pay for it, even indirectly," Mary Sue said, grabbing her winter coat from the coatrack behind the door.

"No, I'm sure he doesn't. I don't know what he's doing, Mary Sue, I really don't. First the—well, never mind that, that's separate, or at least I hope so. Maybe he really does want to decorate his home sweet home, and the rest—that would be me, I think—is just a little added incentive. Who understands how rich people operate? Certainly not me."

"First the what?" Mary Sue turned up her collar as she looked carefully at her friend and boss. "Does this have anything to do with the van you gave to Lark Summit? Because I still don't get that one. We've got two vans, one not looking so good and the one that's on life support half the time. I like the orphanage, honey, I understand your connection there. But I don't get it. Why a van? And why now? Oh, and another biggie—why doesn't the purchase show up anywhere on our books? Because it doesn't. I checked."

"You might need these, and you're going to be late if you end up hitting rush hour traffic," Paige said, fishing the step–side keys out of the drawer and tossing them to Mary Sue.

"That's your answer? *No* answer?"

Paige gave it up. It was either that or just prolonging the agony, because Mary Sue wasn't going to stop until she had the whole story out of her. "The van was a gift, all right. Well, not that exact van. Another one. But I traded it in for the passenger van I gave to Lark Summit. And, no, I don't know who gave me the gift. It was…it was anonymous. To thank me for my work at Lark Summit."

"Damn, that was clear as mud."

Paige dug into the center drawer of her desk and pulled out the letter, still in its envelope. "Here. Now you know what I know."

Mary Sue took the single sheet of paper from the envelope and read the words. "Oh, wow. *To give is more blessed than to receive.* I think I see your problem. Somebody gave to you, and you figured the only *good* thing would be to give as *good* as you got. Am I right?"

"Something like that, I guess. I don't know. Maybe.

What's it called? Paying things forward? Somebody does something nice for you and you do something nice for somebody else? I just know that when I saw the van this person had given me, all I could think was that I have a van. Two. And the truck."

"None of which is exactly in the greatest shape anymore, and we've only budgeted to replace one of the vans next year. But go on. I'm listening. You saw the van *and*…?"

"I saw the van, and I remembered how bad the Lark Summit van is. Was. They were going to cancel the trip to Rockerfeller Center scheduled for next week, because they couldn't trust it on such a long trip. So I was thinking about that, and how much I loved going on day trips like that. Christmas isn't always the happiest time of year for orphans, you know? I mean, people show up, people donate gifts, but it's still not like having a family."

Paige lifted her hands rather helplessly and then let them drop into her lap. "I don't know, Mary Sue. I think I was in shock, a little, and my mind just kept whirling around and around. And the next thing I knew, I was talking the sales manager into a trade. I'm an idiot, right?"

"Not really. Sometimes you're just a little too good to be real, but you're not an idiot. So where does our handsome billionaire come into this? He delivered the envelope? Have I got that much right?"

Paige nodded. "We seemed to…we seemed to hit

it off, you know? There was some sort of spark, some sort of connection."

"Chemistry. Pure animal attraction. Got it. Loving it. Go on."

"He said he'd be back, or he'd have to see me again, something like that. But he didn't come back. Not until today. If I were a calculating woman, I'd say he stayed away just long enough for me to start feeling insecure, like maybe I'd overreacted, and then, when he showed up, I'd be really pleased to see him. Grateful, even."

"That would be pretty cold and calculated on his part," Mary Sue said, handing back the envelope. "Maybe you'd better rethink this decorating job. I know it's the sort of thing you've dreamt about doing. I know it will bump us right up there with the top designers in the city. But will it be worth the hassle?"

"He can hassle all day, for all I care. It's not like he's going to get what he wants. Not when I know what he wants."

"Really? But how much trouble is it going to be for you? Hang a ball on the Christmas tree, get chased around that tree by our handsome billionaire on the make, hang another ball on the Christmas tree? Sounds pretty nerve-racking, not to mention exhausting. I mean, unless you're only trying to convince yourself that you haven't already considered going to bed with him."

"Trust me here, Mary Sue, I'd already considered

that last Friday. No man has never had that instant an affect on me. It was wild," Paige admitted, sighing. "Now I'm not so sure. And there's still the van in there somewhere, you know? I really want to know how he's connected to that, because I don't get it. People don't just give other people things without wanting something in return."

"Sure they do. You just gave Lark Summit a new van."

"Yes, but I did get something from it. Personal satisfaction, I guess you'd say, even if that sounds hokey. It felt good, Mary Sue, watching the kids pile into that van. I felt really *good*."

"So maybe it made your anonymous Santa Claus feel good, too, giving you that van. How come you can feel good, giving, but you suspect the motives of someone else who just might want to feel good, too? That doesn't seem fair."

Paige shrugged. "Okay, point taken. But I don't think Sam Balfour is exactly Santa Claus. When he gives, he expects something in return."

"Like you, served up on a silver platter. He'll provide the platter."

"Exactly. Except that I don't think I'm worth all this intricate planning and chasing."

"No, you wouldn't, would you, honey? That's one of the things I like best about you. You haven't got a clue that you're a pretty unique and terrific person. See you tomorrow morning, all right? And if you think you won't remember everything that happens, for God's sake, take notes, because I'll be expecting a full report."

Four

"Here, try this now."

Paige looked at the vaguely round, segmented gray thing caught on the tines of Sam's fork. "What is it? And this time tell me before I'm chewing on it."

"You said you liked it," he reminded her.

"Yeah? Well, that was before you told me it was a mussel. I don't eat mussels."

"You do now. You asked me for another one. Now, come on, be daring. Open up."

She looked at the whatever-it-was a second time and then closed her eyes and opened her mouth, closing it again around the tines of the fork. Her eyes opened wide as the spiciness of whatever the whatever-it-was had been marinated in hit her taste buds with the impact only slightly less powerful than being slapped upside the head with a two-by-four.

She swallowed without chewing, even as she grabbed her water glass and drank deeply. Even the inside of her lips were on fire. She could feel little beads of perspiration forming under her eyes and wiped at them with her napkin. "Admit it, you're a sadist, aren't you? What...what *was* that?"

Sam looked entirely too happy, so she was pretty sure she wasn't going to like his answer.

"Squid. Marinated squid. So?"

"Oh, *yuck*. So now I understand why they soaked it in cayenne pepper. It was so a person doesn't have to taste it. How can you eat that stuff?"

"It's considered very *avant-garde* in some circles, I believe. A true seafood medley salad. Although you're probably right. Mostly, it's greens and spices. But, congratulations for being so willing to try something new. You're very daring."

"I learned fairly early to eat what's put in front of me. But I think I just hit the wall on that one. I'll stick to my French onion soup from here on out, okay?"

"So that rules out the octopus I was going to offer you next?"

"I think that would be a safe deduction, yes." Paige looked across the large yet strangely intimate dining room. Every table was occupied, and it was only Wednesday night. She wished yet again that she'd had time to go home, to shower and put on another outfit, but she couldn't spend time worrying about what couldn't be changed. "I've never been here before. It's a very lovely restaurant."

"Thank you. I suppose I should tell you that I own it," Sam said, lifting his wineglass to his lips.

"Well, then, how very *lovely* for you," Paige said as the waiter removed the soup bowl and replaced it with her entrée. Why on earth had she ordered lamb chops?

"I had no choice. Bertran's is one of the premier restaurants in the city. It was either buy it or take the chance of not being able to get a reservation."

"Yes, I see the logic," Paige said, trying hard to keep a straight face. She couldn't do it. "It must be terrific fun to be so filthy rich. You probably giggle all the time."

Sam leaned his chin in his hand as he and his wonderful brown eyes smiled at her across the table. "You have no idea. But being filthy rich does come with certain drawbacks."

"The Laura Reeds of this world," Paige said, knowing where he was going, although she didn't know why she knew. It seemed as if they could say only a few words to each other, yet know exactly what the other person meant, where the conversation was headed next. It was almost…spooky.

"Yes, the Laura Reeds of this world. Beautiful women throwing themselves at me, day in, day out. It's a burden I carry."

"Because you don't know if they're throwing themselves at you or at your money."

"Oh, it's the money, Paige. I have no illusions there. I've learned to dread the day the *Fortune 300* is published every year."

"But you're also very handsome. And even nice, when you want to be."

"Why, thank you, Ms. Halliday." He sat back in his chair, feigning embarrassment. "Am I blushing?"

"Stop that. I'm not saying anything you don't already know. No man walks the way you do, dresses the way you do, without knowing the impact he's making on women."

Sam put a hand to his chest as he looked down at his clothing. "It's just a suit, Paige. All businessmen wear suits."

"Not the way you wear them," she said, wishing she could shut up. But this was fun, this back and forth. "And the hair? Just mussed enough to know that it was cut to look just the way it does."

"Oh? And how does it look?"

She swallowed her first bite of perfectly grilled lamb chop, praying she wouldn't choke on it. "Like you just got out of bed. Like you'd be more than willing to go back to bed, with the right company. Oh, God, did I just say that?"

"You did. Looks like I'm going to have to buy my hair salon now, too. I like your hair, you know. There aren't many women with the bone structure to wear their hair so short. Although I might miss the silver glitter, just a little bit."

She looked at him, unable to look away. His eyes smiled into hers, and her stomach did a small flip.

Paige dipped her head, to concentrate on her plate. "This lamb chop is huge but really delicious. You're not eating."

"I'd say I was feasting on you, but then I'd have to shoot myself for being so corny."

She smiled, relaxing again. "And I'd have to cock the pistol for you. That was really bad. Lame, actually."

"I know. Sorry," he said, slicing into his New York strip steak. "I usually don't order red meat when I'm out with a woman, but you gave me hope when you ordered the lamb. You don't mind that I'm a carnivore? No lectures coming my way, on either my clogging arteries or cruelty to animals?"

"Not from me. I'm a simple person, happy with meat and potatoes, neither of which I have time to cook very often. If I were home right now, I'd probably be eating a peanut-butter-and-jelly sandwich over the sink. Jelly drips, if you use enough of it, and I do—and on unhealthy white bread, which is the only way to eat PB and J. So, personally, Sam? No, I don't care if you march an entire cow in here and take a bite out of it."

Once again, Sam leaned forward, his chin in his hand. "Ah, this is interesting. I don't believe I can remember having such an honest conversation with a woman. Truthfully, I don't remember the last time I sat across a dinner table and watched any woman eat more than a few bites of anything."

"And, ignoring the fact that I obviously don't eat like an undernourished canary, that makes me wonder what sort of conversations you do have with women. Politics, global warming, the latest Hollywood gossip—the best place to have your Rolls Royce detailed?"

"I don't think the women I see would be interested in any of that. Mostly, they ask questions. 'Do you like my dress? Does my hair look all right?'" His grin widened. "Later in the evening, it's more like, 'Don't wrinkle my dress…. Be careful of my hair.'"

"Really? Well, you won't hear any of that from me," Paige warned him, and then caught herself. The man was maddening! He was only teasing her, and she knew it, but for some stupid, unexplainable reason, he was also beginning to turn her on. It *had* been a long time between turn-ons, apparently. "I mean…because the…the situation wouldn't arise."

"Never say never, Paige," Sam told her. "I know I never do. But let's get back to our discussion. The man in your life would be trusted to make his own diet choices?"

Paige relaxed yet again. "Mostly. Although I'd probably make him swear off squid or else never kiss me. My lips are still burning."

"Point taken. Let's pursue this, all right? Drawing

from my memory of complaints I've heard from some of my married friends, how many rounds of golf is a reasonable number for the man in your life? Per week."

"The *hypothetical* man in my life," Paige was careful to clarify. "You play golf?"

"No, it's just a question. Yes, I play golf. Do you?"

"Only the kind where you have to hit between the rotating blades of a windmill, or get the ball into the lion's mouth. But I'm very good. Three."

"Three what? Oh, three times a week. That seems reasonable. What about sex?"

This time Paige did choke, a little. "You asked me about golf *before* you asked me about sex?"

His eyes were all but dancing in his head. "A man needs to keep his priorities straight."

"You apparently *do* talk to a lot of married men, to say that." Paige pretended to give his silly question serious consideration. "Okay, I've got a number. Once a day, I imagine."

"All right then, good enough, that takes care of days," Sam teased. "And how many nights?"

She looked at him sternly. "You know what I meant, Sam. To clarify, I meant once in every twenty-four hour period. Or was that question meant as just a sly way of bragging? Because I'm not impressed."

"Damn. I keep working my way up to a full count, and then I strike out again. Tell me, Paige, how do I get to first base?"

Paige popped a small oven-roasted potato into her

mouth and chewed on it for a while before she swallowed it, delaying her answer. He watched her closely, as if truly interested in what she would say next. So she told him the truth. "Persistence?"

She watched as his left eyebrow rose slightly, giving his handsome face a rakish look, rather like a clean-cut Jack Sparrow as played by Johnny Depp in *Pirates of the Caribbean*. She reached for her wine glass to cover her sudden nervousness.

Sam lifted his own glass and held it out toward hers. "A toast then, to persistence."

It was after nine when Sam drove through the gates and up the long, curving drive to Balfour Hall. His uncle went to bed at nine. A person could set his watch by Uncle Ned's bedtime habits, so there were no lights showing in the second floor of the east wing.

Beside Sam on the front seat, Paige was leaning forward, her eyes wide. "The photographs I've seen don't come close to showing how massive this place is," she said in some awe. "You grew up here? I'll bet hide-and-seek was a bunch of fun. Unless you starved to death before anybody found you."

"I'm an only child, Paige. I didn't get to play hide-and-seek. Just hide, which I was extremely good at, by the way. But I had a pony, so maybe we can consider it a draw?"

"More than a draw. A pony trumps just about anything else I can think of. What was his name?"

"*Her* name was Susie." Sam pulled the car into the circular area of the drive, parking it in front of the door. "I haven't thought about Susie in years. We still have the stables, but there hasn't been a horse in them for a long, long time."

She didn't wait for him to walk around to her side of the car, but was standing on the drive, waiting for him. "How much land do you have here, Sam? Obviously enough to keep your own horses. I didn't think anyone owned that much land this close to the city, not anymore."

"The original Balfour was a farmer way back in the seventeen-hundreds, which explains the amount of land, I suppose, and a descendant didn't much like farming but discovered that he was a whiz at figures, which explains the house and fortune. I've never really thought about it much, which probably makes me shallow and unappreciative. I've just never known anything but this house, this way of life. Come on, it's getting cold. Let's go inside."

He slipped his arm around her shoulders and led her up the wide steps to the massive front doors.

"If you ring the bell, will an English butler in an old-fashioned tuxedo open the door? And do you think I could ask any more stupid questions before I learn to keep my mouth shut? I should have stopped at one glass of wine."

Sam smiled as he slipped a key in the lock and ushered her into the massive foyer. "You didn't finish the second glass, and I like your questions. Most people try so hard to look bored and unimpressed that it's obvious they're just dying to gawk and stare. So go for it, Paige. Be it ever so humble, there's no place like a mansion."

She didn't have to be asked twice, it seemed, as she walked into the center of the foyer that was really more of an enormous marble-floored room, complete with fireplace and a double set of curving, ornately carved wooden staircases that climbed the side walls and met in a gallery more than thirty feet wide.

If he looked at the great foyer through her eyes, as he found he was doing now, he would have to say he was pretty damn impressed himself. Funny how a person doesn't notice what's always just, well, just been there for all of his thirty-six years.

She turned in a circle, her head tipped back, looking up at the chandelier, an eight-foot-high mass of rubbed brass and crystal prisms hanging high above a parquet wood round table currently holding a large vase filled with hothouse flowers.

"Someone changes those flowers every week, I think," he told her. "Different vases, different flowers. It used to make me feel like I was living in a hotel. You can either have the florist take care of that or do something of your own for the table."

"Every week? I guess that beats the hell out of a bunch of silk flowers picked up on sale at the local hobby shop and then just changed out with the seasons," Paige said, still turning in slow circles. "Not that you'd know that, of course."

He had to say one thing for Paige Halliday. She didn't watch every word she said around him, was obviously not out to impress him. He liked that. "Sorry. I've lived a deprived life."

"Uh-huh, sure. Do you think you have ladders anywhere? I don't think I own any long enough to reach that chandelier, and I'd kill to decorate it." She stopped moving around and looked at him. "You said you have photographs. I'd love to see them. See what was done with these fantastic staircases. I mean, I have some ideas, but I'd rather stick with tradition as much as possible."

"Why don't we finish the tour first and then look at the photographs." Sam motioned for her to follow him through the archway to the left of the foyer, and into the first public reception room. The baseboards and wainscoting were painted a creamy ivory, the walls above the wainscoting a deep maroon, the furniture plentiful, massive and overstuffed. Uncle Ned called it the main saloon. Sam's mother, when she'd wanted to tease her brother-in-law, called the room the Bordello Reception Parlor.

Sam smiled at the memory. He didn't even remember the last time he'd been in this room, let alone thought of his mother's old joke.

Now he was seeing the foyer, the drawing room,

which they entered next, and the other rooms they walked through, through Paige's eyes. Her eyes were filled with wonderment, and she was not too proud to show her delight or too jaded to realize that Balfour Hall was a treasure trove of things to see, to marvel at and enjoy.

These were the public rooms, those built and maintained entirely for show, to host the huge parties, celebrations and even charity balls that once had been so much a part of Balfour Hall.

Now they were just pretty rooms, filled with furniture, with fine art and priceless antiques collected by Balfours for several generations. But they also were rooms more dead than alive, like the silk flowers Paige mentioned, and not *real* anymore.

Somehow, without even trying, Paige was making them come alive again.

For the most part, Uncle Ned lived in a few rooms, which were more than sufficient for his needs. Sam had his wing, the wing that had been his parents' before him—before his father's sudden death, before his mother pulled herself together and moved to their winter home in Sarasota, to try to pick up the pieces of her life.

He'd actually had to hunt up the key to the front door before meeting Paige for dinner, because he usually entered directly into his own wing.

Sam heard a small voice in his brain, asking him a question, one dripping with sarcasm, or maybe tinged with regret: *Welcome home, Sam. Where the hell have you been?*

They were in the library now, and Paige was looking at the life-size portrait above the fireplace. "You look like him. Are those your parents?"

Sam stepped closer, looking up at the portrait. "You know, I'd never noticed a resemblance. You really think I look like him? He was probably about my age when this was painted."

"Oh, yes, definitely. I mean, not *exactly* like him. But there's something about the eyes. Your eyes smile, did you know that?"

"That's the devil peeking out of them," Sam told her. "At least my mother swears that's who it is. Both with my father and with me. He's been gone for a while now. He died unexpectedly only a few months after I'd finished grad school. One day he was diagnosed, and two weeks later it was all over. My mother lives in Florida now. She said she couldn't stand to stay here, without him."

"I'm sorry. It must hurt so much, to lose a parent."

"It isn't easy, no." Sam took Paige's hand and walked her toward the enormous oriel window that looked out over the grounds. "This is the window I told you about."

"Where you want the poinsettia tree, yes. It's going to be magnificent. I can up-light it at night. It's terrific that this window faces the front of the house. The tree will make a definite statement."

"It sure will. Hey, look, it'll say—big red tree!"

"Don't mock me. I could use pink poinsettias and spray snow on them." She looked at him. "But I really want to see this banquet hall for millions that I'm supposed to make intimate enough for a small dinner party. And then I'm going to need a chair and another glass of wine, because I think I'm going to have a small nervous breakdown. This is a *huge* job, Sam."

"I trust you. Come on, the banquet hall is this way," he said, taking her hand, which felt good, which felt natural. He was going to have to give this whole thing more thought. The woman was beginning to get to him. He hadn't expected that. In matters of romance, it was usually the other way around. And if Sam knew one thing about himself, it was that he needed to be the one in control.

They walked back to the great foyer by way of the morning room, the sitting room, passing by the short hallway to the family dining room, all while Paige marveled at the decorated ceilings, the distinctive fireplaces that, in most cases, had been imported from bankrupt estates in England and France when Balfour Hall was built.

He showed her the pianoforte in the music room, an antique supposedly once used by Mozart to entertain guests during some English country house party.

"That harp in the corner looks pretty old," Paige commented. "Is there a story behind that, too?"

Sam smiled. "There is, yes. A cautionary tale, one filled with warnings about what happens to little boys when they try to stick their head between the strings. I nearly sliced off an ear. A house like this can make for a dangerous playground for little boys on rainy days."

"I can't even imagine growing up as the only child in a house this large and ornate," Paige told him, squeezing his hand. The gesture seemed natural, not planned. "You were lonely?"

"No, although I could lie and try to play on your sympathies by telling you what a poor little rich boy I was. What I was, Paige, was hell on wheels."

"*Was?* As in the past tense?"

"Oh, yes. I'm much better now." He stopped in front of the pair of thickly carved doors more than fifteen feet high that stood directly beneath the balcony of the great foyer, between the two stair-cases. "Are you ready for this?"

"Barely," she said, her eyes wide. "I'm already getting that bitten-off-more-than-I-can-chew feeling, so this should probably put me over the top. I mean—oh…my…*God*."

Once again, Sam felt himself looking through Paige's eyes as he gently pulled her along into the cavernous room. "Up there?" he said, pointing with his free hand. "That's the Balfour imitation of a minstrel gallery. Terrific for hiding out in and watching the dinner party going on down below, when everyone thinks you've gone to bed. Oh, and also unparalleled for launching paper airplanes."

"Paper airplanes? In here? That's just plain sacrilegious, Sam, shame on you. But I'll bet they sailed really well," Paige said, letting go of his hand and walking across the expanse, to the dining table. "How many does this seat? Forty?"

"Close. Forty-two."

She was lightly running her hands over the shining surface of the table. "And how many will make up this intimate dinner party?"

"Eight or nine. I'd like to set places for nine, in any case. How's that glass of wine sound to you about now?"

"Like a really, really good idea." She turned to look at him, those green eyes wide and faintly frightened. "It can't be done, Sam. Nobody could make this place feel intimate. Not unless we pitched some sort of fancy tent in one of the corners."

"A tent? You know, that idea might have possibilities. Which corner?"

Paige rolled her eyes at this remark. "I wasn't being serious, Sam. A tent would be…al-*though*…"

"I think I hear gears turning. Think out loud, Paige."

"I'm not thinking," she told him, beginning a circuit around the long table. "I'm musing. There's a difference. *But,* if I could sort of, you know, *disguise* this massive table with some sort of tablescape? It's so huge, maybe a couple, three, different tablescapes, you know? Then it would lose some of its overpowering *hugeness*. And not a tent, but…but a series of *canopies*."

"Canopies." Sam shook his head, trying to ignore the notion that she was too far away, when she was only standing at the opposite end of the table. "Nope, sorry. I don't get it."

"Yes, you do. Or you will. Canopies, Sam. Striped. Festive. The corners held up by what look to be long swords, or halberds, or whatever they're called—fancy axes with really long handles, okay? The material puddling on the floor, the tops all peaked and everything. A large-as-life English village, decked out for a Christmas Fair. Almost medieval, you know? These paneled walls, that high ceiling? Those *beams?* They just scream medieval."

Now Sam put a hand to one ear. "I don't hear any screaming."

"That's all right, Sam, you don't have to hear it. As long as I do. I can already *see* them, lined up against the walls. The tent, the one for the intimate dinner party, would fit right in, yet be it's own small world, and then the village itself would be perfect for the open house. Each canopy would be its own shop, its own stop in the buffet." She pointed at him. "Tell me the open house will include a buffet."

"I'd be afraid not to. So a buffet it is."

"Great! I know a caterer who'd be perfect. One of the stalls—they were called stalls, you know. Anyway, one of the stalls would be the carving station, for the Christmas joint of beef or whatever it's called. Two stalls set up as bars, one at each end of the room. Excuse me, each end of the *village*. Vendors dressed in medieval costumes wandering the crowd with trays piled high with pastries and things like that. Jugglers. Strolling minstrels. Wait! Not just strolling minstrels. Minstrels in the minstrel gallery, too. I mean, isn't that what a minstrel gallery is for?"

"So rumor has it, yes."

Sam was beginning to really like this idea. Lord knew the room was large enough to accommodate Paige's elaborate plans, measuring forty feet across and with a length of over seventy feet. He'd been in smaller houses. More importantly, Uncle Ned would like this idea. He might even like it enough to want to be a part of it. Uncle Ned and Maureen had thrown some damn good parties, years ago.

"So that's what we do. You can't just stick a table in here and say, hey, we're having a party. Not in a place this size. You've got to go big or stay home, right? Travel the whole nine yards, Sam. Please, Sam. *Please* tell me I can do this."

She looked so appealing as she walked toward him down the length of the table. He especially liked the way she was actually hugging herself now, her eyes shining like emeralds. You'd think he'd just given her the Hope Diamond, when what he'd really handed her was a damn whole lot of work.

"If you think you can handle it, all right. Go for it."

Her relief was obvious, as was her delight. "Oh, Sam, this is going to be *so* good. I can't believe how excited I am. Pink Christmas trees? Gilded hula hoops? From that—to *this?*"

"So this is where I get to say that I'm glad you're happy? Better yet, is this where you thank me?"

Paige dropped her arms to her sides for a moment and then walked straight toward him, to wrap those arms around his neck as she smiled up into his face. "Thank you, Sam. I mean it. Thank you so much. Right now I don't care why you're doing this, I simply *can't* care why you're doing this. Not when it's all going to be so great. You can't know what this means to me. Balfour Hall is like…like a magical playground. A fantasyland. The sort of thing I dreamed about as a little girl."

And then, as if she couldn't do anything else that would adequately show her thanks, she went up on tiptoe and kissed him on the mouth.

All right. He'd never thought of Balfour Hall as an aphrodisiac but what worked, worked.

Sam felt an immediate kick-start to his libido and began to slip his arms around Paige…just as she broke contact and pushed away from him, her eyes still shining.

"Come on, Sam, show me those photographs. You said you kept them in the library, right? Let me see if I can find it again without getting lost. And then tomorrow, I want to come back and see the decorations you told me about. Where are they?"

"Uh…in the storage rooms above the garages," Sam said, watching as Paige all but danced toward the doorway, eager to see the photographs he'd promised her, her high heels clicking against the wood floor, that ridiculously long scarf flying out around her and somehow accentuating her long, long legs. All golden blouse and beige slacks and scarlet scarf; again the slightly naughty Christmas angel.

She was so obviously genuine, so unconsciously beautiful. And so completely oblivious to the impact she'd just had on him with that impetuous kiss.

Well, damn. If he'd never thought of his family home as being an aphrodisiac, he'd never thought of Balfour Hall as competition, either….

Five

Paige accepted the snifter of blackberry brandy Sam had told her she'd enjoy more than another glass of wine, willing her hand not to shake. "Thanks."

Then she covertly watched him as he returned to the cleverly hidden small bar to pour a snifter of golden-looking brandy from another crystal decanter. He'd told her that blackberry brandy was too sweet for his taste, and more suited to hers, as she'd liked the wine he'd picked for her at dinner.

She'd answered him in nods and monosyllables, because she was still trying to figure out why the hell she'd hugged the man. Worse, she'd kissed him.

So much for that metaphorical chastity belt she'd strapped on with such conviction.

Not that the hug and kiss were all that bad. In theory. A gesture of thanks, that's all. In theory.

In practice? In practice, she was pretty sure that in another ten seconds she would have been prone on that baronial dining table, with her legs wrapped around the man's back.

Paige took a sip of the brandy. Sweet. Sort of thick in a way. Syrupy, even clingy. And, she hoped as she took another sip, medicinal. As in it might be a cure for transient stupidity.

She looked up from her seat on the leather couch as he walked toward her again, the snifter in one hand, a large photograph album tucked beneath his other arm.

"There are a dozen or more albums, but we can start with this one. It contains what my mother calls an overview of Balfour life, then and now. In other words, she got tired of trying to organize all of the thousands of photographs in chronological order."

"Are there any of you on a bearskin rug?" she asked him as he sat down beside her. "Or is that something parents don't torture their kids with anymore?"

"Torture?"

"Yes. You know. It's your first prom, and your mom pulls out the old photo album for your date, and turns straight to that picture of you bare-assed on a rug? It happens all the time on TV sitcoms."

"I guess I lucked out there," Sam said, putting his snifter down on the edge of the coffee table before laying the book down, too, and opening it. "But there is an empty space in here somewhere, because I ripped up the photograph—the only one in existence, by the way—of me smiling openmouthed at the camera with a mouth full of braces. Mostly, I frowned for about two years."

"Really? I'd wondered about that," Paige said, and then caught herself. "Uh, I mean, not the frowning, because you really don't frown, but how kids feel about braces. I didn't need them."

"You're lucky. I couldn't chew gum for two years, and that drove me crazy. What's strange is that I haven't chewed gum now for about twenty years, and I don't miss it."

"No, that's reasonable and very human. We often want most what we can't have," Paige said, and then inwardly kicked herself again. If the man commented on the weather, would she still be able to put her foot in her mouth with her response?

He captured her eyes with his own slightly mocking gaze. "And then, when we can have it, when we finally get it in our grasp, we don't want it anymore?"

"Okay. I suppose that also seems reasonable," Paige said, reaching for the top corner of the first page of the photograph album, and hopefully finding something she could use for a change of subject. "Oh, look, who is that? And would you take a look at that collar? You'd think he'd slice his ear off if he turned his head."

"I think that's called a celluloid collar," Sam told

her, his voice close to her ear. "That might be Samuel Edward Balfour II. Junior Balfour. Or else he's the third. Anyway, he's one of the numbered Sams. I should know this, shouldn't I?"

He'd touched a nerve, even if he couldn't know it. "Yes, Sam, you should. Family is important. Family is your heritage. Who they were helps make up who you are. This house, Sam? It's wonderful, it truly is a treasure to be proud of. But at the end of the day, it's family that really counts. Knowing your roots."

Then she shut up, because she was doing it again. Saying things she shouldn't say. They weren't swapping life stories here. The man was a client. Period.

"I suppose you're right," Sam said, reaching in front of her to turn another page. He kept turning pages, looking for photographs showing the house at Christmas. "My mother was into genealogy there for a while. I'll have to send these albums down to her so she can label some of these photographs. Okay, here's one. The great foyer."

Paige leaned forward, directing her gaze to the photograph Sam had indicated with his finger. What she saw was a little boy in a white shirt and short dark blue velvet pants, a bandage on his knee, smiling into the camera as he proudly held up a fishing pole with a big red bow on it. The little boy's eyes were *smiling*.

Something inside her chest went sort of spr-r-o-ing. *My, wasn't that sophisticated...*

"So, what do you think?"

Paige snapped back to reality a lucky heartbeat before she said, "About what?" She cleared her throat and said, "It's a good photograph, very inclusive. I think I can re-create that look. It's quite simple, actually, the live evergreen swags and bows and all. Old-fashioned, very traditional. I'll probably have to replace the bows, however. Those really don't hold up for too many years unless they've been stored very carefully. Who…um…is that you?"

"In all my glory, yes." Sam was still looking at the photograph, a small smile playing around the corners of his mouth. "I loved that fishing pole. I haven't thought of it in a long time, but I did love it." He turned to look at Paige. "There's a stream that runs through the property. Nothing but minnows and a few almost generic-types of fish too small to bother with in it, but that never stopped me from thinking I was going to reel in a whale. Mostly, I brought home frogs Mom wouldn't let me keep."

He wasn't trying to be charming, Paige was sure of that. Well, pretty sure of that. He simply *was* charming. Charming came naturally to him, like the air he breathed.

As battles of the sexes go, she had come into this one seriously underarmed and without a clear strategy. Time to back up a bit.

"A pony, your own stream to fish in—what else made up your childhood, Sam? Is there an indoor swimming pool or tennis court somewhere?"

He raised one eyebrow as he looked at her. "The tone is amused, but the question is a little pointed. What's going on here? I was doing pretty well there for a while. Did I just lose points because I had a happy childhood?"

"No, of course not. Don't be silly," Paige said, turning back to the photograph album. She hadn't meant to sound so sharp. "I had an imaginary friend when I was little. An imaginary sister, actually. Her name was Gretchen, and she was the brave one, the one who checked under the bed and in the closet every night, to make sure there were no monsters waiting to jump out and get me."

"Did she ever find any?"

Paige frowned as she looked up at him again. "Any what? Oh. Any monsters? No, she never did. But that didn't mean they weren't there. She just kept them away."

"Who keeps them away now that you're all grown up? Has Gretchen been replaced by a knight in shining armor? Should I be watching out for him and his great white stallion?"

This conversation was getting ridiculous, as well as increasingly uncomfortable. "I'm thirty years old, Sam, and hardly a child anymore. I slay my own dragons now."

"So no boyfriend," Sam continued. He was a very persistent man. "No one particular man in your life."

"No, Sam, no one particular man in my life," she

answered, tension bubbling along her nerves. "And, just in case you were going to ask, I'm not looking for one, either. My life is quite complete as it is. Now, either find me some photographs of the banquet hall or take me home, because this conversation is over."

"I thought we were talking too much, too," he said softly as he slipped one hand behind her neck and drew her closer. "Much, much too much talking…"

Paige could have resisted him. He wasn't holding her that tightly as he slipped his fingers into her hair.

But she was also intensely curious. Would Sam's kiss, in reality, be even remotely close to as devastating as she had already half decided it would be?

Besides, she rather liked the feeling of the shivery goose bumps his touch immediately raised on the back of her neck, an instant, pleasurable reaction that skittered down across her shoulder, a tingling that reached all the way to her fingertips.

Her lips parted, just a little, almost involuntarily, and she closed her eyes.

It had been a long time….

She lifted her arms to hold on to him as he eased her down onto the decorative cushions that were piled against the arm of the couch, their mouths clinging, his tongue initiating a sweet, welcome invasion she had no intention of denying.

His strong, hard thigh was between her legs, and she felt an instant tightening, a near burn of concentrated physical reaction of her most intimate being to the stimulus he provided, that the mere thought of what would come next provided.

Sam's moves were practiced, extraordinarily smooth, but Paige didn't care. She'd think about that later, think about all the other women who had succumbed to him at some other time.

Right now, it was her turn.

And it had been a very long time....

He had her blouse hem free of her slacks now, and she felt him expertly easing open the buttons of that blouse, one by one, as he kept his mouth fused to hers, his tongue working small miracles of arousal.

Her heart was pounding as he efficiently dealt with the front closing on her bra, freeing her breasts. He pressed the palm of his hand between them and held it there, as if to tell her that, yes, he could feel that frantic beat, too.

And that he liked the feeling.

Paige heard her soft moan of loss when his mouth left hers, but then arched her back as he turned his attention to her breasts, capturing first one nipple, then the other, leaving a trail of warm, moist kisses even as she felt the snap of her slacks release, even as her mind registered the soft sound of her zipper sliding open.

Oh, he was good. He was very, very good....

His mouth was next to her ear now. "Nobody wins, Paige, nobody loses."

"That's...that's not always true." She closed her eyes as the soft whisper of his voice seemed to send off small vibrations inside her ear, down the side of her neck.

"Are you planning to break my heart, Paige?"

She pushed gently at his shoulders, and he obligingly moved back so that she could look into his eyes. "I don't think that's possible."

"You'd be surprised at what's possible, Paige," he said, his gaze hot and dark and capable of curling her toes inside her shoes. "You feel it, don't you? You wouldn't be here if you didn't feel it. We both knew this was inevitable the first time we met."

Paige averted her eyes. "I…I don't know what you're—yes. *Yes,* all right? Inevitable."

He stroked the back of his hand down her cheek. "And that makes you angry? With me? Or with yourself?"

"With myself," Paige admitted quietly. "I know who you are, what you are. And yet…and yet, here I am."

"I'm not the bad guy, Paige. I'm a man, and a man who wants you. Very much. It's not just the sex, and that's not just a line. I think you could be…important to me. Necessary to me."

"You don't even know me."

"Correction, sweetheart. I've never known anyone quite like you. There's a difference. A difference I think we should explore."

Paige tried to summon a smile. "This is ridiculous. You're lying on top of me, I'm half dressed—"

"Half undressed. But I'm working on it."

"Don't interrupt. We're lying here, and we're having this deep, and deeply strange conversation. Part of me wants to continue that conversation, but the rest of me has totally different plans for the evening."

Sam's smile melted what was left of her resolve. "We can stop now, postpone that inevitability, or we can enjoy each other now. Just tell me what you want."

She raised her arms to press the palms of her hands against his cheeks as she lifted her hips suggestively. "I think…I think I want you to shut up and come here. If you're done talking, that is."

This time when he took her mouth she more than met him halfway. *In for a penny, in for a pound*—that was the old saying, wasn't it? He wanted her. She wanted him. As he'd said, some things were just inevitable.

When he put his hand between them to push down her slacks, she helped him by raising her hips. When he fumbled with his belt, she pushed his hand away and did the job for him.

All the while, their mouths were fused together, anticipating, simulating the act—his tongue thrusting, withdrawing, her mouth capturing, holding. Never had she felt such an intimacy of passion, this extraordinary *need*.

Paige was swallowed up by the soft cushions that insulated her from the weight of Sam's body as he made short work of protecting her, even that brief interruption bringing a moan to her lips.

And then he was inside her, filling her, and she wrapped her arms and legs around him in her effort to take all that he would give her.

Vaguely, as passion, want and sweet, escalating need replaced everything else, Paige wondered who at Holidays by Halliday was going to win the pool....

Sam made his way to the greenhouse that stood on its own some thirty yards away from the rear of the east wing of the house, checking the watch on his wrist and measuring the hour against rush hour traffic and the beginning of his meeting with several international bankers at the Balfour Building on Chestnut Street downtown.

But as he'd told Paige, you're gonna have to serve somebody, and Uncle Ned had called this meeting, named the time and place and Sam had no choice but to attend.

He opened the door to the greenhouse, closing it again quickly against the morning chill that had frosted the lawns of Balfour Hall, and called his uncle's name.

Uncle Ned lived for his flowers, and the greenhouse had been expanded several times over the years, until it now rivaled some of the local nurseries for size and capabilities. But what was money for, if it couldn't buy you a few toys?

Sam passed by a long table crowded with pots of a flower he suddenly recognized. It was tall, a little spiky, and with its flowers exactly like those he'd seen last night in the great foyer.

"Son of a gun," he said under his breath, feeling like a fool. Now he knew who put those fresh flowers in the great foyer once a week. Who put fresh flowers all over the house, for that matter. "I really have to slow down, start paying more attention to what the hell goes on around here.... *Uncle Ned? Where are you?*"

"Over here, Sam. Turn left at the table of amaryllis."

"I would, if I knew what the hell an amaryllis looked like! Keep talking, Uncle Ned, and I'll just follow your voice." Sam pulled the handkerchief from his back pocket and wiped at his forehead before shrugging out of his cashmere topcoat. You could roast an ox in this overheated building with no problem.

"Ah, see that you found me," Uncle Ned said, smiling. He was seated on a high stool, a rubber apron tied around his spreading waistline, the bib of the apron held in place by the loop of material slung around his neck. He had on bright green rubber gloves, and he was snipping at a sad-looking plant with a small pair of clippers. "Emergency surgery," he said, snipping off another small, limp branch.

"Really. Will the patient live?"

"It'll be touch and go for a while, but I think so, yes." Uncle Ned put down the clippers. "You didn't listen to me, Sam. I'm extremely disappointed in you. *Extremely* disappointed."

"I don't know what you're talking about," Sam

said, knowing damn full well what his uncle was talking about. *Whom* his uncle was talking about.

"Don't insult me. Paige Halliday isn't like your other women, Sam."

Sam nodded. He'd been thinking the same thing almost constantly since last night. The woman had gotten to him. How, he didn't know. He had already planned to see her again today, even if he had to make up a reason. "I agree. She's nothing like any woman I've known. That's her attraction. I'm allowed to be attracted, aren't I?"

"No, Sam, you aren't. I had Bruce investigate Ms. Halliday thoroughly before I chose her to receive one of my anonymous gifts. Did you bother to read Bruce's report?"

"Not really, no. Are you going to tell me what I missed? She's one of your do-gooders and a winner. She's also beautiful, desirable, unattached and—" Sam caught himself before he said, *willing.* "What else is there to know?"

Uncle Ned carefully eased himself off the stool and picked up the ailing plant, carrying it over to a table sparsely populated by other plants that looked like they'd seen happier days. "I shouldn't. You should care enough to read the report on your own. But I suppose you were too busy figuring out a way to…don't make me be crude."

"I wouldn't dare," Sam said, bending down to pick up a trowel he saw hidden half-beneath one of the tables. Uncle Ned was really upset. Why this sudden interest in his nephew's lifestyle? He'd never seemed to have any problem with it before. "What's going on here, Uncle Ned?"

Uncle Ned stripped off his rubber gloves. "I'm getting older, Sam. I'll be seventy-six on my next birthday. Your father, if he'd lived, would be seventy-two now. You'll be thirty-seven on your next birthday. Meaning, if you're counting, that your father was your age when you were born."

Sam only nodded. He nodded, because he had nothing to say. Uncle Ned was going to say it all. He knew his role for the morning, and it was that of listener.

"Maureen and I were never blessed with children, Sam. You were the only child born to carry on the Balfour name, the Balfour legacy, if you want to call it that, and sometimes, when I'm feeling particularly maudlin, that is what I want to call it. Before I die, I want to hold Samuel Edward Balfour VI in my arms. I want to see you happy, Sam, see you settled. You're the son I never had. Now I want a grandchild. I want to see the legacy."

"Grandchildren? You're talking about grandchildren? But there's plenty of time for all of that, Uncle Ned. After all, you're not going anywhere." Sam's deliberate smile faded as he waited for his uncle's answer, and his heart stuttered for a moment. "Are you? Uncle Ned?"

* * *

Okay, so she was an idiot. Perhaps even bordering on certifiable. What else could explain her behavior last night? After swearing to herself—hell, after swearing to *him*—that she wasn't going to get involved, wasn't going to become another of his transient love affairs, she'd folded like a house of cards as his laughing brown eyes had gone suddenly intense and mysterious.

And sexy. Sam Balfour had sexy down to an art form, no question. From his look, to his voice, to the way he smelled, to the way he slanted his mouth just so as he zeroed in for the kill. Oh, yeah. *Expertus-romanticus,* as the ancient Romans might or might not have said. He had it nailed, the whole routine.

"And then he nailed you," Paige heard herself say, and winced as her knuckles whitened from her tight grip on the steering wheel of the van. *Did you just hear yourself? One night with the guy and you're saying things like that? Thinking things like that?* She closed her eyes. *Already wondering when he'll drop you like a used car he's going to trade in for a new model but hoping he'll decide to get a few more miles out of you first? God, Halliday, you're pathetic.*

What was probably more pathetic was the way she was hunkered down in the driver's seat of the van that was parked out of sight behind a billboard just off the main highway, waiting for Sam's car to pass her on his way into the city.

He'd told her about a meeting he had downtown this morning when he'd dropped her off last night—after one last, long, searing kiss obviously meant to keep her thinking about him until she saw him again (and it had worked).

He'd also given her the code to the front security gates, obviously as a show of trust, which was nice, and told her to stop by any time to check on the decorations, measure staircases, whatever she needed to do.

It was all so smooth, so easy. She could slip into his life without a second thought, fall into his arms, his bed. He made it easy. He made it simple. No wonder none of his women saw the ax coming until it was too late.

Except they all knew the odds were that it was coming, Paige reminded herself as her stomach did a small flip at the sight of Sam's luxury car passing by on its way downtown. *You know it's coming—and he knows you know it's coming, because you have a big mouth, Paige Halliday, and you told him so. He has to figure that you know the rules and are okay with them.*

She put the van in gear and eased it toward the highway, now that the coast was clear. *When am I going to learn that I'm not as damn sophisticated as I'd like to think I am?*

Although Paige believed she had pulled it off pretty well with Mary Sue earlier, when her friend had demanded a minute-by-minute recap of the big date. By concentrating on describing the job, the sheer magnitude of the project, she had steered Mary Sue away from too many personal questions and then grabbed the digital camera and her favorite measuring tape. She'd escaped the office before Mary Sue stopped being giddy about how much money they were going to make on the job.

Now she was heading back to Balfour Hall, sneaking there like some thief in the night, avoiding the guy who had eased her back onto the soft cushions of an overstuffed couch and made love to her as if she was the most beautiful, desirable woman in the world.

Or at least for this week, she was.

And that's what Paige knew she had to remember every single moment she was in his presence. He was temporary, just like this job.

She stopped the van and leaned halfway out the window to punch in the code and then pulled the van through the opening and proceeded halfway up the drive before stopping once more to look at the imposing structure ahead of her.

Sam was right. The facade did put her in mind of Biltmore House, in its coloring, in the shape of its windows. But, large as Balfour Hall was, she could probably drop three of them into the Biltmore and have room for a five-car garage and a tennis court. So it wasn't *that* big. It wasn't ridiculously huge.

Yes, she could see it as somebody's home, although Sam must have rattled around in it a lot while he was growing up. A dozen children could have spent their days sliding down those banisters and playing hide-and-seek in the maze of rooms, and the place still wouldn't have been overcrowded.

That, she decided, was because of the design. The center block of the three-story building consisted of that immense foyer and its twin staircases in front of the banquet hall, which would soon house her miniature medieval village. Except on formal occasions, that center block was nothing more than a passageway from one wing of the house to its identical twin on the other side.

Sam said he lived in one wing, and as Paige drove around to the back of the house, she wondered which one it was. After all, they hadn't made it past the first floor, had they?

Now that she'd been *initiated,* would she make it to the second floor? And would she please, please stop thinking that she had somehow sold herself in exchange for a great job and some even greater sex?

Paige pulled the van next to the five-bay brick garages and checked her makeup in the rearview mirror before climbing out and going in search of Mrs. Clarkson, the housekeeper, to alert her that the designer would be poking around the premises.

Smoothing down the wool, three-button kelly green jacket she wore over a cream silk blouse and atop lightly pin-striped charcoal slacks—the ultimate professional look, she hoped—Paige was almost to the door Sam had told her she'd see directly across from the garages when the sun glinted off something in the far distance.

Curious, Paige turned away from the door and re-thought her idea of leaving her coat in the van. Then, since the sun was fairly warm, she shrugged and headed off across the grass, making her way around the large jut out of the banquet hall and toward the far wing. As she walked, she couldn't seem to stop turning her head left and right, to admire the enormous, curving terraces and the swimming pool that came complete with its own stone waterfall.

And, if she wasn't mistaken, there were two, no three, flags out there on the rolling grounds. Flags stuck on top of poles and the poles standing in the center of— Good Lord, the man had his own mini chip-and-putt golf course!

"Well, now, *that's* just obscene," she said, laughing.

The greenhouse she'd been steadily making her way toward, however, was not obscene. It was simply unbelievable. How could anything so modern, so huge, look as if it had been there since the house was built? The glass all looked old, the fittings aged copper and ornate, even as she heard the soft whir of modern machinery.

She was feeling the chill now and decided that it would be warmer inside the greenhouse. She'd just pop inside for a minute, and then she'd head back to see Mrs. Clarkson.

Well, at least it would sound like a good excuse if she was caught being so nosy.

Paige knocked on the door, doubting that knock would be heard above the sounds of a voice she recognized as Sarah Brightman's, singing her "Wishing You Were Somehow Here Again" solo from Phantom of the Opera, the lonely Christine lamenting the loss of her father.

That song, the poignancy of the words, Brightman's voice, always made Paige cry. There were a lot of people Paige wished could be somehow here again, most definitely her father and her mother.

She tried the door, and the latch depressed soundlessly, so she stepped inside, struck immediately by the heated, moist air, the heady scent of rich peat and what had to be more than one thousand flowers, and Brightman's voice climbing to a crescendo that threatened to shatter the glass panes above Paige's head.

"Hello? Is there anyone here? Hello!"

"'...help me say goodbye.'"

The glorious voice faded away, the music stopped and Paige heard someone call from deep inside the greenhouse. "I'm back here, two tables beyond and to the left of the amaryllis. Do *you* know what an amaryllis looks like, young lady?"

"I do, sir, yes," Paige said, making her way toward the strong male voice.

"Then you'll be a refreshing change from my last visitor," the not-quite-elderly man said, smiling at

Paige as she turned the corner to see him standing there, holding an empty clay pot in one hand and a trowel in the other. "And most definitely easier on the eyes. Hello, I'm Uncle Ned."

Paige's answering smile was quick and genuine. What a pleasant-faced man, from his shock of mussed silver hair to the smudges of rich black earth on his cheek. "And I'm Paige. Hello. Please excuse me for barging in on you like this. I was drawn in by the beauty of the building. And that marvelous music." Her smile widened. "And the flowers. You've got your own little heaven on earth here, Uncle Ned, don't you?"

"I do, yes. Just me, my music, my flower friends… and a few aphids, I'm afraid. But I'll vanquish them. I always do. You're the one who's going to deck the halls for Sam, aren't you? Big job. One could almost say too big a job for a pretty little girl like you."

"Are you flirting with me, Uncle Ned?" Paige asked as she leaned a hip against one of the sturdy metal tables.

"I could be," he said, winking. "But, at my age? How about I only offer you my flowers instead? I've got poinsettias back there, you know. All shapes and sizes. You'll be wanting the red ones."

"I'll be wanting lots and lots of red ones, Uncle Ned. How many do you have?"

"Enough. You'll need forty-seven of them to make up the tree. It has been some years, but I still keep those same plants going, year to year. It's all in knowing when to cut them back, when to hide them from the sun." He shrugged his shoulders. "And a little like the mother who still cooks for a small army, even when all the children are grown and gone, I suppose. It will be nice to put the poinsettias to work again."

"Sam said it's been a lot of years since Balfour Hall was decorated for the holidays. So that must mean you've worked here for a long time?"

Again, Uncle Ned smiled, and something about that smile told Paige she might have taken in the clay pot and the trowel and the smear of dirt and added them together to come up with the wrong impression. "You could say that, yes. I feel as if I've lived here for all my life. Is Sam paying you enough?"

The abrupt shift in conversation caught Paige unawares, and she only nodded. "More than enough some would say."

"He'll get his money's worth," Uncle Ned said, picking up the clay pot again and then looking at it as if he'd forgotten what he'd planned to put in it. "He always does…"

Paige looked at the man suspiciously. Were they having one conversation or two? There was a subtext there, maybe even a warning. She decided to test her theory. "Mr. Balfour's reputation precedes him, Uncle Ned. And I'm a big girl."

"And that was meant to tell me that you can take

care of yourself. Yes, I understand," Uncle Ned said, putting down the pot once more. "Let's go see those poinsettias."

Six

Sam had never in his life cut short a meeting for personal reasons, but he did that morning. It seemed only fair, as his mind wasn't on financial globalization but centered much closer to home.

His uncle had played his little game earlier and then watched to see how high Sam jumped before admitting that he was fine medically, just feeling old and lonely. But the exercise (that jumping to a worrying conclusion part) had set Sam's mind off in directions he didn't think it needed to take until he'd turned forty, at least. Wasn't forty the new thirty? He was just now entering his prime.

But Samuel Edward Balfour VI? Sam wasn't so

sure that Samuel Edward Balfour V was quite ready for that yet.

Although he probably shouldn't have said as much to Uncle Ned, who had immediately pointed out that then just maybe it was time Samuel Edward Balfour V "grows the hell up."

Marvelous.

Which brought Sam back to the subject, the person, who had been occupying his thoughts even more than his uncle's words—Paige Halliday. There was just something about that woman….

He'd screwed up last night, definitely. She'd pretty much thrown down the gauntlet, challenged him with her poor opinion of his lifestyle, and he'd used every trick in the book to break down her defenses, get her where he wanted her.

He couldn't complain that it hadn't worked. The dinner, Balfour Hall, giving her what she knew was a dream project, softening her up with endearing stories of his childhood. Luckily, he'd been a pretty cute kid. Talk about a good use of props; the photograph of himself and his fishing pole was one of his mother's favorites and would have melted the heart of a stone. And then, his timing perfect, he'd moved in for the kill.

What the hell was *wrong* with him?

Better questions: Why had he been so reluctant to take Paige home last night? Had he really thought about taking her upstairs to his bed, a bed no other woman had ever shared with him because he'd always kept his women separate from his private life? Why had he kissed her good-night and then walked away, only to turn back halfway down the walkway to go back and kiss her yet again?

When had he ever done that? When had he ever felt the need to do anything even remotely close to any of those things? When had he ever made love to a woman and then not automatically begin figuring out ways to get rid of her?

But she was different. Sam had told his uncle as much, and he meant it. There was just something more *real* about Paige Halliday. For one, she worked for a living. He couldn't say that about many of the other women he'd ever—

He'd ever *what?* Enjoyed? Used?

"Son of a bitch, I don't need this self-analyzing, navel-gazing crap," he grumbled to himself as he pulled the car around to the garages and saw Paige's van parked there. "I'll go in, I'll see her, I'll be pleasant because I'm stuck with her until Christmas Eve—something I should have thought about before I started this. But that's it. She's the wrong woman at the wrong time, showing up right as Uncle Ned starts messing with my head. There is absolutely nothing else going on here. Except that I'm talking to myself, and that can't be a good thing…"

Sam's resolve lasted until he ran Paige to ground in the banquet hall. He'd entered through the door to the second floor minstrel gallery, figuring he could stand up there, unobserved, and watch her as she worked. He'd have time then to really look at her, observe her as she was unaware of him, her guard down. She might not stir his blood today the way she had last night. Hell, since the first time he saw her with silver glitter turning her into a sexy angel.

He didn't know what watching her this way would prove, but it was the only idea he had, so he went with it.

But when he opened the door to the minstrel gallery, it was to see Paige standing at the curved railing, her back to him.

The woman definitely looked good from the back, her slacks curving enticingly over her buttocks and then dropping a long way toward the floor. She had great legs, and now that he knew what they really looked like, the slacks, no matter that they were gray and tailored, teased him with the fact that they were covering a true treasure.

The green jacket was all right, too, but Sam saw it as armor, hiding more treasures from view. A sweater would have been an improvement, losing the jacket. A soft fuzzy one, like the one she had on that first day.

Cripes. She was here on business. What did he expect her to wear, a satin gown that plunged to her waist front and back, a Come Hither sign pasted to her forehead?

Besides, the tailored gray slacks were just as successful as any satin gown.

So all right, so he could stick with Paige until Christmas Eve without considering it a sacrifice, a hardship. As long as they both—no, scratch that. As long as *she* knew their association would be temporary. *He* already knew that. Right?

Shaking his head slightly, because he was pretty sure some of the marbles inside it had come loose and needed a good rattle back to where they belonged, Sam quietly walked up behind Paige and bent to place a kiss on the side of her neck. "Found you at last," he said, whispered, into her ear. "Sometimes this house is just too big."

"Sam…hello," Paige said, keeping her back to him. "I, uh… Mrs. Clarkson told me you wouldn't be back until six."

Sam stood back, feeling rebuffed. Kissing her neck had felt good to him, but she didn't appear moved at all. "I know. I'm playing hooky. I figured you might need someone to hold the other end of the tape measure. What are you doing up here?"

"I, uh…just…nothing."

He stepped to the railing, looking toward her as she seemed to be sliding something inside her jacket. "What do you have there?"

"Nothing. Really. Just some notes I was… Oh, hell. All right, you caught me." She pulled the something from beneath her jacket and handed it to him.

Sam grinned, first at the paper airplane she was holding and then at Paige—who blushed very prettily. "Have another sheet of paper? You didn't fold this one quite right. You get more lift if you give it more wingspan."

"Really?" Paige turned to a tablet and pen he hadn't seen on one of the musician chairs and tore off another sheet. "Show me. I knew I was doing something wrong."

Sam looked over the railing and smiled again. There had to be a half dozen crashed paper airplanes littering the parquet floor of the banquet hall—and one more stuck in one of the quartet of large, antique crystal chandeliers.

Paige pointed vaguely out over the banquet hall as a whole. "That was actually looking like it would be my best effort, if the chandelier hadn't jumped into the way."

"Not nice to blame your failure on an inanimate object, Ms. Halliday. I can see you had a sadly deprived youth if you were never taught how to make paper airplanes. I, on the other hand, never make excuses. Of course, I am an expert in the area of paper airplane flying."

A shadow slid in and out of Paige's eyes almost too quickly for Sam to catch it. "Yeah, yeah, you talk a good story, Balfour," she said, handing him the paper. "Now let's see what you can do."

He took the sturdy page she handed him, glancing

down at the printing on it. Graph paper—a good weight for paper airplanes. "You use these to draw out your designs?"

"To scale, yes. I'm not that far with this project. I'm sorry to say that I'm still at the I-think-I-may-have-bitten-off-more-than-I-can-chew portion of the program."

"Which explains the paper airplane launch?" Sam asked as he deftly folded the paper.

"What can I say? I don't smoke and seldom drink. I have to have some sort of vice, don't I? Mine is wasting time doing things I shouldn't be doing when I'm not sure of what I should be doing."

Sam lifted one eyebrow as he smiled at her. "Would I be wrong if I thought *I* fell into that category? Something you shouldn't be doing?"

Paige screwed up her face at what he knew was a very bad joke. "Actually, you top the list. Now, show off your skills—not that you don't have skills in… I mean, show me what you can do. No! Scratch that. Just launch the damn airplane, all right?"

Sam's grin widened at her obvious frustration with herself. "You want me to go hunt up a shovel for you, or do you think you've dug deep enough all by yourself?"

"If I haven't disappeared yet, I'm not deep enough. I'm sorry, Sam. It's just… Well, I feel a little awkward. After last night…"

"All I've been able to do is think about you,"

Sam said as she lowered her eyes. "That's not a line, by the way, and honestly, all by itself, that doesn't make me happy."

Her head shot up. "Excuse me?"

Deciding he had a big mouth he'd be smart to keep closed for a while, Sam turned and launched the airplane. It dipped dangerously at first and then rose as it flew out over the banquet hall, making it to within ten feet of the other end of the expanse before landing almost gracefully on the parquet floor.

He rubbed his hands together in satisfaction. "I've still got it," he said teasingly.

"You've got something," Paige agreed. She made a circular motion with her hand, as if urging him to "spill it" if he had been about to confess to something. "You were saying…?"

"Nothing. I say nothing quite often. So, tell me about your plans for the big night. I've been giving some thought to the idea of roasting a pig in the fireplace, you know. But I doubt there's been a fire in there for over five years, so if you want roast pig, let me arrange to have the chimney checked out first."

"I already have that on the list. The cleaning, I mean, not the pig roast. I'd rather stick with a great hulking Yule log, if you don't mind. It seems traditional in a setting like this."

As she spoke, she tore off another sheet of paper and began folding it, mimicking the folds he'd made in his own paper. She was a quick learner…which maybe wasn't a good thing, not if she was dedicating herself to learning about *him*.

He put his hands over hers as she tried to make another fold. "No, not that much. Remember, you want to have lift. And how's your delivery motion?"

"Not as smooth and practiced as yours, that's for sure," Paige shot back at him, and once again they were in dangerous territory. It certainly didn't take much to get them there, either. Sam was getting the idea that they could begin a conversation about the weather and within moments be slinging double entendres back and forth about high pressure zones and prevailing winds.

"Touché." He stepped behind her and slid his left arm around her waist as he covered her right hand with his own. "All right, here's how you do it." He moved in closer, caught her subtle scent. "What's that perfume you're wearing? You smell good."

"Soap, I think," Paige said. He felt her taking in a deep, almost shuddering, breath.

"Only soap? Really?" If he could feel her pulse, he was pretty sure it would be racing. His ego, which frankly had been feeling a little bruised, took heart.

"Maybe my shampoo? I don't often wear perfume."

"You don't need it," Sam said quietly, slipping his right hand down over her wrist. "All right, here we go. Draw your arm back like this, hold nice and steady, don't forget to keep your preferred trajectory in mind as you bring your arm forward again, and—"

"What does that mean, exactly, when it comes to paper airplanes? Trajectory?"

"It means the same no matter how you use it. It's the path of a projectile or other moving body as it passes through space. In other words—never mind. Just launch it where you want it to go."

"Well, duh. That wasn't exactly helpful, Sam. I want it to go *out there,* of course. I'm not going to turn around at the last minute and throw it against the wall behind me."

Sam brushed his lips against the skin behind her ear. "If I'm going to teach you how to play golf, I can see I'm going to have to first stock up on patience and then maybe a couple of stiff drinks."

The words he'd just said replayed themselves in his head—golf? He'd just said he was going to teach her to play golf? Not in December, he wasn't. So did that mean he was thinking of Paige and at least several months into the future at the same time? What the *hell* was happening to him? Was this all Uncle Ned's fault, or hers? It couldn't be his. He was just an innocent bystander. Oh, all right. Not entirely innocent and not exactly a bystander. Not after the explosive passion of last night and certainly not after he couldn't get the memory of that passion out of his head today.

He let go of Paige's wrist and stepped away from her. "Why are women so prickly when a man tries to tell them something? Just toss the damn thing, all right?"

Paige kept her back to him. "Yes, sir. As you command, sir." Then she turned to look at him, paper airplane still held in her hand, poised for flight. "Are you trying to pick a fight with me, Sam?"

Sam was about to say *don't be ridiculous*. But maybe she was right. "I'm not sure. You?"

"It might be easier," she said, taking hold of the paper airplane with both hands, totally ruining the wings. "Oh, now look what I did! Go away, Sam. You make me nervous and stupid." She crumpled the airplane completely as she rolled her eyes. "Well, wasn't that a *sophisticated* thing to say?"

"It was an honest thing to say, and I think I'm flattered." He held out his hand to her, and she deposited the crushed airplane into it. "Not exactly what I had in mind," he said, smiling. "Come on, let's go down to the library and talk about your plans some more. I am your research source, remember."

"Not completely," Paige told him as she picked up her tablet and pen and followed him out into the hallway. "Uncle Ned has been very helpful. And he's so sweet. He guided me around the second floor of the garages, where all the decorations are stored, and showed me his poinsettias, which are absolutely gorgeous, and more than enough to give you a poinsettia tree that will knock your socks off."

Sam thought he kept his composure very well, considering that his mind was spinning in several directions. He knew he had to hear more. "Is that right?

Uncle Ned? *Sweet* Uncle Ned?" he asked, taking her hand and leading her toward the narrow staircase that led from the minstrel gallery to the ground floor.

"Your gardener, yes. I was looking around for— Okay, I was *snooping,* and saw that magnificent greenhouse and walked in. And found Uncle Ned. He likes you, you know. And I think it's wonderful that you keep him on, even though he certainly can't do heavy work around the grounds anymore. Then again, I'd say he's worth his weight in gold for the way he has with plants."

"Worth his weight in gold?" Sam hid a smile. That crafty old man! "Yes, I think we could safely say that. So, you met Uncle Ned. My gardener. What else have you been doing, besides getting paper airplanes stuck in chandeliers?"

He stood back to let her pass ahead of him into the Library, and then watched as her shoulders stiffened momentarily as she looked at the couch.

Thirty-five rooms in this place, and he had to pick the library. There was no question about it, he was losing his edge. And since Paige Halliday was the only new thing in his life—the only real complication in his life—he had only her, or himself, to blame.

She lifted her chin and turned to smile at him. "So? Did you find more photographs? I'd really like to know what was done with the crèche, where it was placed. It's gorgeous, and Uncle Ned told me each figure was completely hand carved in Spain. How you could have had it packed away above a garage for years is amazing to me."

"I know. I'm ashamed of myself. But you're going to correct all of that, remember?" Sam rubbed at the back of his neck, trying to concentrate on something other than the way sunlight was streaming in through the large oriel window and backlighting Paige in a way that made her seem outlined in gold.

"You haven't really given me enough time, but I'm going to try." She tipped her head to one side. "What are you doing?"

"Doing? Nothing."

"Yes, you are. You're looking at me that way again. Like I have a piece of spinach stuck between my front teeth, or like I'm an alien that just stepped out of its spaceship. Whatever you're doing—stop it."

"You don't want to be in this room, do you?" Sam asked her, as she hadn't moved since stopping a good ten feet away from the couch that was positioned in the middle of the library. "That's my fault."

Paige turned her back to him and walked around the couch, sitting herself down very deliberately and looking up at him in some defiance when he followed her. "You could *not* be more wrong. I'm perfectly comfortable in this room." She crossed her legs even as she spread her arms wide, relaxing back against the soft cushions. "See?"

He had to give her credit for guts.

He'd removed the photograph of Uncle Ned from

the album he'd shown her last night, and told her a
photograph might be missing because he'd destroyed
one of himself looking bad in braces. At the same
time, he'd made sure she'd seen the adorable little kid
with the bare knees and the brand-new fishing pole.
Every move he'd made last night had been planned,
cold and calculating, and like the district attorney
always said in television drama courtroom scenes,
with malice aforethought.

All in all, he'd played Paige like a fish he'd wanted
to land with that new fishing pole. He was a shallow,
manipulative bastard out for his own pleasure,
through and through. That it had taken him nearly
thirty-seven years to figure that out didn't make him
any happier. Well, that thought didn't make him any
happier right now, either.

"I seduced you, Paige," Sam said, feeling the
rush of honesty flowing through his veins—or
draining out of his head. Something was going on,
he knew that much.

He pushed the photograph album to one side and
sat down directly in front of her on the coffee table,
looking levelly into her eyes. "Nothing about last
night, nothing about anything that happened after
we met in the coffee shop and you told me you knew
me by reputation was spontaneous on my part. The
offer to decorate this place, the intimate dinner, the
house tour, the photograph of the cute little kid in the
short pants, the whole nine yards. I planned it all,

Paige, and it all went down just the way I'd planned. And I'm sorry."

Paige didn't move. Her long legs remained crossed, her arms flung out casually along the back of the couch. Her gaze never left his; she never blinked.

The hands on the mantel clock paired up at the Roman numeral twelve. For the count of twelve, there was no sound in the room but the clear bell chimes of the clock striking out the hour.

Finally, Paige spoke.

"You must think I'm the lamest, most gullible female you ever met."

"No, no," Sam said quickly, leaning forward, his elbows on his knees. "I pulled out all the stops. After what you said to me? After what you told me about…about your college roommate…"

"Laura," Paige said, ice in her voice. "Her name at the time was Laura Reed."

Sam mentally winced, knowing he'd screwed up again. "Exactly. Laura Reed. I remember." Was Paige ever going to blink? He pinched at the bridge of his nose. "Where was I?"

"Digging your own hole this time. Let me help you out with that, all right? You were telling me you think I'm too stupid to know what we were doing last night—what *you* were doing last night, at least," she said calmly. "Have you ever done an IQ test on any of your dates, Sam? Because I'm guessing that my IQ wouldn't have to be much higher than that of tapioca pudding in order to beat out your usual play toy, Laura included. *Of course* I knew what you were doing. Now stop hovering like some penitent about to go down on his knees, and get out of my way. I want to stand up."

Sam was on his feet before everything Paige had said to him had fully registered in his brain. "Wait a minute," he said, taking hold of her arm as she tried to move past him. "I want to be clear on something here. Did I seduce you, or did you seduce me?"

Her smile landed a figurative punch to his gut. "Nice girls don't tell."

"No? Well, let me tell you something, Paige. You may look like an angel sometimes, but I don't think the nice girl defense is going to work here. Now. Are we having some kind of contest here, or is something else going on?"

For the first time, Paige looked apprehensive. "Contest? I...I don't know what you mean. We... we're both adults. We...enjoyed each other last night. You're the one trying to read more into it."

"Am I?" Sam reached up a hand and cupped the back of her neck. Tilted his head slightly as he brought his mouth close to her full, slightly parted lips. "This is all just...casual for you?" he asked her in a near whisper.

A small smile began to play around the corners of her mouth. "Let's just say I knew what I was doing."

He settled his free hand around her slim waist,

beneath her jacket. Their mouths were still only a whisper apart. "In that case, Miss Smarter-Than-Tapioca-Pudding…would you like to do it again? Only this time, you can pretend to seduce me."

And she was gone. Just like that, as he closed his eyes and moved in for the kill, he was holding air and probably looking like a major jackass.

"Not right now, thank you," she said from ten feet away, standing in front of the fireplace. "Tell me more about your father. You really do resemble him a lot."

Sam suddenly felt like a rank amateur. Smooth? He'd thought *he* was a player? Paige Halliday made him look as clumsy as a high school junior out on his first big date—with his second cousin, because his mom fixed him up after he couldn't get a prom date on his own. "Sure. What do you want to know?"

"Well…you told me he passed away some years ago and that your mother lives in Florida. Surely there's more."

"Uh-huh," Sam said, joining her in front of the fireplace, the two of them now looking up at the oil portrait of his parents. "Next question, *Why* do you want to know?"

"Idle curiosity?" Paige said, shrugging her shoulders. "Families…interest me. That's all."

"While kissing me doesn't."

"Not right now, no," Paige told him, amusement clearly in her tone, and then she actually patted his cheek. *Good dog. When we're done here, maybe you can have a little treat, all right?*

"My father was a teacher," Sam said, giving up. "Well, not exactly a teacher, not in the usual way. He was a world-class engineer, and he traveled overseas, teaching people how take care of themselves, drill wells, clean up their water supplies, avoid diseased food. He liked being an engineer, but he loved helping people, not just by writing a check, but by giving of himself. With as much Balfour family money as he had behind him, Dad could afford to love both what he was and what he did with what he was."

Paige stepped closer to Sam, actually leaned her head against his arm. "That's beautiful, Sam. Did you and your mother travel overseas with him?"

"Not me, no. Just my mother. Many of the places they went were considered too primitive and dangerous for a young child, and then I was in school and it was impossible for me to travel with them anyway. So I stayed here."

Paige lifted her head to look at him, her eyes wide. "By yourself in this huge house? With what, a nanny or something like that? Or did they ship you off to some boarding school? Oh, I'm sorry. You don't have to answer that."

"Why? I was fine. They were home for weeks at a time before they were gone again, and I wasn't exactly without people to watch over me until, yes,

I was old enough to go to boarding school. Which I liked, by the way."

He figured he might as well tell her everything. Sam took hold of Paige's hand and led her back to the couch, pulling her down with him but not letting go of her hand. "When Dad got sick, they came home. He had the best doctors, but he'd picked up some damn exotic bug somewhere, and by the time they'd figured out what it was, it was already too late. He couldn't beat it. And that's the story of my father."

"It's a sad story, Sam," Paige said, squeezing his hand, "and yet somehow beautiful. Clearly your father was very dedicated to what he was doing. You must have been devastated to lose him."

"Yes, I was," Sam said, looking across the room at the painting one more time. Maybe that's why he normally avoided this room. Because, as devastated as he'd been by the loss of his father, he'd been pretty damn mad at the man, too. Just as Sam had been coming into his own as a man, able to be on a level playing field with his father, the man was gone, and Sam's mother was as good as gone. They'd always been so complete in themselves, just the two of them, do-gooders on their lifelong mission—with Sam never really fitting into the mix very well.

But it had worked out. Uncle Ned and Aunt Maureen had in Sam what they couldn't have on their own. He'd been as much their son as he'd been to his own parents. Maybe more.

"Do you know something, Sam? I like you, and I have since I first met you. But I think I like you even better when you aren't trying so hard," Paige said, leaning in to kiss his cheek.

He laughed in a self-deprecating way and shook his head. "I've never had to work so hard before meeting you. My good looks, my natural charm—my money. They've always been enough. Mostly, the money. I'm not that vain, you know."

"You forgot to mention those sexy, smiling eyes or how modest you are with it all," Paige pointed out, smiling. "Ask me to go to dinner with you tonight."

He enjoyed seeing her smile. "All right. Will you, Ms. Halliday, do me the pleasure of joining me for dinner this evening?"

"Will squid be on the menu, Mr. Balfour?"

"Definitely not."

"I see. Will *you* be on the menu, Mr. Balfour?"

"I think that could be arranged."

Paige stood up before he could grab her and kiss her until her eyes rolled back in her head—because she was driving him crazy, and they both knew it.

"In that case, I'd be delighted. Now, if you'll excuse me, I have to get back to work…and figure out how to get a paper airplane down from a chandelier."

He remained on the couch, swiveling to watch her leave the room, her long legs doing something to his insides that probably wasn't a good thing this early in the day. "And no tapioca pudding for dessert!" he called after her and then smiled as he heard her clear laugh from the hallway.

He spent five minutes looking at the portrait of his parents and then went upstairs to find the green folder with Paige's name on it....

Seven

Anxious to get away from Balfour Hall and its owner, Paige drove back to Holidays by Halliday pretty much on autopilot.

If she'd had anything to drink, she'd have to say she was drunk. What else could explain how she behaved whenever Sam was within ten feet of her? When he was within five feet of her, she turned into someone she barely recognized. When he was closer than that, the sensible, reasonably intelligent, modest, normally morally upright and at least marginally uptight Paige Halliday disappeared completely.

She had to get a grip here, remember who she was and who he was.

Maybe after tonight…

Paige blew in through the front door of her shop, her mind still anywhere but on business, to see Mary Sue wrestling with an enormous garland that seemed to be getting the best of her.

"Here, let me help you," she said, picking up one end of the garland that was constructed of fake greenery and decorated with pretty red cardinals and golden Christmas balls. "What's this for, anyway?"

"Well, damn," Mary Sue said, hefting the garland onto a worktable. "Here I was hoping you knew the answer to that one. I couldn't find an order form anywhere in the box. All I know is it came from Claire and the box was marked Rush."

Paige frowned. "Oh, wait, I remember now. This is the staircase drape for the Henderson house. Remember, Mary Sue? First it was white doves, but then some helpful pain in the neck told her white doves in a house were bad luck, or something. Her big party for her husband's employees is this Saturday night, so thank God this arrived, or I was going to have to go hunt up three dozen red cardinals and replace each dove by hand in the first garland. Is anyone free to take it over there to switch the garlands out, or do you want me to do it? Because I can do it. Trixie Henderson could talk the ear off a donkey, and she'd drive you crazy."

"No, that's all right, Paul can handle it, and he could probably talk the other ear off the donkey, so he and Mrs. Henderson should cancel each other out," Mary Sue said, the garland finally wrestled back into the carton. "How's it going at the mansion? We've been having a real ball here, I have to tell you."

Paige headed for the back room and the coffeepot. Mary Sue made great coffee, and Paige had decided she needed to *sober up* before she saw Sam again. "Do you have to tell me? Or would I be happier in my ignorance?"

"Oh, no, you're not getting away that easy. If I have to suffer, you have to suffer. I got a call at home at three o'clock this morning, since I'm your alternate emergency number and you, it would seem, were unavailable. I take it last night was a success— for somebody."

Paige turned back to the coffeemaker, pretending to top off her cup. She knew exactly where she had been at three o'clock this morning, who she'd been with and what had been happening at that time. "Three o'clock? Really? I must have slept through the phone ringing. I'm really sorry, Mary Sue. What sort of emergency? This building's still standing, so obviously not a fire. Although," she added, looking around the room and the controlled chaos it contained, "it might be hard to figure out whether or not we've been robbed."

"Very funny, but if you want to see chaos, come to my house. I'll be ready for Christmas, oh, around next February. Anyway, nothing happened here,"

Mary Sue told her, motioning for Paige to move so that she could pour herself a cup of coffee. "The mall, however? That's a whole other story. You do remember the Twelve Days of Christmas tableau-type thing we set up, right?"

"Right," Paige said warily. "Is this going to be like the turkey thing? Something fell over and hurt somebody? At three o'clock in the morning?"

"No, not quite, but thank you for playing our game. Unless you'd want to give it another shot—no, don't. You'd never guess, and let me tell you, the night watchmen or security guards or whatever they call themselves have some big 'splaining to do. As in, where the hell were they?"

Paige headed for a worktable and one of the stools. "Oh, boy, what happened?"

Mary Sue grinned. "Remember the eight maids-a-milking mannequins, Paige? They were still milking, all right, but not the cows. Let's just say the ten lords a-leaping—having somehow lost their pantaloons—were all wearing big smiles on their faces, okay? Making two of the maids ambidextrous, in case you're wondering about the math, or just overachievers. Our only good luck was that the mannequins aren't ana-tomically correct—but anyone with half an imagi-nation could easily fill in the, well, the missing parts."

Paige got a sudden mental picture she was sure would be burned into her retinas for a long time. "Oh, God…"

"Yeah. You're getting the idea, I guess? There were other bits of rearranging—weird crossbreeding going on with the geese and the hens and swans—although I probably don't have to spell that all out for you more than that. I will say that two of the piping pipers definitely would get a double-X rating. But, relax, it's all fixed now, finished before the mall opened for the early-bird walkers. I'm thinking college prank or fraternity initiation, or something like that. This was all a little too well done for high school kids."

"I should have been there," Paige said, guilt flushing her body. "I shouldn't have taken the job Sam offered, no matter how terrific it could be for us. We were already too busy."

"Oh, right—about the Balfour job?"

Paige closed her eyes for a moment. "Is this more bad news?"

"That depends on your idea of bad news. Your timetable—I looked at it—has you completing that job by the twenty-third, in time for this Christmas Eve party our handsome client is giving, right?"

"Right," Paige confirmed carefully. "I hadn't seen the place yet so I was flying by the seat of my pants when I wrote up that schedule yesterday afternoon. I built in a couple of extra days, but that's my target. Ten days, probably working Sundays, too."

"Well, don't look now, but the target just moved. I would have told you right away, but I figured the

Twelve Days of Christmas thing would relax you, make you laugh, before you went into panic mode."

"And here you thought you knew me so well," Paige quipped, rolling her eyes.

"Sorry about that. I agree, I shouldn't have waited. I got a call two hours ago from our favorite Philadelphia newspaper. They want to do a full-color spread on Balfour Hall in the Style section on the twenty-first. Complete with an interview with the designer, which is the icing on the cake. That call ended when Channel Six beeped in, and they've now got us for a video segment on the same day. Twenty minutes ago I got another call, this one from—*ta-da!*" Mary Sue held up a copy of the most important women's magazine in the country. Not just Philadelphia or the Tri-State Area—the entire *country*.

Paige felt her eyes nearly popping out of her head. "Don't play with me, Mary Sue. That's not funny."

"Do you see me laughing here? I'm already planning exactly when I should ask you for a huge raise, because we're taking off now, Paige, straight into the big time. They'll wait until the twenty-third, since their article won't come out until next October, in time for next Christmas. They plan ahead, you understand. I got all the dope from my new friend Mandy, the managing editor."

Paige sat very still for a full minute, her mind racing, and then got to her feet. "Get me a complete rundown of the projects we've still got on the burner—there can't be that much left to do on any of them, public or private—and a guesstimate of how much maintenance you think any of them will need between now and Christmas. Watering the live plants and making sure nothing fell over, nothing blew away, nothing got ruined by the weather, that somebody's dog hasn't chewed on it or that somebody's kid hasn't popped all the glass balls with a baseball bat—that sort of thing. The usual. Check last year's records. They'll give you a good idea."

"Wait a minute. Slow down," Mary Sue ordered, grabbing a pen and a notepad and scribbling furiously for a few moments. "Wait until I tell my kid that he's having Christmas in late February this year. Okay, ready, fire away."

"Get me another list of how many people we have, how many more we'll need. I'm hoping none. Get Sally Burkhart on the phone—you know, from the design school. I'm betting she'll loan me some of her students since they'll be going out on Christmas break soon anyway. I want a full team of strong backs assembled and waiting for me outside the gates of Balfour Hall at seven o'clock tomorrow morning, and tell them to bring bag lunches, because we're going to be there all day. There's two mountains of stuff in the rooms over the garages, and it all has to be brought to the house, unpacked, sorted, cleaned up and put where it belongs as soon as I know where it all belongs. And greens! Order greens, and have them delivered straight to Balfour Hall."

"How many greens? Can you give me a ballpark figure?"

Paige pictured the mantels, the double staircase in the great foyer. "Call somebody and take whatever they've got in stock, all of it. Only then can we start on the village in the banquet hall. Oh—I need a Yule log. Think giant redwood, and then go just a little bit smaller. And then find someone else to man the phones here, because you're coming with me. I can't do this without you."

Mary Sue grinned as she made a snappy salute. "Yes, fearless leader. I hear and I obey. I knew you'd come through on this. Oh—and I just decided that *now* would be the perfect time to ask for that raise."

An hour before Paige was scheduled to show up at Balfour Hall, Sam went in search of his uncle, who had done a pretty good job of avoiding him all afternoon.

He found him in the library, one of the photograph albums open across his knees. "Hello, Sam. I've found a good number of photographs that should prove helpful to Ms. Halliday. They're already stacked up on the desk over there."

"Good for you. Good for her. Why didn't you tell me?" Sam asked, walking over to the desk and leaning against it as Uncle Ned sat at his ease on one of the wingback chairs.

"I don't know, Sam. Why didn't I tell you *what?* There's such a multitude of subjects to choose from, you know."

Sam rubbed at his forehead; his headache had been on its way out until he realized his uncle was going to make him do a verbal dance before he told him anything.

"I read her file."

"Did you now?" Uncle Ned said, closing the photograph album. "A little tardy, but better late than never, I suppose. Is this going to be a general discussion, or is there something specific in Ms. Halliday's file you'd like to highlight for me?"

"You may look like the proverbial jolly old man, Uncle Ned, but at the bottom of it you're a real piece of work. You picked her on purpose, didn't you?"

"On purpose? In what way, for what reason? Go on. I'm certain you have formulated an interesting theory. Why don't you expand on it so I understand where you're coming from?"

Sam set his jaw for a moment, and then gave it up. You didn't win with Uncle Ned, nobody did, not in his heyday and not now. The most you could hope for was to break even. "Bruce is very meticulous, Uncle. He puts a date on everything. That file originated nearly two years ago, and it's been regularly updated ever since."

"I'm also very meticulous," Uncle Ned suggested, smiling at Sam.

"I would have said devious. Then I checked the other files from this year's crop of do-gooders. Those files were started this year and ran for no more than a month before you had me send off the gifts, the money, whatever."

"I see nothing untoward in that. Sometimes it takes longer for me to make up my mind about a subject. Pour yourself a drink, Sam, and sit down. Tell me what's bothering you."

Deciding that might not be such a bad idea, Sam poured himself two fingers of Scotch and returned to lean against the front of the desk. "You picked her."

"You're repeating yourself now."

"You picked her—*for me*."

Uncle Ned's smile grew slowly. "Oh, very good, Sam. Frankly, I was beginning to worry about your powers of deduction."

Sam pointed his glass at the man. "Thank you, you old conniver, but I'm not done. There's more. She's local, so you could have Bruce keep pretty close tabs on her until you were satisfied with your choice. And, because she's close, it even made it semilogical for me to take Bruce's place and deliver the letter."

"Getting the two of you face-to-face, yes. I worried that it might be too obvious, but you didn't catch on, did you? I think you were too angry with me for saddling you with my project—which you loathe—and too captivated by my Ms. Halliday."

"*Your* Ms. Halliday. You admit it." Sam shook his

head. "God. How could I be so stupid? You've been leading both of us around on leashes, haven't you?"

"Not really, Sam. I only found her and then also devised a way to put you two together. Anything after that was—and remains—a bit of a crapshoot. You do realize that the problem I had to wrestle with was that, in the normal course of your social life and your incessant womanizing, your paths never would have crossed."

"What would you have done if I'd just met her, handed her the letter, and walked away?"

"You did, Sam, at least for a few days. I'll admit that I was about to fall back on my Plan B and hire Ms. Halliday to decorate Balfour Hall, when you finally gave in and went after her on your own. Also having the annual dinner party here was your invention and probably looks now like at least a small payback for my intervention. Please consider me duly chastened."

"You're not even close to *chastened*."

"True. I'm fairly happy, as a matter of fact, especially after meeting Ms. Halliday, speaking with her. She's delightful."

"And nearly as complex as you, although you probably won't believe that," Sam interrupted, remembering his and Paige's earlier sparring match. "She might even be smarter than I am in a few ways."

"Is that so? Good, then she's even a better match for you. I won't even point out that, while I was—to be blunt—*playing* you, you were happily believing that you were playing *me*. Using my project to get to Ms. Halliday and at the same time slip in the bonus of forcing me out of my doldrums? What a coup it must have seemed to you. Neither of us is free of sin in this, Sam. You're definitely my nephew."

Sam looked at his uncle through narrowed eyelids. "I just thought of something else. Where's Bruce?"

"Bruce? After bringing me the photograph of you standing in an alleyway, covered in imitation snow, you mean? In Hawaii. His…let's say his flight was unexpectedly delayed a few days."

"Until I came to my senses and went after Paige and ended up executing your Plan B for you. But you fought me on the idea of decorating this place, having the dinner party here. You might have even looked frightened about the prospect."

"Yes. I'm good, aren't I? You're also good, Sam. You run our companies very well. But I still have some moves left that you haven't seen before."

Sam drained his glass. "Like letting me think you might be ill."

"That was pretty low, and I apologize. But I woke you up, didn't I? Life moves on, whether you want it to or not. Someday I won't be here, Sam. I love you, and I want you settled in time for me to enjoy seeing your happiness."

"And Samuel Edward Balfour VI," Sam said quietly. "You really spooked me with that one. And you're obviously serious, or you wouldn't have decided to open up Balfour Hall after all these years."

"I can listen, Sam, as well as give out advice. It is time. Maureen would be angry to know I've dug myself in here so deeply that I'm afraid to come out again. She might even have called me a coward, as she was the bravest woman I've ever known. Paige Halliday is right for us both, Sam, in many ways. And you do like her, don't you?"

Sam looked up at the portrait of his parents. "She gave the van to an orphanage. Lark Summit."

"Yes, we've established that," Uncle Ned said quietly, as if he knew they were now treading dangerous waters.

"I saw the newspaper clipping about the little girl at the orphanage who's undergoing chemo. Paige's hair is as short as it is because she donated her hair two months ago, to have a wig made for the child."

"Leaving little or no question as to her fine heart, her dedication or her character, I know. Did you read the entire file?"

Sam studied the bottom of his empty glass, as uncomfortable now as he had been when he read the file. "She grew up at Lark Summit. Parents unknown, never adopted, only two tries at foster parents that didn't work out. She…ah…she asks a lot of questions about family. She has told me that family is very important. And I laughed her off, even said something asinine about her having a deprived childhood because she didn't know how to fly a paper airplane. She never let on how that comment must have hurt her. She never said a word about her gift, what she did with it."

He lifted his head and looked at his uncle. "I'm a real ass here, Uncle Ned. I'm not looking good here at all, not to me, not to her, not to anybody. I tried to treat her the way I treat other women."

"Interchangeable. Dispensable. Convenient."

Sam held up one hand, smiling wryly. "That's enough. Nice of you to keep a list, but yes, you're right. So my question is—why did you subject Paige to me, since I'm such a bad ass?"

"Timing is everything, Sam, in business, in life. When I first learned about Ms. Halliday and her devotion to Lark Summit, you weren't ready for someone like her in your life. But I've sensed a restlessness in you this past year, even the slowly dawning realization that your life isn't as perfect as you'd like to believe it is, as it seemed to you when you were in your twenties, your early thirties. As long as we're being truthful here, I was holding the young lady in reserve, until I thought you were ready."

"Funny, I never noticed the strings," Sam said. "But that doesn't mean I'm not your puppet."

"You're angry," Uncle Ned said, getting to his feet. "You have every right to be, son, and I'd be sorry if I didn't think I've done the right thing. You're seeing Ms. Halliday again this evening? And, according to Mrs. Clarkson, she's coming here? That's a first for you, Sam, what with your belief that a smart bird doesn't—well, we both know the rest of that statement."

Sam nodded. He really didn't trust himself to speak, not just yet. Anger might make him say something they'd both regret.

"Good. Now here's a bit of either timely or unfortunate news for you. Tomorrow morning I need you to leave for Singapore. You should be back in time for the party, if you work very hard."

Sam's head shot up. "Singapore? There's nothing going on in Singapore."

"Don't say that until you check the folder I had Mrs. Clarkson put on your desk upstairs. Chang Industries has unexpectedly come on the block, or it will, in three days. I want you there, I want the inside track before the general announcement. Better yet, get our offer in before anyone else even knows the company is for sale. We've wanted Chang for a long time, Sam, and now's our chance. We could find someone else to go in your place—it would take three of our people to replace you—but I think a little distance between you and Ms. Halliday might not be a bad idea at the moment. After all, she's going to be very busy for the next two weeks. But I'll be here, to watch over her."

"Right, that's another thing. She thinks you're one of the gardeners."

His uncle suddenly looked ten years younger, his smile wide, his eyes nearly dancing in his head. "Our Ms. Halliday is in for more than one surprise on Christmas Eve, isn't she, Sam? I find that I'm quite looking forward to the evening." Then he sobered. "Try not to screw this up, Sam. You've got tonight and then two weeks to think about what's been holding you back from finding real happiness. I've every confidence you'll know what you need to do to secure that happiness after being on your own to think about it all."

"Absence makes the heart grow fonder?"

Uncle Ned shrugged. "There's another one. Out of sight, out of mind. No matter what happens or doesn't happen between you and Ms. Halliday, I think you might finally begin to understand what makes Sam Balfour tick."

"With the women I—let's just say I know who they are, what they are. I'm up front with them, and I know what they're about, what they're after. Men or women, in business or socially. I just don't like— no, scratch that. I'm not comfortable around do-gooders. I don't—present company excepted, of course—I don't trust them."

"Yes, son, I know. Did you ever ask yourself why?"

Paige held up two bags when Sam met her at the side door of Balfour Hall at six-thirty. She put a bright smile on her face, trying to ignore the small flip of her stomach as he stood in front of her, dressed casually in navy slacks and a soft knit shirt open at the neck. "I didn't know if you were a Geno's Steaks person or a Pat's King of Steaks person. Since they're right across the street from each other, I picked up cheesesteaks from both places, and you can pick your favorite. Is that all right?"

"Sounds and smells good to me," Sam said, standing back to let her come in to what turned out to be a very nice foyer, certainly smaller than the great foyer, but impressive anyway. "Let's go upstairs. I asked Mrs. Clarkson to set out napkins and an assortment of drinks for us."

Paige nodded, suddenly at a loss for words. Once she went up those stairs, the conclusion of their evening was pretty much a given, and they both knew it. "It might be less messy if we ate in the kitchen?" she suggested, hesitating.

Sam took the bags from her tight grip as he leaned in to lightly kiss her cheek, and kept his mouth close to her skin. "You don't want to come upstairs to see my etchings, little girl?"

"Very funny," Paige shot back at him and headed for the staircase. She was halfway up the flight before she realized the score was already Sam, one, Paige, zip. Not that she was keeping score, but it probably wasn't a bad idea to at least remain alert.

She stopped at the top of the stairs and looked around at a second small foyer, splendidly decorated in deep, rich woods and antiques. She tried to get her bearings and then headed through the open archway into what looked to be a living room. A very large living room, comfortable and welcoming.

Sam was right behind her. "Keep going. Dining room is on your left, through those double doors."

"This is nice," she said as she joined him at a dining table that probably could seat twelve at the most. "A real family dining room. Not at all like the banquet hall."

"Right. It doesn't have an echo," Sam said as he dumped the bags, one after the other, onto a bone china platter. "God, these really do smell good. Cheesesteaks are all ours, you know, just as much as Ben Franklin and hot pretzels and Rocky Balboa. Often imitated, never duplicated. If you ever see the words *Philly cheesesteak* on a menu anywhere else in the world, don't fall for it. Nothing comes close."

Paige began to relax. He was Sam, no matter that they were sitting here in his mansion, no matter that he was going to be no more than a temporary blip in the radar of her life in a few days or weeks, no matter that she thought they should have a chance for so much more. There was always time for regrets. For now, she'd live in the moment.

"You should do TV ads. Except who would you do them for, Geno's or Pat's?"

"I'd have to stand in the middle of Passyunk Avenue and just point in both directions, I guess." He grabbed a steak in a Geno's wrapper and put it on his plate. "Your turn."

"It only seems fair that I take a Pat's," Paige said, reaching for another wrapped steak sandwich. Then she got to her feet. "You said there were drinks. Let me get you something."

His mouth full, Sam pointed toward the far corner and the bar setup there, and Paige grabbed them each a longneck bottle of beer out of a silver bucket crowded with ice. Beer, in a silver champagne bucket. It was true: the rich *were* different.

As they ate, Sam gave her more information about the house, how it had always been decorated for the holidays, and promised her more photographs before she went home. She told him about the phone calls from the media and thanked him for arranging the publicity. He said it was the least he could do and reached for a second cheesesteak, this time a Pat's.

She caught him looking at her a little bit strangely a couple of times, but then thought she was overreacting, reading things into his glances that just weren't there. In her turn, she had to remind herself to stop looking at him as if he was on the dessert menu.

When Paige couldn't eat another bite, she pushed back from the table and put her hands to her stomach. "I probably shouldn't say this, but I think I liked tonight's dinner even better than last night's, in the restaurant. You can't eat with your hands in restaurants."

"You like to do things with your hands?" Sam asked,

winking at her before downing the last of his beer, and they were immediately back in "uh-oh" territory.

"I run a design business. Very hands-on. So, yes, I suppose so," she said, deliberately playing dumb. Then she smiled. "I like touching things…tactile, you know? The different textures, the varying shapes, and how to best combine them, make them fit together in satisfying ways. I love the softness of goose down, the deep caress of velvet, the coolness of silk slipping through my fingers, the almost sensual warmth of fur."

She thought that would do it…and she was right. After all, they were adults—consenting adults. They both knew where this was heading, so why not cut to the chase?

Sam held out his hand to her, and she took it, allowing him to draw her to her feet and out of the dining room, back into the living room. He stopped in the middle of the room and turned to face her. "So that's your favorite of the senses?" he asked her, putting his hand to her cheek, lightly stroking her skin with his knuckles. "Touch?"

"It…it, uh, seems a good place to start, yes," Paige said, knowing that from here on out it was probably best if she didn't think too much. "You?"

"I'm a fan, yes," Sam said, moving his face close to her ear. "Smell is also all right. Like, you smell really good, Paige." He drew back and smiled. "A whole new advertising strategy for Pat's and Geno's. *Eau de cheesesteak.* It could be a big seller."

Behind them, a fire blazed in the fireplace, but Paige was pretty sure that wasn't why she felt so warm. "I was going to mention the sense of hearing, but I think the cheesesteak perfume as a turn-on line sort of lost me. How about moving right on to taste?" She went up on tiptoe and pressed her open mouth against his, their tongues instantly dueling as his arms went around her, as her hands sought out the strong planes of his chest.

Her eyelids fluttered closed as he lifted her into his arms while still kissing her and walked with her back to the foyer and beyond.

Sensations both familiar and alien delighted and frightened Paige as she felt herself being lowered onto an already turned-down bed, Sam leaving her only long enough to kick off his shoes and remove hers…kissing the arches of her feet before moving up on the mattress, to end with his forearms braced on either side of her head.

He smiled down at her, although, just this one time, that smile didn't seem to reach his eyes, which remained deadly serious. "Number five, Paige. Sight. I knew you'd look good here," he said quietly. "I've been imagining you here for most of my life. I just didn't know it."

She wanted to believe him, longed to believe him. Maybe even needed to believe him.

"I don't know what's happening here, Sam," she said, perhaps revealing more of herself to him than she should. As she'd told him before, she knew who he was, what he was. She'd heard the stories, read a few of them on the Internet. Seen the photographs of all the beautiful women he dated. "I thought I did, but I don't. I mean, I talk a good story but—"

"Shh," he whispered, his fingers busy unbuttoning her blouse. "If we're starting over, you're going out of turn. Talking—hearing—was third. Touch comes first." His hand closed around her breast, the heat of his palm radiating down, down, setting off an answering warmth deep between her legs. "Touch me, Paige…"

Her heart pounding, her breaths becoming shallow and quick, Paige welcomed his invasive kiss as she tugged at his shirt, pulling it free of his slacks before pressing her hands against his bare back.

His skin was on fire, fevered. Like hers.

He shifted slightly, brought his mouth to her breast, captured her nipple through the sheerness of her silk bra, and she was able to slide her hands forward, undo his slacks and push them out of her way.

Touch. He wanted touch.

She wanted touch.

Touch…and taste.

And the sweet sound of his sigh, more nearly a groan, when she found him, grasped him in her hand. Warmth, heat, silkiness, softness, strength. Velvet over steel.

Sam put his arm beneath her back and pulled her

up with him so that they were sitting closely together, facing each other on the bed. His brown eyes had gone dark as night, and she watched him watching her as he slid her blouse from her shoulders, rid her of her bra.

She saw a quick flicker in his eyes as he reached for the front opening of her slacks and helped him push them and her panties down over her knees and beyond. He was so intent on what he was doing, and he did it so well.

That part she would forget about, his obvious expertise. She only wanted to know what he was doing to her, now. He was undressing her with his hands, yes. But it was more than that. He was undressing her with his eyes, with the way he touched her, as if worshiping every new revealed inch of her.

He drew her lower against the small, supporting mountain of pillows and now his mouth followed the trail his hands had blazed, kissing the hollow between her breasts, lightly tonguing her sensitive navel, skimming the tip of his tongue across her lower belly. The sensitive flesh between her thighs tightened and released, her every nerve ending tingling.

In anticipation.

He eased her legs apart and moved lower, slipping one of the pillows beneath her buttocks as he raised her up even as she bent her knees and braced her feet against the mattress, opening herself to him. There was no modesty, no shame. There couldn't be, not when Sam kept looking at her that way, as if filled with wonder.

Paige felt tears pricking behind her own eyes, so awed by the worship in his, and then let her eyelids flutter closed as he joined her in the most intimate kiss lovers could exchange.

His mouth was hot and moist against her, his tongue magical as he explored, flicked, lightly suckled. He used his fingers to spread her, invade her, and followed each foray into new territory with his warm breath, his curious tongue. Paige gritted her teeth as he took her high, then higher, sending showers of delight through her that she'd never known were possible.

And then the urgency took over, a *want* so elemental, so strong, that she gave up dominion over her body and ceded all power to him. His fingers, his mouth, were doing things to her that sent her flying so high she forgot to breathe, could not breathe. All she could do was cling to the ecstasy he brought her, until the effort became too much and she let go, her body pulsing and clenching, racked with pleasure.

"Sam!" She reached out blindly, begging him to come to her, to hold her, to let her hold him as she tried once more to anchor herself to reality.

But then a new sensation overcame her, and she knew she wanted to give. She had taken, and the taking had been wonderful. But it wasn't enough.

"Sam…?" Paige swallowed hard on the tight knot

of tension and passion rising in her throat. She wanted him, every bit of him. She wanted to crawl inside him, become a part of him. She dared again to reach her hand down, to touch him intimately. "Sam. Let me…"

He looked at her, looked deeply into her eyes, his own naked and vulnerable. And something else. Something she couldn't put a name to, was afraid to attempt to identify—because if she was wrong, her heart just might break.

"Please," he said quietly, holding on to her as he rolled onto his back, ceding her the power now. She kissed his chin, his chest, pushing herself slowly down the length of his body, her fingertips tracing his every muscle, all the fascinating ridges and small valleys that made up his personal landscape.

She didn't have Sam's expertise, really wasn't sure what he'd like, how to please him, but what she lacked in expertise she hoped would be overshadowed by her very true desire to give back at least some of the pleasure he'd given her. Tentatively, she cupped him in her hands. Tentatively, she kissed him. Dared to touch him with the tip of her tongue.

Above her, she heard Sam sigh her name as he said, "Yes, yes," and she was lost….

Eight

Sam tore up the stairs to his quarters in Balfour Hall, cursing as he went, stripping off his tie as he took the steps two at a time. Late. Late. He was late.

Don't let him be too late....

He'd promised Paige he'd be back in plenty of time, time he needed to explain what couldn't be explained long-distance, during their daily talks on the phone. Those wonderful, long, intimate and sometimes carefully worded talks.

She hadn't told him about her anonymous gift.

He hadn't told her why she'd received it or what tonight was really all about.

He'd decided that was something he had to explain to her face-to-face.

Now he was running out of time. His flight had been delayed because of the weather. He shouldn't have chanced I-95, not at five o'clock. Not with a slick coating of snow slowing the highway to a near crawl and then going to full stop after some jackass with four-wheel drive thought the Caution: Bridge Freezes Before Road Surface sign was meant for everybody but him.

Wealth and reputation had some perks. The private jet from Singapore and little more than a wink and a nod got him through customs. But nobody winked at Mother Nature or could protect you from idiots.

Like himself. When it came to idiots, Sam had decided he just about topped the list. Close the deal with Chang Industries—no problem. Close the deal with Paige? Big problem.

Because first he'd had to close the deal with *himself,* and a lifetime of stupid ideas and conclusions, childhood, childish conclusions that had no place in his adult world.

As Sam stripped and got into the shower, not waiting until the water heated, he cursed himself for the millionth time for not telling Paige the truth, all of the truth, about her gift, his part in it, Uncle Ned, what was going to happen tonight, his private revelations—all of it.

Mostly, he should have told her about Uncle Ned. Definitely. Sweet old Uncle Ned. The *gardener.* Would he actually show up for the party? Of course he would. He wouldn't want to miss the fun of watching his nephew eat three or four straight courses of crow.

Fifteen minutes later, his hair still damp and his bowtie crooked, Sam was back downstairs and heading for the banquet hall.

At least, during one of their phone calls, he'd had the common sense to ask Paige to be here early tonight, to act as his hostess for the dinner party. So she would already be there, wondering where the hell he was.

Sam stopped, pushed up the sleeve of his tuxedo and looked at his wristwatch. "Wrong," he told himself, wincing. "Not wondering. Pacing…and *pissed*."

"I still don't understand why Sam didn't want place cards," Paige said, wringing her hands together as she gave the elaborately set table one last inspection as Mary Sue slid one of the crystal wine glasses a half inch to the right.

"Relax," Mary Sue soothed, although there was a hint of tension in her own voice. "He said *hostess,* right? That means he's at the head of the table and you're at the bottom—the other end. Unless he wants you to sit at his right hand side, of course, because I've read that it's also done that way sometimes. Besides, you're going to knock his socks off when he gets a look at you in that gown, and he'll probably want you to sit on his lap."

Paige smiled, feeling heat run into her cheeks. "I

still think it's too low-cut," she said, touching a hand to her cleavage. "I mean, there's being subtle and then there's *come to mama, big boy*. I think this gown might have crossed the line."

"Okay, I've tried to convince you, in the store when you tried it on, while the gal was wrapping it up and again tonight. Be a prude if you want to, because that's it for me. I'm done. I'm outta here. I've got this kid, and he has this thing about wanting *his* mama home on Christmas Eve. But I'll give it one parting shot, since I know you're really nervous. You look terrific, Paige, like a woman in love, waiting for her man to come home. This place looks terrific. It looked terrific on TV last night, it looked terrific in the magazine and in the newspaper. It's going to look just as terrific next year when Holidays by Halliday is the cover shot seen on every newsstand in America."

"Yeah," Paige said, casting her gaze over the rest of the banquet hall, unable to keep a shiver of excitement from dancing up her spine. "Terrific. Thanks, Mary Sue. And you're right, you should go home now. Sam will be here soon. He landed over two hours ago."

"It's the snow, it held him up. A typical Pennsylvania white Christmas, more trouble than it's worth," Mary Sue said, gathering up her purse and the large canvas satchel stuffed with scissors, tape, glue and anything else that might be needed for a last-minute on-site repair of one of their decorations. "If you guys are lucky, it held up everybody else who's coming, too."

Paige hugged her assistant and kissed her on the cheek. "Thank you, Mary Sue, for everything, and Merry Christmas. Come on, I'll walk you to the door."

They passed by the "village stalls" with their gaily striped canopies, a centerpiece of greens and thick white candles in glass sleeves set on the plank counter of each serving station tonight. During the open house on New Year's Day, those stalls would serve as stations for the lavish buffet, everything served on the newly polished silver plate Mrs. Clarkson had shown her a few days ago. An entire room lined with shelves, each shelf filled with gorgeous antique silver. The job may have been the largest Paige had ever taken on, but it sure had come loaded with materials that couldn't help but give the whole thing that *wow* factor.

"It's a whole other world, this house, isn't it?" Paige asked as they entered the foyer. She stopped, her breath caught yet again by the splendor of this towering space. Uncle Ned had outdone himself with the tall floral centerpiece on the round table and the exotic, weeping greens wrapping up the double staircases filled the room with the smells of Christmas.

"Holy...*whoa.*"

Paige tore her gaze from the enormous chandelier almost directly above their heads. It was hung now with dozens of looping strings of real Austrian crystal garland that cast a rainbow of sparkling light everywhere. The fifty-two little ivory shades had been replaced with the red velvet ones Paige had discovered in one of the boxes. Perfect. It was just perfect. But Mary Sue was looking toward the hallway. "What?" she asked. She turned her head, and then froze. "*Sam.*"

"Merry Christmas, Paige," Mary Sue whispered as she quickly slipped into her parka. "Good luck unwrapping *that*."

It was almost like the first time he'd seen her. She wasn't covered in glitter this time, but she shone like an angel just the same as she stood beneath the chandelier, her gown a slim column of shimmering silver silk. Simple, elegant, whispering sex in its every line and curve and yet entirely classy and classic. Just like her.

"Hello, Paige," Sam said, his legs finally able to move again, so that he could approach her, slip his hands onto her hips. "I've missed you. Very much."

Paige lowered her gaze for a moment and then looked up at him, her eyes shining with what he was afraid were unshed tears. She raised a hand to his cheek as she searched his expression. "I was so afraid of this moment these past two weeks. And…and now it's here."

"And are you still afraid?" Sam asked her, stepping closer to her, pulling her hips gently against his.

Paige slowly shook her head. "No. I don't think I am. You're not going to say goodbye, are you?"

"No, sweetheart. Not this time. Not to you. Not ever."

He lowered his lips to hers, capturing her sigh as she opened her mouth for him. There was passion as he kissed her, as they held each other, but passion was only a part of what Sam felt. He was *home*.

"Come to the library with me," he said moments later against her ear. "We have to talk."

"But your guests will be—"

He grabbed her hand, cutting her off. "I know, Paige. That's why we have to talk now. There's something I have to explain to you before they arrive. I've already put if off too long, hoping to let you go first and—*damn!*"

The sound of the door chimes brought Mrs. Clarkson and her simple black dress into the foyer, where she hesitated with her hand on the latch, looking to Sam. "Will you greet your guests here, sir, or should I wait until you and Ms. Halliday retire to the banquet hall?"

"Just a moment, please, Mrs. Clarkson. Hoping I'd go first with what, Sam?" Paige asked as she reached up to straighten his bowtie. "But it's all right. Your guests come first right now. We can talk later, although you really should see the poinsettia tree. It's gorgeous. I want you to see all the rest of the house, too. Not that you've said anything about this space. I think they nailed it, Uncle Ned and the gang. He was such a huge help. I don't think we would have made it without Uncle Ned."

"Yeah, he's always a big help. A regular Santa

Claus." Sam held up his hand toward Mrs. Clarkson, silently telling her to continue to wait. "All right. Just promise me something first, Paige."

"Sam? What's wrong? I thought we were—"

"All right? You thought we were all right? We are. *I* am, and I hope you are. But there are things you don't know about—"

The chimes pealed a second time.

Sam put his hands on Paige's shoulder. "Do you trust me?"

"*Trust* you? Sam?"

"Just trust me. No matter what you hear tonight, no matter how this all goes down—and God only knows what Uncle Ned is planning—just remember that it doesn't matter. Nothing matters here tonight, Paige, except you and me."

"Uncle Ned? What would Uncle Ned be planning? You're scaring me, Sam," Paige said quietly.

"But you'll do it?"

"Trust you, you mean." She nodded. "I will, Sam. I promise."

Sam expelled a breath and dropped his arm, indicating that Mrs. Clarkson could open the door now.

Sam introduced her as "the genius behind these magnificent decorations," as "my very good friend, Paige Halliday."

Paige listened closely each time he introduced her to a new arrival, wondering what she hoped to hear and wasn't hearing. Still, he kept his arm around her waist, kept her close to him as drinks were poured, polite conversation was conducted and a variety of canapés were offered from silver trays.

She stopped counting after three couples had arrived and been introduced, as there would be only one extra place setting at the table, one Sam had already informed her may or may not be needed. If it came time to be seated and their last guest had not yet arrived, the place setting would be removed.

Finally, Mrs. Clarkson came up to quietly say something to Sam, and he went off with her, leaving Paige to circulate without him. She loved the attention he was paying her, the way he kept her beside him, but she was beginning to believe they were joined at the hip—or that he was afraid to let her out of his sight. But if she was the hostess, she needed to mingle more with his invited guests.

Paige accepted the compliments everyone heaped on her, and she explained that there was to be an open house on New Year's Day, and how the tented stalls would be employed as small carving stations, bar setups, and the like.

Emily Raines, a petite blonde with an infectious enthusiasm, actually went so far as to suggest that Paige was an artist. "And, as an artist myself, please let me say that I'm extremely jealous. It takes real vision to take a space this huge and make it seem so…intimate."

"My fiancée knows whereof she speaks, Paige," Cole Preston told her as he put his arm around Emily's shoulders. "You should see what she did with one run-down old building and a big dream."

"And a lot of luck in the form of a great big, anonymous check," Emily said as if reminding him of something. "That's how Libby describes what happened to both of us." When Cole looked at her questioningly, Emily laughed. "Libby Jost, that pretty Sissy Spacek look-alike you were manfully trying not to ogle a minute ago. Five minutes together in a powder room, darling, fixing our lipstick, and we women can cover a lot of ground. Besides, we're all pretty sure we know why we're here. To meet our mysterious benefactor. I'm just so happy that I can finally thank him."

Paige smiled as Emily and Cole went on to talk about her arts center for senior citizens and then drifted off to speak with the Sissy Spacek look-alike. But a thought had begun to form in her mind, and her heart was racing in her chest.

Libby and her fiancé, David Halstrom, were deep in conversation with the third couple, a very distinguished and yet devastatingly handsome doctor, Seth Andrews, and his bride, Becca. Paige hesitated to interrupt, but Becca quickly motioned for her to join them.

"Isn't this exciting?" Becca asked Paige. "You know, all three of us—six of us, really—have been wondering since the day our gifts arrived just who could be so very kind, so very giving. And then we got those invitations? I can't tell you how nervous I am."

"Nervous about meeting our reclusive billionaire Santa Claus," Libby Jost clarified, and her fiancé shook his head.

"Excuse her, please, Paige. She saw some gossip column about there being a Santa Claus somewhere out there who rewards the good or the true, or something like that."

"It was in Leticia Trent's 'This 'N' That' gossip column, and when I checked on the Internet, I learned that she's been writing about this Santa Claus for a long time now."

"Which, of course, makes it all fact," David said, winking at Paige. "Or do you know something we don't know? Sam seems like a nice guy, and this place is certainly impressive. But he doesn't look much like a Santa Claus."

Paige kept her smile, even as her stomach dropped to her toes. "Um…exactly what does this Santa do, please? I'm afraid I don't quite understand."

Libby happily explained as Emily and Cole joined them. According to Leticia Trent, some anonymous billionaire (Sam? He qualified, Paige supposed) picked people to present with a gift, monetary or otherwise, to reward them for something generous and unselfish that they'd done. If the person kept the gift, used it the way ninety-nine percent of people probably would—for themselves—that was the end of the story.

"But," David told her, "if the person uses the gift for the good of others, then there is another gift. According to this Trent woman, that gift is one million tax-free dollars."

"*What?* I mean—pardon me?" Paige shot her gaze around the banquet hall, madly searching for Sam. Who she was pretty sure she then planned to kill. Slowly.

"It's all rumor, gossip. But, if it *is* true, David and I have already decided not to keep it. Not that you guys have to do something like that, of course. It's just what we decided, once I read the articles."

Dr. Seth Andrews looked at Becca. "This is…interesting. Isn't it? I only thought we would be meeting the anonymous giver tonight. We didn't plan on anything so bizarre, did we, sweetheart? I don't know that I want to stick around for this."

Becca only sighed. "Don't go all proud on me, Cole Preston. Somebody did a very nice thing, and I want to thank him." She turned to Paige. "Besides, I highly doubt the man is going to play Santa to the tune of three million tax-free dollars. That story is nothing but sensationalistic gossip. It has to be."

"Yes, of course. I'm sure that's all it is," Paige agreed and then mumbled an excuse about needing to check on some last-minute details before they sat down to dinner.

Her smile left her face the moment she'd turned her back on the six guests, and her eyelids narrowed as she searched the shadows of the large room for any sign of Sam. Who, if he had a brain in his head, was hiding somewhere.

All the pieces were falling into place for her now. Sam was—Paige closed her eyes for a moment—*Sam*-ta Claus. *He* had written that letter he'd delivered. *He* had set up this whole thing, *investigating* her, monitoring what she'd done with his anonymous gift, hiring her to decorate his house, watching her like a bug under a microscope to see how she'd react, which way she'd jump.

It was sickening.

Disgusting.

Maybe even a little bit creepy.

Except…

It was also a new van for the kids at Lark Summit. It was a great art center for senior citizens in Kansas. It was expanding a health clinic in West Virginia and a wonderful children's park in Missouri.

And none of it sounds anything like the Sam Balfour I know, Paige told herself as she turned around once more, just in time to see everyone else looking at Sam, who had asked for everyone's kind attention.

She watched as he sought her out with his rather troubled-looking brown eyes, and she fought not to turn on her heels and run out of the banquet hall. But he'd asked her to trust him, so at least she could listen to whatever it was he had to say.

He'd better start talking, though. Fast.

"I want to thank you all for honoring your invitations and coming here tonight," he said, and then smiled. "Not that it wasn't a command request, was it? I'm sorry about that. By now I'm sure you've all compared notes enough to know that you've all been the recipients of anonymous gifts this year, and you may even think you've been invited here tonight to thank your benefactor. But that's not why you're here. You're here so that your benefactor can thank *you*. You've made him very proud, warmed his heart and, although it pains me to admit this, shown me how right he is and how wrong I was. You are, all of you, quite remarkable human beings. Some might even say you're members of a vanishing breed, although your benefactor doesn't believe that."

Paige wet her lips, wishing her throat hadn't gone so dry. Sam looked quite imposing, and his speech, the genuine humbleness in his voice, made her feel that she didn't really know him at all.

"There will be lawyers and legal formalities later, I'm afraid, necessary forms covering the confidentiality of this evening. But for now, let me say that each of you four recipients—Libby, Becca, Emily…and Paige—out of many who received similar anonymous gifts during the course of this year, have earned not only your benefactor's admiration, but also tax-free checks in the amount of one million dollars."

There was a gasp from one of the women, and Paige heard a whispered "I *told* you so" from Libby.

"In the normal course of events," Sam went on, "your benefactor would still be anonymous, but I was fortunate enough to convince him that, after many years of, as some people may call it, playing Santa Claus, it was time he came out of the shadows and met the people he so admires. And so, ladies and gentleman, please allow me to introduce my uncle, Samuel Edward Balfour IV."

As Sam gestured toward the far archway, Paige turned along with everyone else, to see...

"Uncle Ned?"

His silver hair shining in the light of several dozen candles and the crystal chandeliers, his smile brighter than any of them, dressed in a wonderfully fitting tuxedo rather than overalls and a plaid flannel shirt, Uncle Ned walked into the large room, stopped, sought out Paige with his twinkling eyes and waved rather sheepishly in her direction.

Paige slowly shook her head even as she began to move backward, away from the facts that had just been flung in her face. "No...no..."

She turned and ran toward the foyer.

"Paige! Paige—wait! Damn it, Paige, you promised you'd trust me."

Paige skidded to a halt in the middle of the great foyer, remembering that her coat and purse were in the library and that it was snowing outside. She wasn't going anywhere, so she might as well have her say. She whirled around to face him.

"And you promised me that...that you'd—oh, forget it! You didn't promise me anything, did you? You gave me your line, and I just folded like a house of cards. You and your uncle, the both of you. Just lie after lie after lie. You're a real pair, and I'm a real jerk!"

"I should have told you sooner," Sam said, approaching her carefully, as if she might bolt at any moment, just open the front door and go running out into the snow. "I was wrong. I know that. I wanted to tell you. But Uncle Ned wants to be anonymous... wanted to be anonymous. And you never said anything. I kept hoping you'd feel you could tell me on your own, but you didn't."

Paige looked away, hating that he was actually making at least some sense. She could have told him. She just hadn't. "I was worried the van might be involved in something illegal."

Sam smiled—and she longed to hit him. She loved him, but that didn't mean he wasn't ripe for a good right cross, darn it! "Illegal, Paige? Still? How could the van be illegal?"

"I don't know! I said money laundering, but that didn't make sense. Nothing made sense. And you said you were acting only as a delivery person for a client, or something like that. How could I tell you what your client wouldn't tell you? *Especially* if there was something weird going on with the whole thing. Because I wasn't going to have you tell me that I needed to give the van back, Sam. Those children need that van. So I…I just tried to put the entire thing out of my mind and forget it had ever happened."

"And now you're angry because you're one million dollars richer?"

"Yes! No!" She scrubbed at her face with her hand, without a thought to her makeup. "I mean, I'll just give it to Lark Summit. I make my own way in life, I always have."

"But you never forget where you came from," Sam said, edging even closer.

She looked at him intensely. "You—Uncle Ned— you had me investigated, didn't you? You probably know more about me than I know about me."

"I know what you are, Paige. A good person. Not a do-gooder. You're so much more than that. You're like my father, although I didn't realize why I was so angry with him or why I was fighting buying into Uncle Ned's beliefs. You're a good person who does good things."

She shook her head. "No, that's not right. I mean, not about your father, but about me. Don't try to fit me with a halo, Sam. I'm a selfish person. I give to Lark Summit, decorate the residence for holidays and things like that, because I'm a *selfish* person. I like the way I feel when I'm helping those kids."

"We'll argue some more later." He reached out and took her hand. "Come on, let's go to the library while Uncle Ned covers for us. I want to see that poinsettia tree."

Paige let him guide her back through the house to the library, where the poinsettia tree, backlit with spotlights half buried in the snow outside, stood as her favorite decoration out of anything she'd done. "It's beautiful, isn't it?"

"It's just the way I remember it," Sam said, leaning in to kiss her cheek. "Thank you, Paige. You can think what you want, and I'm certain you will, but you've made a huge difference in my life, and in Uncle Ned's. When I started this, I had no idea how it would end up, but that's what happened. Uncle Ned would say, undoubtedly will say, that I've finally grown up. So stay or go, that's entirely up to you, but please let me say this first. I love you, Paige. I love you, and I want you in my life if you'll have me. Now and for the rest of our lives."

If there was one thing Paige had learned growing up "in the system" it was how to choose her battles, when to fight and when it was simply easier to give in and go along with the inevitable.

Sam was inevitable.

"Oh, Sam…"

"I know this is happening quickly for you. It is for me, too. But when I saw you standing under that chandelier in the great foyer? My first thought was, my God, I love that woman. My next thought was that there should be children sitting together on the steps behind you, allowed to stay up late and watch their beautiful mother and their proud father as they hosted their annual Christmas Eve reception. For a moment, Paige, the image was so clear in my head that I had to stop and remember that it wasn't real. But it could be. If you can forgive me for being such a—"

Paige put her hand over his mouth. "Too much talking, Sam. Much, much too much talking. Please, just shut up and kiss me...."

Epilogue

Sam and Paige entered Uncle Ned's private study. They were still smiling about the way Sam had carried her across the threshold of their own quarters a few minutes early, and then had nearly dropped her when a startled maid who was vacuuming the foyer carpet shrieked in surprise and tried to pull the vacuum cleaner out of the foyer with her—the cord catching at Sam's ankles.

As Sam had said, that would show them to cut their honeymoon short and come back two days early, unannounced. But Easter would arrive in three weeks, and an apologetic Mary Sue had phoned to say that Paul had fallen off a ladder while stretching to reach a four-foot-high Easter egg that had been the second straight purple one in a row of suspended eggs that was supposed to alternate between purple and yellow. Now Paul was purple, black and blue and even turning a little yellow in spots, and Paige was needed back on the job at Holidays by Halliday, ASAP.

"Sam! Paige! You're home," Uncle Ned exclaimed, waving them into his presence like some king who must be obeyed. "You look wonderful, both of you. How was the honeymoon? How was Barbados?"

"Come with us next time, Uncle Ned, and find out for yourself," Sam told him as Paige crossed over to the desk to give the older man a hug and kiss. "You did promise us you'd stop staying cooped up in here, remember?"

"I'll have you two know that I commandeered Bruce, and we went for a drive just the other day." He looked up at Paige. "To Lark Summit. It seems they'd like a baseball field."

"Yes," Paige said, smiling at Sam. "I know."

"And did you know that Bruce once played semipro ball, Sam? He's not only agreed to help with the planning but has also volunteered to help coach."

"Really? Does that mean you're not going to have him running all over the country investigating people for your Santa project anymore, hiding behind trees and invading people's privacy, as Paige described it?"

"I'm afraid there's no more Santa project. You were right, Sam. That Trent woman was getting too close. Part of the joy Maureen and I got over the years was being anonymous, and if that is lost to me, why not simply go completely public? Paige, there will be papers for you to sign in a few weeks, but I'd be greatly pleased if you'll help me run the Maureen Balfour Foundation. If part of the fun for us came from being anonymous, the greatest majority of our satisfaction was in the giving itself."

Paige hugged the man again. "I'd be honored, Uncle Ned. Thank you so much." Then she leaned past him, to pick up a newspaper clipping on the desktop. "What's this? Isn't that—Sam, look. It's a photograph of Libby Jost."

Sam took the clipping from her and read the caption out loud. "'Plans were announced today for a proposed major addition to the newest children's park in the area. Libby Jost, seen here presenting a check for one million dollars to Mayor Cliff Hagen, says the money is earmarked for the construction of a one-of-a-kind carousel and other improvements. The hope is that renting the carousel and an adjoining building for parties will supply a steady income for the park.'"

"It's the last entry for my scrapbook, at least for this one," Uncle Ned said when Sam handed back the clipping. "Emily Raines has underwritten two more senior citizen art centers in towns not far from her original project. And Becca and her new husband, as you know, immediately donated her check to that same clinic in West Virginia. Now we begin a new scrap-book, Paige, and fill it with bouquets to my Maureen."

"Oh, Uncle Ned, that's the perfect name for the foundation."

"And what's my job, Uncle Ned?" Sam asked as Paige came around to the front of the desk, to slip an arm around his waist. "Or do I just get to watch?"

Uncle Ned blinked up at his nephew. "I didn't think you'd want to become involved in—do you really want to help, Sam? From your heart?"

"From my heart, Uncle Ned. I can't think of anything I'd like to do more, from my heart. Except kiss my bride, that is."

So he did.

* * * * *

Turn the page for a sneak preview of
High-Society Secret Pregnancy
by
Maureen Child

This glamorous first story in the
PARK AVENUE SCANDALS mini-series
is available from
Mills & Boon® Desire™ in October 2009.

High-Society Secret Pregnancy
by
Maureen Child

"Damn it, Julia, answer the phone," the deep voice growled into the answering machine, and Julia Prentice winced when the caller hung up a moment later.

She'd been dodging Max Rolland's phone calls for two months now, and he still hadn't given up and gone away. Not that he was stalker material or anything, Julia reassured herself. No, he was just an angry male looking for an explanation of why she'd been refusing his calls since their one amazingly sexy night together.

The reason was simple, of course. She hadn't been able to think of a way to tell him she was pregnant.

"Whoa." Julia's roommate and best friend, Amanda Crawford, event planner extraordinaire, walked out of her bedroom. "He sounds royally pissed off."

"I know." Julia sighed. And she could even admit that Max had a right to be angry. She would have been, too, if she'd been in his shoes.

Amanda crossed to her, gave her a brief hug, then said, "You've got to tell him about the baby."

Sounded good in theory, Julia thought as she dropped into the closest chair. She looked up at her friend and saw the gleam of sympathy in Amanda's gray eyes. "How'm I supposed to do that?"

"Just say the words." Amanda sat down, making their gazes level, which she pretty much had to do all the time. Julia was short, at five feet two inches, and Amanda was eight inches taller. Built like a model, Amanda had short, choppy blond hair, beautiful gray eyes and a loyal heart.

"Easier said than done," Julia said, smoothing one hand over the sharp crease in her pale green linen slacks.

"You can't wait forever, honey," Amanda told her. "Sooner or later, you're going to show."

"Believe me," Julia said, "I know. But that night I spent with him was an aberration. I mean, things got all hot and heavy so quickly I didn't have time to think and then the deed was done and Max was telling me he wasn't interested in anything more than a mutually satisfying sexual relationship."

"Idiot," Amanda offered.

"Thanks for that." Julia smiled. "Anyway it seemed that that was the end of it, you know? Max wanted uncomplicated sex and I wanted more."

"Of course you did."

She dropped her head against the chair back and stared up at the ceiling. "Now everything's different and I don't know what to do."

"Yeah, you do. You just don't want to do it."

"I suppose." Blowing out a breath, Julia said, "He deserves to know about the baby."

"Yep."

"Fine. I'll tell him tomorrow." Decision made, Julia actually felt a little better about things. After all, it wasn't as if she was going to ask Max to be involved in his child's life or even to pay child support. She could afford to raise her baby on her own. So, all she had to do was break the news of impending fatherhood, then let him off the proverbial hook.

"Why have I been obsessing about this?"

"Because you're you," Amanda said, smiling. She gave her friend's knee a pat. "You overthink everything, honey. You always have."

"Well," Julia said wryly, "don't I sound exciting?"

Amanda laughed. "Hey, don't knock it. You overthink and I act on impulse too often. We've all got our crosses to bear."

"True. And it's time to pick up yet another cross." Julia pushed herself out of the chair, then tugged at the hem of her white linen blouse. "I've got to go to that residents' meeting."

"Lucky you."

"I really wish you could come with me," she said.

"Not me, thanks," Amanda countered. "I'm meeting

a friend for dinner, where I will have a lot more fun than you will tonight. Personally, I'm glad to be only a roommate, with no place at those meetings. I'd be bored to tears in ten minutes."

Sighing, Julia said, "Five."

* * * *

Don't forget High-Society Secret Pregnancy
is available in October 2009.

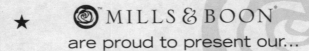

are proud to present our...

Book of the Month

Expecting Miracle Twins
by Barbara Hannay

Mattie Carey has put her dreams of finding
Mr. Right aside to be her best friend's surrogate.
Then the gorgeous Jake Devlin steps into her life...

Enjoy double the Mills & Boon® Romance
in this great value 2-in-1!

Expecting Miracle Twins by Barbara Hannay and
Claimed: Secret Son by Marion Lennox

Available 4th September 2009

*Tell us what you think about
Expecting Miracle Twins
at millsandboon.co.uk/community*

Fabulous new talent introduced by international bestseller
PENNY JORDAN

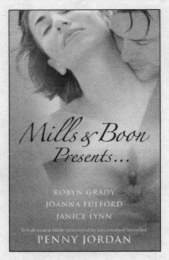

Mills & Boon Presents...

ROBYN GRADY
JOANNA FULFORD
JANICE LYNN

Fabulous new talent introduced by international bestseller
PENNY JORDAN

Three exciting new writers – three fabulous new novels:

BABY BEQUEST
by Robyn Grady

THE VIKING'S DEFIANT BRIDE
by Joanna Fulford

THE NURSE'S BABY MIRACLE
by Janice Lynn

Available 18th September 2009

www.millsandboon.co.uk

M&B

From No. 1 *New York Times* bestselling author Nora Roberts

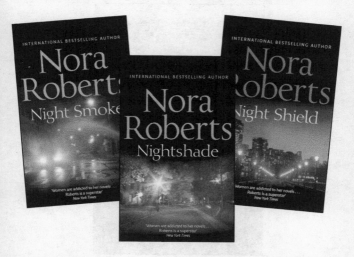

Nightshade available 2nd January 2010
When a teenager gets caught up in making sadistic violent films, Colt Nightshade and Lieutenant Althea Grayson must find her before she winds up dead...

Night Smoke available 5th February 2010
When Natalie Fletcher's office is set ablaze, she must find out who wants her ruined – before someone is killed...

Night Shield available 5th March 2010
When a revengeful robber leaves blood-stained words on Detective Allison Fletcher's walls, she knows her cop's shield won't be enough to protect her...

Passion. Power. Suspense.
It's time to fall under the spell of Nora Roberts.

His innocent mistress

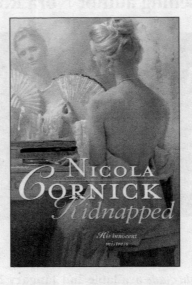

Orphaned and vulnerable, Catriona is doing
her best to resist the skilful seduction of the
scandalous heir to the Earl of Strathconan.
Then her newly discovered inheritance
places them both in terrible danger.

First kidnapped, then shipwrecked with only
this fascinating rake as company, her
adventure has just begun…

Available 18th September 2009

millsandboon.co.uk Community

Join Us!

The Community is the perfect place to meet and chat to kindred spirits who love books and reading as much as you do, but it's also the place to:

- **Get the inside scoop from authors about their latest books**
- **Learn how to write a romance book with advice from our editors**
- **Help us to continue publishing the best in women's fiction**
- **Share your thoughts on the books we publish**
- **Befriend other users**

Forums: Interact with each other as well as authors, editors and a whole host of other users worldwide.

Blogs: Every registered community member has their own blog to tell the world what they're up to and what's on their mind.

Book Challenge: We're aiming to read 5,000 books and have joined forces with The Reading Agency in our inaugural Book Challenge.

Profile Page: Showcase yourself and keep a record of your recent community activity.

Social Networking: We've added buttons at the end of every post to share via digg, Facebook, Google, Yahoo, technorati and de.licio.us.

www.millsandboon.co.uk

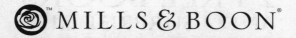

2 FREE BOOKS
AND A SURPRISE GIFT

We would like to take this opportunity to thank you for reading this Mills & Boon® book by offering you the chance to take TWO more specially selected books from the Desire™ 2-in-1 series absolutely FREE! We're also making this offer to introduce you to the benefits of the Mills & Boon® Book Club™—

- **FREE home delivery**
- **FREE gifts and competitions**
- **FREE monthly Newsletter**
- **Exclusive Mills & Boon Book Club offers**
- **Books available before they're in the shops**

Accepting these FREE books and gift places you under no obligation to buy, you may cancel at any time, even after receiving your free books. Simply complete your details below and return the entire page to the address below. You don't even need a stamp!

YES Please send me 2 free Desire stories in a 2-in-1 volume and a surprise gift. I understand that unless you hear from me, I will receive 2 superb new 2-in-1 books every month for just £5.25 each, postage and packing free. I am under no obligation to purchase any books and may cancel my subscription at any time. The free books and gift will be mine to keep in any case.

Ms/Mrs/Miss/Mr_____ Initials _____

Surname _____

Address _____

_____

_____ Postcode _____

Send this whole page to: Mills & Boon Book Club, Free Book Offer, FREEPOST NAT 10298, Richmond, TW9 1BR